rainbow, no end

a novel
by
lloyd knight

Order this book online at www.trafford.com
or email orders@trafford.com

Most Trafford titles are also available at major online book retailers.

Print information available on the last page.

ISBN: 978-1-4120-5448-5 (sc)
ISBN: 978-1-4122-3457-3 (e)

Trafford rev. 07/02/2019

 www.trafford.com

North America & international
toll-free: 1 888 232 4444 (USA & Canada)
fax: 812 355 4082

Author's Note

Although this story may appear somewhat biographical, it is not. It is a short novel. The work does contain some events from my own experiences, but most are imaginary. Apart from some references to a couple of true identities, all characters are fictitious.

For cipher buffs, in **Chapter 21** there is a coded message, devised by me. All information necessary to interpret the message is available within the text of the story. The decoded message is shown in full. Even so, I would be interested to hear from anyone who manages to *crack the code*.

You will find a useful **glossary** after the end of the story. Please refer to it as you come across terms requiring explanation. These are usually indicated by the use of *italics* or 'quotes'. The glossary contains some anecdotal material.

Kamsa hamnida
Lloyd D Knight

To Bonnie,
my life partner

Proem

Leo rushed out of the pub into the cold, clear night, fearful of the ogre at his back. His mind was racing. The taste of fear was on his breath. Bright lights flashed inside his brain. Apart from the sound of his shoes clomping on the pavement, there was silence all around. He did not want to be in this place. There were too many other times, when he had succumbed to the powerful influence of the demon drink. Tonight he would run from it. He must escape! His legs would not work properly. His knees felt as if they would buckle under his weight.

He felt a panic attack coming over him. Instead of running evenly, he lurched across the road. Confusion blurred his vision as the storm water drain came up to meet him unexpectedly. It should have been further away! He slipped on the rim and crashed into the black, bitumen smelling ooze at its bottom, banging his head on the solid clay side of the metre-deep ditch.

Stunned and hurting, he felt himself drifting back, his mind regressing to another time and another ditch. He passed out.

It was now 1952. He was back in South Korea and the air-raid sirens were screaming. In the dark he had fallen into a storm-water drain beside the dirt road leading from the squadron club back to his tent. All hell broke loose in the night sky above him as the anti-aircraft guns opened up. His stomach squirmed. Not so much from the fear of being killed or injured, but from the gut-full of liquor. It was his 20th birthday. His Flight Commander had told him he would not be flying the next day, so he had hung one on, with considerable help from his fellow pilots.

Now he lay in four inches of sump oil, a legacy from the Air Service Squadron which, late at night, sprayed the stuff on the base's roads to keep down the dust for a couple of days. He knew that the black, stinking oil would ruin his khakis, but he had more urgent matters to worry about. If he didn't get back to the billet area and into his assigned trench soon, he would be up before the CO in the morning on a charge. Failing to be at one's post while the unit was under attack was a serious matter.

The intruder was 'Bed-check Charlie', an old Russian PO-2 biplane. The Chinese pilot had come in at low-level, under the radar and would, if following his previous practice, fly around the base about a mile outside the perimeter. He would repeat this for the next four or five nights. As soon as the alarm was raised, almost everyone on the base would go to the trenches, where they would spend most of the next four or five hours. The tactic tended to be very disruptive to an aviator's sleep pattern. It was a very effective form of harassment and didn't cost the enemy much either. This form of attack was a copy of the technique used by the Russians against the German army during WWII.

Of course the base defences would swing into action and put on a display to rival the 4th of July. But the ack ack never managed to shoot down the interloper. Every so often he would fly over the airfield and drop a few mortar shells, just to ensure that everyone was still dutifully spending the night in the trenches. From these vantage points they could enjoy the splendid exhibition of red, green and white tracer, interspersed with bright flashes of exploding projectiles from larger ordnance. The noise, the 'pyrotechnic' display, and smell of burning cordite made for quite an impressive, even exciting show. In the long run though, it was one experience all could well do without.

After a couple of nights of this harassment the CO's instruction was: 'When the air-raid sirens start their wailing, stay in your sack and try to get some sleep. If the bombs start to fall, rush to your trench.'

One night one of the lads in the squadron lines reckoned he had a bead on the intruder and cooked off a magazine of .303 rounds from his rifle, in the general direction of the aircraft. All he got for his drunken initiative was a reprimand from the old man the next day.

They tried everything to get that bastard ... F86 Sabres and Navy Panther jet fighters. You name it! The jets were too fast and kept overshooting the target aircraft. They even sent a radar-equipped C47 Dakota transport plane up to ten thousand feet to shadow 'ole bed-check'. When the Dak was over the enemy, he'd drop a myriad of parachute flares in a vain attempt to illuminate the biplane for the gunners below. It's a wonder they never brought down the 'gooney bird' instead. Nothing seemed to work! However, they finally shot down a couple of them, with the radar equipped, night-fighter version of the F4U, Chance Vought Corsair. These were slower, piston-engine aircraft. At the lower closing speeds, the US marine pilots were able to show their sharp-shooting skills to better advantage.

Leo managed to drag his six-foot frame out of the ditch and staggered, puking all the way, to his trench. As he stumbled down the ramp in the dark, he bumped into Jack Hogan, one of his flying training course classmates. Jack was about the same height as Leo. He had a mop of black curly hair and brown eyes, whereas Leo's hair was sandy and he had pale blue eyes. Despite his Scottish complexion Leo had developed a golden tan in the Korean summer sun.

'Hey Leo, mate!' Jack exclaimed. 'Whatever happened to you? Last time I saw you, you were trying to escape from the clutches of that big fat USAF nurse. Boy! Did she have the hots for you! Did you make out?'

'No,' he mumbled.

There was no way he was going to admit that he was still a virgin. And the thought of being seduced by a bleached, smelly, and probably poxed dame who was at least 15 years his senior frankly repulsed; no, frightened him.

Leo remembered the experience of one of his USAF friends, a 4th Fighter Wing jet-jockey. He came back one day, all shot-up after a stoush in 'Mig Alley', along the Yalu River, which formed the border between North Korea and Chinese Manchuria. This was where the Russian built Mig 15s, piloted by Chinese and North Koreans, did battle with the UN, mainly USAF F86 Sabres. Rumour had it that Russian pilots took part in some of these battles.

Leo's friend banged out just north of Kimpo after his

Sabre jet lost most of its hydraulic fluid and all of its fuel. Initially he had thought to put it down on a straight stretch of sand in the Han River. But when he turned onto his final approach, he could see that the area was too small.

By the time he pulled the lever on his ejection seat, he was too low. The 'chute deployed a moment before he landed. He rolled up in a ball and broke both his legs and one arm and dislocated his other shoulder. He spent three weeks in the base hospital before they shipped him Stateside. Would you believe a guy in that situation could get the 'clap'? Sounds like one for Ripley! Well, it happened. Some polluted little ward aid had rewarded our warrior by climbing on top and banging him while he was in full traction.

No way would he get caught like that. His mother had instilled into him the value that he should save himself for the right person; someone he could love and cherish as a partner for life. So, even in his drunken state, he did not succumb to the temptation.

The all clear sounded at 0100 and he made his way, with a little help from his friends, back to his tent. Leo crashed onto his foldout stretcher and lay there staring at the ridgepole, trying to stop his world spinning out of control. He lurched out of his cot at least twice to stagger outside and dry-retch. There was nothing left in his stomach. He sat out there staring at a distant point of light until he brought the dizziness back in check. Then, he crawled into bed again to doze until the next bout came over him. He finally fell asleep to wake up later in the morning, with a rather sick headache. He wondered whether it was really worth it to 'celebrate' to that extreme.

1

'What the hell am I doing here?' he mouthed. He realised he had passed out in the ditch while trying to get away from the pub and had been dreaming, or hallucinating. His head hurt from the bump and the stench of the stagnant muck he lay in almost made him throw up. It was rather ironic that in his dream, or flashback, he should be worried about the CO putting him on a charge, because, if the Director could see him now, he would be drummed right out of the service.

Leo climbed up out of the ditch on the side opposite the hotel and crawled into the bushes. From there he could watch to see if anyone, or anything, followed. Was he in a hallucinatory state? Or was there really some sort of monster chasing him? Right now he wasn't sure of what was going on. He sat there in the dead silence, trying to regain his bearings and his self-composure. He could feel his heart pounding and hear the blood pulsing through his head.

There was a movement in the bushes to his left. He drew his weapon and readied himself to repel an attack. A low hissing sound came from the direction of the movement. He remembered that Harold Thwaites, his partner, was out here as his back-up during the surveillance of the publican across the road. He was obviously trying to get Leo's attention.

'Hey Leo! Whatever happened to you?' Harry asked, as he shone his pinpoint torch in Leo's face.

Was this déjà vu, or was he hallucinating again.

'You look like you've been on the slops for a week, but you were only in there for twenty minutes.'

The light dawned. The publican had been onto him and slipped him a Mickey. He muttered a garbled explanation to Thwaites.

'I think I've been drugged. I fell into the drain down there and knocked myself out. That creep must have cottoned onto me, so now I've blown my cover.'

'Well, we'd better call it a night and hightail it out of here,' said Harry. He checked the area was clear and they stealthily made their way back to where they had left the car, several blocks away.

Leo considered Harry as one of his friends; as much as you could expect a colleague to be a friend in his uncertain world as an operative in the Australian Secret Service. Harry was a little shorter than Leo, slightly podgy in build, with balding, grey hair and a somewhat complaining nature. Leo thought he had been a one-time police detective, but people in this business didn't want or need to know too much about their colleagues' past lives. He did know that Thwaites had been in security intelligence for about fifteen years. They had been partners for about two years and Leo assessed him as a fairly trustworthy soul. He was, however, a bit weak and indecisive and easily led. Leo didn't mind this though. It allowed him to be the decision maker and made for fewer hassles.

Harry drove them back to the office. They knew the Director would be waiting for a debriefing on the night's activities. He had ordered them to refrain from electronic contact for the time being and explained the reason for this blackout. The security section had discovered that some outside group had intercepted communications on the agency's operations two days before. They had not yet been able to identify the culprits.

This could explain how his cover had been blown at the pub earlier in the evening. Now he was personally compromised and didn't see how he could possibly continue his involvement in this mission. His head felt like it was going to explode.

Barely able to focus on the road or the buildings that were flashing by, he muttered to himself, 'Must stop his heavy drinking.'

Except that this time, the consequence was not of his doing.

As they drove in silence through the narrow winding streets, Leo pondered this recurring problem.

Janine, his daughter, had warned him many times, 'If you don't pull yourself together, you will not be able to hold down any sort of responsible job.'

It had only started since his divorce from Gloria and her subsequent demise. How long had it been? Must be about twenty years! Her death was almost like something out of a second-rate movie, bad braking, or worn tyres on a wet and winding coastal road. Losing control on a hairpin bend, the car had plummeted into the gorge. She had been heading for Sydney to visit her mother after having a nasty telephone argument with him.

He thought the quarrel, which was about his leaving her without any explanation, might have affected her driving. He had always partly blamed himself for the accident. Janine believed the accident was just misfortune. He had never discussed this with her, but one day he would set the record straight with his loving daughter.

As Harry drove on in silence, Leo wondered what she was doing at this time.

2

Janine had a tall willowy figure, with blond hair like her mother's, and her father's blue eyes. She was single, approaching forty and lived alone in a northern Sydney suburb. She often thought about her dad and wondered what he was doing. Right now, she hadn't heard from him for several weeks, which was a little unusual. She hoped he wasn't back on one of his binges. These lapses seemed to her to be less frequent. She prayed that he would soon overcome the need to imbibe.

Janine didn't really know what her father's job was. Most men of his age would be retired. She knew he had completed a long air force career and had seen active service as a fighter pilot in the Korean conflict. In Vietnam he flew C130 Hercules transports and later, helicopters in the combat role, during that terrible war. He hardly ever talked about those episodes in his life. He had never really confided to her anything about work matters since her mother died.

Now it seemed as though he was still his ever-secretive self. At times, when things appeared to get too tough, he would go on three-day binges and make an awful mess of himself. This had bothered Janine deeply over the years. However, the last time they had discussed his problem, he had approached it differently from his usual defensive attitude. He told her he was really working hard to beat the demon, and was applying some of his old military discipline to take better control of his life and emotional weaknesses.

No, he hadn't always been so secretive. When she was younger, before her mother's death, they had been very close. Her father had an intrinsic love of the outdoors and the Australian bush. He had always been a bush-walker and nature lover. He used to take her everywhere.

The most memorable excursions were the hiking trips, filled with mystery and adventure. He would always set some goal, like finding a lost cave or relic, or solving some tricky orienteering problem. He taught her all sorts of bushcraft, navigation, survival and even the

Morse code. She sometimes wondered if he wished she had been a son. He never intimated in any way that this might be the case.

Janine had wanted to fly, like him, so she joined the local aero club during one of his postings to Canberra and took flying lessons. She eventually gained her private pilot licence, which made him rather proud of her.

She often flew with her father and although he wasn't her formal instructor, he gave her many good pointers to safe flying, airmanship and navigation techniques. She learned to love the feeling of freedom that aviators can get hooked on when they soar up to meet the fluffy white cumulus clouds. Sometimes they flew into the overcast where he showed her the nuances of controlling the machine solely by reference to the flight instruments. She always found it exciting to fly, and understood completely why he loved it so much. They had been wonderful years.

On one of their excursions into the bush, he had set her a problem that required her to de-cipher a rather simple code from map references. They had a couple of secret codes, which he had devised, and only the two of them knew. The aim of this particular exercise was to try to locate a secret piece of equipment, a *black box* that had been hidden by an imaginary downed fighter pilot before he walked out of the bush. She had figured out the co-ordinates, and they had set out to hike to the spot in a rather remote place down the South Coast of New South Wales. The terrain here was fairly rough going. They needed to traverse a rocky plateau covered with scratching tea tree. This area had few helpful landmarks. Then they descended into a deep gorge with taller saplings and *black boy* grass trees. This was much more pleasant trekking.

The final five or so miles was up a long spur-line, which was broken by false summits. They were like long, sloping steps, each of which gave her the impression that she was almost at the pinnacle. Having pushed herself almost to the limit to reach the top of one, it was *shattersville* to find there was yet another long haul to the next. As she progressed up each of these, she prayed that it would be the last. Her father told her at the time that life was just like that. Each time you think you have *made it* and can begin to rest on your laurels, a new challenge presents itself and you have to virtually start all over again.

He suggested that each level strengthens you for the next, and if you don't give in you will eventually reach the top, a stronger and better person. He always tried to instil his philosophy of life into her. She was only fourteen at the time, but she managed to navigate, with very little prompting from him, right to the site.

Part of the cryptogram indicated that the subject of the search was 'somewhere between a rock and a hard place'. After one and a half days of solid hiking, she finally led them to within spitting distance of what must be the spot. Sure enough - there was a shallow cave with a smooth sandstone wall at the back and a large boulder toward the front. Instantly she knew the object of their search was behind that rock. She ran to it in eager antici-pation and there, jammed under the back of the rock was indeed, a black box.

It was actually a black-painted biscuit tin that looked rather worse for wear. She was amazed! How did it get there? What did it contain? He didn't let her succumb to the desire to rip off the protective sealing tape to open it, and discover it's hidden treasure. She had to secure it in her backpack and carry it until they found a suitable place to camp for the night. This was all part of his method of discipline training that he had learned from *his* father.

She always remembered a story that he had told her one night as they sat by their campfire after a hard day's hike. When he was six, his father had taken him on one of his many wood-gathering trips into the Blue Moun-tains to the west of Sydney. They were not far from North Richmond in New South Wales where the family lived. His father was a Wireless Operator Mechanic in a Royal Australian Air Force bomber squadron at the RAAF Station, Richmond. The year was 1939, just before WW II started and it was only a couple of months before his father was killed in an air crash near the base.

As his father was loading a rather heavy log into the back of his Model A Ford he slipped, jamming his hand between the log and the far door of the car. He passed out. Leo tried in vain to open the door or pull the log back, while his younger sister, the only other person present, tried to wake their father. All was to no avail. Now the father came round, but he feigned continued unconsciousness to see what the children would do. Leo had proceeded to calm his sister, sit her next to her father to comfort him, and set off down the road to seek help.

His father made a rapid recovery and called Leo back. Much hugging and assuring followed and father commended son for the way he had handled the situation. It was a fairly tough test for a six-year-old, and maybe even harder on the little girl.

So now Leo was applying a similar teaching technique to his daughter. He believed in the truth of the old adage, 'patience is a virtue'. She would have to wait.

Once they had pitched camp, the fire lit and supper taken, they set about opening the box. It was hermetically sealed and had a faded notice printed on the lid.

THIS IS PART OF A BOY SCOUT EXERCISE
PLEASE DO NOT REMOVE

After peeling off the many protective layers, she prised it open and found a can of peaches, and chocolate bars sealed in alfoil. There were similarly wrapped toffees and beef jerky, and a small bottle of lemon drink concentrate. The box also contained a letter of congratulations to the members of the Charles Darwin Patrol, who were supposed to find it. It had been there for over four years, but the contents were all still edible. The careful preparation of the package and the coolness of the south-facing cave had preserved them.

Leo told her the story of how it came to be there. While based at Canberra in a helicopter squadron, he had become an Assistant Venture Scout Leader with a local troop. She remembered this well because, apart from being an old scout himself, he was *blackmailed* into taking on the task as part of an agreement to let her join the associated Girl Guide Company.

The scout leader and he often planned adventures for the teenage lads in the patrol. This had been part of one of those excursions, planned during one of Leo's quixotic moods. He had prepared the box and secreted it during a helicopter navigation training flight. Circumstances had prevented the completion of the scouting exercise and soon afterwards he was posted to Vietnam. The package had remained there undisturbed until that day.

3

Harry turned into a laneway and parked. Leo's mind returned to the present and the job in hand. They climbed the three flights to the solicitor's office in the crummy, old, back-street commercial building in downtown Redfern. A rat scurried down the dingy hall that was littered with torn papers and smelled dank. Most of the offices were unoccupied and everything was in a state of disrepair. This was their temporary HQ, set up by the agency as a command post for this operation. The translucent glass panel in the door at the top of the narrow staircase carried a faded sign:

BROWN, BROWN and DUNSTAN
Barristers and Solicitors

How corny can it get? They were used to this sort of old-fashioned cover. Perhaps the rationale was one of reverse psychology. Something so obviously fake would have to be construed as being genuine. They let themselves into the darkened office.

The *old man* was sitting behind the desk, his feet up, puffing on his infernal pipe. The Director was several years younger than Leo. He was about Harry's height but quite slim, with steel grey hair, a cold pinched face and grey, penetrating eyes. Leo did not like him very much. He was certainly a pro and had served in a long, successful career, but there was an evil streak in his nature. This had really come to the fore during the Cold War days. He maintained a dogged pursuit of communists and *fellow travellers* long after the censuring of the old McCarthyism era. He was not above using torture to gain his interrogation outcomes and at times appeared schizophrenic.

'So, why are you back so soon?' he asked gruffly.

'We were sprung!' offered Harry

'What happened?'

They proceeded to tell him of the night's activities and how Leo's cover had been blown.

'Well, I half suspected that might occur.'

'What!' whined Harry. 'Why weren't we warned? All we knew was that there was a break-down in coms security.'

'Yeah. Well I didn't realise it had gone outside the government set. I thought it was the Feds or the NCC trying to cut into our action.' After a pause he added. 'Okay, Kirkland, you're off this case. I know you've put time and effort into it, but your cover's gone. Now they know they're under surveillance, they'll go further underground and we'll possibly lose them altogether.'

He looked at Harry, scratching his head. 'Thwaites, I'll keep you on it, but we need to rethink our whole approach.'

'Yes,' muttered Harry.

'Leonard,' said the Director, turning to face him squarely, 'I want you to take a month off. You need to get your s... together. I suggest you go bush, no liquor, get yourself laid, have a good break, heaven knows you've earned it.'

Bristling at the reminder of his mother always calling him Leonard, Leo nodded assent, or was it acquiescence?

'OK,' he answered. 'I suppose I could go up to my hangout'

Leo was a little taken aback by the sudden decision. Something didn't gel. He was already wondering why they were surveilling a drug-running suspect. This should have been a job for the State Police drug squad or the Federal Police. He knew however, never to question assignments in this job. There were probably other, national security aspects. Intelligence was always strictly on a need-to-know basis. To seek more information than one needed was not only unprofessional, it could be illegal, or even dangerous.

He had been in trouble in the past for attempting to *buck the system* by trying to apply reason to some of the decisions made by higher authority. In the old days this had meant a severe reprimand that was recorded on his personal file as a misdemeanour. He had accrued a couple of those.

In more recent and enlightened times the *punishment* had been replaced by counselling from the Director or some higher management official. Sometimes the top brass realised that if they'd listened to advice, or even sought counsel from field operatives, the outcome of an operation may have been more efficacious. Most times, however, life was more survivable if he just did the job right and kept his trap shut.

4

A few years earlier Leo had secretly built a small cosy hut, back in the Blue Mountains in the Great Dividing Range west of Sydney. It was in a very secluded spot. For personal security reasons, he had told only Harry and the Director of its existence, in case they needed to find him urgently.

It was a log cabin built with modern materials. The roofing consisted of securely attached shingles and the single room contained all the comforts of home. The cabin had a vehicle hideaway attached to the back wall. This was fully lockable, built into the side of the hill, and camouflaged to discourage vandals. The hut was well stocked with non-perishable foods, warm clothing and fuel. Equipped with an eight panel solar-powered system for charging a bank of batteries, it was a very hi-tech, compact retreat. The electrical system was automatically backed up with a Honda generator. This allowed him to install a freezer/refrigerator and supplied power for his laptop, sat-phone, other battery-operated devices and a modest amount of lighting.

There was a large propane bottle on the back wall of the hut, inside the vehicle hideaway. This supplied energy for cooking, water heating and space heating if he ever needed that.

Apart from freezing some meat, vegetables and ice cream, he had a good stock of frozen bread. He had learned the frozen bread trick for supplying some *fresh* food on one of his early Antarctic trips to the Casey base. They used to take frozen milk back then, enough to see out a whole winter season when the supply voyages from Hobart were suspended. These days, with UHT and a modern kitchen where they can bake fresh bread daily, they wouldn't have to bother carting and storing the frozen stuff.

Leo decided he *would* take the old man's advice and head up there for a welcome break. He could use this time to reflect on his life, his loves and his future. So, with some fresh supplies of fruit, some reading matter, unrelated to work and a much reduced stress level, he made a pre-dawn departure and headed for the hills in his Range Rover.

He took a circuitous route to confound any possible tail. This was always his SOP when he wanted to be sure his destination remained secret, a habit born of his job training. Leo put in several hours of hard driving, including a long stage of negotiating some strictly four-wheel drive tracks. Even so, he reached at his hideout around noon, still relaxed and feeling rather excited at the prospect of getting out into his beloved Australian bush.

It had rained for the last couple of days. So when he climbed out of the car, the overpowering aroma of eucalyptus and wet bracken struck him. Magpies and Currawongs warbled complicated songs from the tall forest gums. The world seemed to be at peace. This was just what he needed. He unpacked the car and drove it into the hideaway to discourage any would-be callers. For the same reason he would neither light fires nor play any music or news on speakers during his stay. It would be headphones only. At this stage he figured on staying up there for about four weeks, in line with the boss's orders.

He thought, 'I must call Janine and tell her I'll be out of the loop for a few more weeks.'

As he loaded the perishables into the fridge he automatically grabbed a can of beer, but stopped short of opening it, remembering the Director's instructions. Well, it might be a good time to start imposing some self-discipline again. An alcohol free day might be just what the doctor ordered. Or, why not make the whole period AF? He could well-afford to make a change in his habits.

Janine had been right about that.

If he didn't take hold of this opportunity, he could blow it all. There was no doubt though, there was no chance of following the old man's other command, the one about getting laid. But that would do him no harm either. He had managed his celibacy quite well since Gloria's death, so he saw no value in any casual liaisons at this time in his life.

After he finished settling in, Leo grabbed his fishing rod and worked his way down the steep hill to the creek. The path was in fact a dried up natural watercourse, lined on either side by tree ferns and *black boys*. This latter specie, which now bore the politically correct name of *grass-tree,* bore a resemblance the yuccas of New Mexico. It was Leo's favourite native plant. It was an amazing coincidence that the New Mexico plant's name came from the Spanish; whereas the alternate name for the unrelated Australian specie, yacca, was of Aboriginal origin. He always marvelled at the unusual beauty of its pluming green fronds, which sprayed out of the rough black trunk. The grass skirt-like foliage surrounded the tall, straight spear of the single flower stem. The attractive red flower was only generated about every five years. The plant made up for this low level of fecundity by surviving flood, fire and drought for maybe a couple of hundred years. Like many Australian plants, it relied on fire to initiate its regeneration.

It was a balmy autumn day and Leo was already feeling an inner, igniting spark to his own regeneration. Finding a suitable spot near the bank, he dug up a few earthworms and readied himself for some serious angling. The creek was about eight metres wide at this point and formed a pond that was quite deep. There was a white sandy beach on the opposite bank where the flow curved around to the right and disappeared beneath the dense, blue-green foliage of the overhanging eucalyptus myrtle.

After casting the baited hook into the stream and setting the rod in a handy knothole in a log, he pulled a book from his backpack and settled down for a pleasant Sunday afternoon's reading and fishing. The book was 'Lion over Korea' by David Wilson. It was a well-written account of his old squadron's wartime exploits.

As he recommenced reading at the bookmark, Leo remembered the strange and powerful dream he had experienced when he took the header into the ditch and his mind returned to that fearsome, yet exciting period in his life. He put the book down and gazed into the smooth, still water.

5

He was remembering 1952 again. He recalled his 45th mission over North Korea – his last one. This was a rocket projectile strike on a railhead near Sinanju. His squadron was mainly involved in that type of attack then.

Their second most frequent mission was the recce and interdiction of the main routes. The aim of those patrols had been to seek targets of opportunity in the form of convoys or freight trains, denying the enemy the use of their means of communication toward the front line. Authorisation for each attack had to be obtained from mission control.

A section of four Meteor jet fighters was split into pairs; one element at ten thousand feet, the other flew cover at twelve thousand. On some of those missions they ran into reasonably accurate anti-aircraft fire. The radar-ranged *flack* bursts would occur at the level of each pair. These deadly black puffs usually trailed behind the aircraft as the gunners set their aim. Luckily, their aiming wasn't as precise as the radar ranging. As soon as the first burst occurred, the pilots would call it and break away, climbing to disrupt the aim, and the height measurement of the radar.

However, on that last raid they flew much lower and were more susceptible to machine gun and even small arms fire, if an enemy soldier got in a lucky shot.

Leo was the twelfth aircraft over the target in the sixteen-ship formation. He switched off the pressurisation as he rolled into the attack at fifteen thousand feet and lined up on his section of the target area. That was a small group of huts in the southeastern corner. Intelligence had identified them, as a troop concentration.

As he steadied his aim at the centre of the huts in the gyro-gun sight, he could just make out the small green-clad figures running from them. Interspersed amongst the green, were several dressed in white. Leo knew that they had been civilians, or maybe even family, accompanying the soldiers.

As the leader's sixteen high explosive rockets erupted in the centre of the target, he had released his eight rockets with their napalm heads. This accurately delivered a forty-gallon fireball, right into the middle of the shattered buildings, completing their destruction, and probably causing death and inflicting horrible injuries to those who had not yet fled the target area.

Leo remembered hearing stories that some pilots in similar circumstances had deliberately mis-aimed their napalm. It would be difficult to make such a decision because ostensibly, it would be a dereliction of duty to take such action. He had never felt any compulsion to do that. For years afterwards, he had suffered nightmares about some of those attacks, reliving their tormenting moments.

He had just pulled out of his attack dive when BANG, the canopy imploded in a thousand pieces. He remembered being momentarily stunned, and hearing, above the roar of the airstream, a small, distant voice yelling, 'Blue Four, are you OK?'

He recalled how he had shaken his head to clear his foggy vision.

'What's happening?' his mind yelled.

Blood trickled down his forehead and into his eyes. Death looked him in the eye and he suffered a moment of sheer panic. His goggles had gone. The turbulent air behind the windscreen tossed his head around and blasted his eyeballs. The Meteor jet rolled and yawed to the right, even though he had automatically applied left aileron. He strained to keep his eyes open. Squinting to keep the wind and cockpit dust out of them, he looked over his shoulder at the right wing and saw the gaping hole in the centre of the engine nacelle. He knew he must have taken a 37mm direct hit.

He recalled that he had applied full left rudder and reduced the power on the remaining engine. It had been no use. The aircraft rapidly entered a spiral dive. He was only about two thousand feet and had insufficient control authority to recover.

Blue Three followed him down calling out, 'Your right wing's shot to pieces Leo. Bang out! Bang out!'

He pulled his feet back off the pedals to prevent his legs being chopped off by the jagged front edge of the canopy. Reaching up with both hands, he grabbed the ring behind the back of his head and pulled the blind down over his face. This action triggered the firing mechanism of the seat. It also protected his face and neck from the three hundred miles per hour windblast as his seat exited the cockpit. He felt the boot in his behind as the cordite cartridges in the Martin-Baker ejection seat propelled him up and out of his disabled machine. The strain on his back felt as though his spine was snapping. He let go the handle as the drogue steadied the seat into its forward and downward trajectory. Without waiting for the automatic separation to occur, he released his seat harness, pitched headlong out of the seat and pulled the ripcord of his parachute.

He couldn't have been much more than a couple of hundred feet above the rocky terrain. The 'chute deployed in a couple of seconds and he found himself swinging violently beneath that heavenly canopy. Messrs Martin and Baker had saved the life of another British airman! Though it was probably a case of, *out of the frying pan and into the fire*. That was the worst-case scenario for going down behind enemy lines; right near the target you had just helped blow to pieces and set on fire. What was the line of the ballad they sometimes sang in the squadron club describing this situation? Something about,

> There were husbands and wives;
> Itty-bitty children sharpened their knives.
> It was sa-ad when the pi-i-lot went down.

He remembered having a momentary vision of being chopped up by the angry citizens below and hoping that if captured, it would be by the Chinese and not the North Koreans.

6

His mind returned to the present, and he saw that the sun was already below the tops of the mountains. His line was swishing to and fro in the creek making overlapping wave patterns in the otherwise calm water. He realised that during his daydreaming, a fish had hooked itself and was just waiting to be hauled in. It was a nicely sized speckled perch that would make a fine meal.

While climbing up the hill to his cabin, Leo wondered why he kept returning to the vivid memories, and his dreaming of his Korean experience. Was it the book? Had reading about his old unit's exploits been some sort of powerful memory trigger?

It was a strange, although not entirely unpleasant experience, re-living those times. He pondered over some of the *what might have beens*. For instance, what would have happened in his relationship with Michiko, his first true love, if fate had been kinder.

Leo cast his mind back, remembering clearly the circumstances of their first meeting and what had eventuated. It had been on his second *Rest In Country*, which was like a monthly, four-day, mini *R and R*. It was really a misnomer, because they didn't have to stay *in country*. It was permissible to hitch a ride with the RAAF transport squadron, back to Iwakuni on the island of Honshu, Japan. This was a USN Air Base and the RAAF Contingent's main support centre for operations in the area.

Jack and he had hitched the ride on that occasion and arrived in Iwakuni on a Saturday evening. On checking the activities board in the Sergeant's Mess, they saw that the Padre's Sunday Excursion was a ferryboat ride to visit the city of Matsuyama. That was an all-day excursion, forty miles across the inland sea to the island of Shikoku.

'Well that looks like a better prospect than spending

a weekend in the haunts along the main street in Iwak,' said Jack.

Leo agreed, so after dinner they had a couple of drinks in the mess and were in their sacks by nine.

Next morning they arose bright and early, and after breakfast were picked up in front of the mess by the air force bus for the forty-minute drive to the ferry terminal.

The scenery during the three and a half hour boat trip was magnificent. There were numerous islands; mostly small, steep-sided, and covered with lush green vegetation. A few of the smaller ones had Shinto shrines on them. Some of those shrines, in the form of colourfully decorated arches or gates called Torii, were standing alone in the water. They were draped in heavy rope decorations. The curving lines of the architecture and colouring were beautiful.

The Chaplains had arranged on-board chapel services for those interested, and a picnic lunch with no charge to the participants. There must have been about twenty officers, NCOs and nursing sisters on board. The weather was fine and sunny with a warm, gentle breeze from the north. This produced a cancelling effect on the relative wind caused by their southerly headway, leaving the deck in a delightful calm.

Although they were only sergeants, Jack and Leo were quite used to mixing with officers. In Korea, because all of the USAF pilots were commissioned, the Australian Sergeant Pilots clubbed and messed with the officers. Over there, they removed their sergeant's stripes and were identified rank-wise only as 'Pilot'. This sometimes caused problems with the USAF 'other ranks' when it came to the protocols of saluting and use of the title 'sir'. The problem was made even worse by the fact that the Americans saluted even when not wearing caps, whereas the Australians did not salute when bare headed. The CO remedied this quandary by instructing the pilots to return salutes as if they were officers. He also had the USAF commanders brief their troops on the fact that Australians, like their own USN, did not salute without headdress. They were encouraged to wear caps as much as possible.

All had a great time taking in the scenery and chatting amongst themselves. It was one of the few occasions when they were permitted to hang up their uniforms for a day. It was great to be able to relax in 'civvies' and mix with all ranks. They welcomed the chance to chat with some Aussie girls instead of those grotty 'B' girls in the various watering holes around downtown Iwakuni. They were mainly prostitutes and held no interest for Leo or Jack.

Some the guys based at Iwakuni frequented those places regularly, despite the warnings from the MO, Service Police and the Padres. Some of them paid the price and were shipped home in disgrace.

When they docked at the small village of Mitsuhama, everyone split up and went their separate ways. This was on the understanding that they must be back at the wharf by three o'clock to catch the ferry.

It was a fifteen-minute trolley ride to the city. Jack and Leo stayed together strolling around the interesting streets and enjoying the peaceful surroundings. After looking at a couple of the local attractions, they searched for a bar to sample some of the local beer. They had heard that 'Kirin' was a pretty good example of a local brew.

As they walked down a narrow street near the centre of town, looking in the brightly painted shops, they came upon a likely looking establishment. Over the doorway was a large neon sign that read in English,

GURAMON BAR AND NIGHT CLUB

It was open for business and through the large windows they saw that about ten of the twenty odd tables were occupied by groups of young men and women. They went in, sat at a table next to the young people and ordered a couple of beers. Leo and Jack talked for a while and listened to the forties and fifties American music. The jukebox kept pumping out Glen Miller and Benny Goodman classics. They made a couple of selections of their own.

As the waitress brought their second beer, a young man from a nearby table came over to them and asked, in reasonably good English, if he could join them.

'Sure,' said Jack. 'Please sit down. My name is Jack and this is Leo.'

'Ah so! Jack and Reo, welcome to Matsuyama, my name is Tsushima Kenje, please to call me, Kenje. Are you American soldiers?'

'No, Kenje.' Jack replied. 'We're Australian air force pilots.'

'That very interesting,' said Kenje. 'Why are you in Matsuyama?'

Leo explained that they were based at Iwakuni and were on a day visit to his beautiful city. He made no mention of Korea. They were well briefed regarding talking to strangers about war matters.

They chatted for a while. Kenje explained that he was studying law at the nearby university; he was twenty-one years old and lived at home with his parents. All of his friends present were uni students, who usually met there about four o'clock several times each week. Today they had come to celebrate the end of semester with a lunch, which they had just about finished. Jack asked Kenje what the name of the club meant.

'You know! Famous US Navy fighter plane, "Guramon".'

Leo and Jack laughed as they recognised the word, *Grumman*. Leo realised that the neon logo out front was in fact a stylised monoplane with a large radial engine and propeller.

Leo had noticed a particularly attractive girl sitting at Kenje's table. He could hardly keep his eyes off her. Kenje noticed this and asked Leo if he would like to meet her.

Leo was embarrassed to be discovered apparently ogling the girl but said, 'Yes, I certainly would.'

Kenje went back to the table, spoke briefly to the girl and brought her, and one of her friends back. Jack and Leo stood as Kenje made the introductions.

'Reo and Jack, from Goshu, this is my cousin, Michiko, and this is Sumiko.'

Leo was now doubly embarrassed to learn she was a close relative of Kenje. He was really off to a bad start. He showed his embarrassment by almost knocking over his beer glass as they all sat down.

Michiko smiled pleasantly, sat down next to him and shyly struck up a conversation. Her English was superb, with a slight American accent. What he found most impressive, was that she pronounced his name Leo, with an 'L' sound. This was the first time he had heard his name pronounced correctly in this part of the world. He asked her how she came to speak such good English.

'Well,' she said, 'my father was in the diplomatic corps and he served a four-year appointment as an assistant to Japan's first post-war ambassador to the Philippines.' She continued, 'I was twelve at the time and accompanied my parents on that posting. I attended an American school in Manila.'

This explained the accent as well as her expertise in the language.

They chatted on for a while. He told her about his early life in Melbourne. He talked briefly about the schools he had attended and eagerly boasted to her about his flying career so far, again not mentioning Korea. She told him that her father and Kenje's were brothers. She also told him they were related to a famous novelist, Dazai Osamu, who was an idol of hers. Although Leo was fairly well-read for a young Australian male, he had to admit he had never even heard of Oriental Literature, let alone read any.

Jack seemed to be hitting it off well with Kenje and Sumiko. He looked around and said to Leo in a rather forlorn voice, 'If we don't leave here in the next twenty minutes we'll miss the ferry and be in all sorts of strife.'

As he spoke, Jack saw a couple of their air force party walking past the club. On the spur of the moment he asked, 'Why don't we tell them we're staying over and will report in tomorrow as early as possible when we return to Iwak?'

'OK,' Leo replied.

So Jack raced after them and squared it away with the timely messengers. As he returned, the uni crowd was beginning to break-up and leave. Leo started to panic. Was their sudden decision going to be to no avail?

Jack quickly explained to their newfound friends that they had decided to stay overnight and asked Kenje if they could all meet later. Kenje indicated he was keen to do that and the girls offered no objections. Kenje said they could all have dinner in the club that night, there would be a good band playing and everyone loved dancing.

He remembered thinking at the time that it was fast heading toward a most favourable outcome.

As Leo approached the cabin, after his long climb, his thoughts returned to the present and the meal he was about to prepare to accompany his fresh catch.

7

For the next couple of days Leo just rested, exercised, read and fished. Although the fish weren't biting very well, he had a couple of reasonable meals from the creek. Everything was functioning normally in the hut and he was starting to get bored. He hadn't had a drink yet and was not finding the stock of beer or the bottle of CC in any way tempting.

Regular hard exercise was part of his makeup and he was fitter than most people half his age. He started a tighter exercise regime, which included running down the hill to the creek, then back up again. He was feeling great!

On about the fifth day, he decided that he needed some diversion. He packed a small rucksack and decided to hike to the north for a couple of days. He had his mini GPS to assist in his return but he left the sat-phone behind. It was safe in the concealed cellar beneath the hut with the other high-tech surveillance gear and weapons. These were usually close at hand.

Next morning he set out at a steady traverse speed of about seven kilometres per hour. After descending into the valley in front of his hut and climbing the far side, he followed a long ridgeline for several kilometres. He then descended into a major northerly oriented valley.

He had never ventured into this territory before and was rather surprised at the change in flora over such a short distance. The trees here were not so tall as the forest gums up near his camp. There was as well, much more scrubby bush beneath the trees. This made the going more difficult. It was a beautiful, sunny day and Leo was experiencing a deep sense of serenity in his green world. After all the rat race associated with his job, he was always keen to get away from it all and go bush.

As he slogged along he thought of some of the good, and not-so-good, times in his life.

During the early years with Gloria, he had been a caring and faithful husband and she, a good wife and mother. But he had been too young and immature to know how to establish or maintain a sound relationship. He was bored with the humdrum of domesticity and his military life took him away from home for much of the time. They were not really sexually compatible and he had almost succumbed to the temptation of being involved in a couple of affairs during the middle years of their marriage.

These dalliances had taken the form of secret dates on several occasions with the unhappy wives of a couple of his colleagues. He had a close scrape with exposure during what was to be the last of these interludes. He then came to realise that these immature and wrongful actions must cease. So he went to the other extreme and *got religion*.

At the time it helped him to remain true and faithful, but it didn't bring him much satisfaction. He put in a few years of diligent study, teaching and preaching and *good works*. However, he found a high incidence of hypocrisy among the Christians in each of the churches that he joined with each new posting. He remembered that he found a majority of them practised what he called, 'Churchianity', not Christianity.

He decided to venture out on his own, outside the church, keeping the main tenets of the gospels and caring for others, but not being party to any formal religious practise. He made a comprehensive study of other religions and came to the conclusion that, although each had unique qualities and flaws, they were basically the same in relation to the worship of God and the treatment of others.

He could not accept the need for people to try to force their own beliefs on others; particularly the way Christians tried to *convert* folks of other faiths. It seemed to him that the worm had turned now, and some extreme elements of the Islamic faith were trying to emulate those earlier Christians by pushing *their* religion onto the rest of the world.

His personal value was, 'Do unto others as you would have them do unto you; but let *them* do their own thing!' During this phase of his life he seemed to alternate between jousting at windmills for good causes, and looking for the pot of gold at the end of the rainbow – neither facing the realities of life, nor gaining any real sense of personal achievement.

He was diligent in his job, reaching high levels of qualification in his flying career. He had completed a one-year training course at the Air Force School of languages, qualifying in Mandarin and picking up a little

Russian as well. He always tried to see other people's points of view and to accept them as they were. He was as well fairly community spirited, joining in activities at his daughter's schools and assisting in scouting activities. But mainly he felt dissatisfied with his life, and longed for more excitement and challenge.

When he returned from the Vietnam conflict, he was very mixed up emotionally and all of his feelings of love for Gloria had gone. He was fed-up with the military life, and wanted some new challenges. He decided to resign his commission and launch into a new career.

He remembered an offer made by a Colonel Johansen, a Special Forces operative. He had met the Colonel during a covert operation in which he had been involved as a helicopter pilot a few years earlier. Johansen had said that he, Leo, had just the sort of attitude and background required to make a good agent in service to his country, and to further the principles for which he had now fought in two wars. Consequently, he contacted the Colonel. He had been in the security intelligence business ever since.

During the cold war years this had taken him into many exciting and diverse situations. Some filled him with extreme ennui, others, with stark terror. One of the sad aspects of that era was that for security reasons, he could not share those experiences with anyone but those directly involved. It was truly the case of, 'I could tell you about that, but then I'd have to shoot you.'

These excursions took him throughout most of Southeast Asia – Burma, Malaysia, the Indonesian Archipelago and Thailand. Then, back to Vietnam working with 'Air America'.

Now, life was much more benign. This current drug dealer surveillance was about the most exciting operation he'd been caught up in for years. Even that had been shaping up to be totally uninteresting. Then, before he could get fully involved, *it* was over.

Stopping at a peaceful billabong around noon, Leo munched on his soppressata and dill pickle sandwich – thanks to his own food preparation expertise, and to his frozen bread. He finished off the repast with a slice of his homemade muesli bar. All was washed down with a small carton of frozen milk that had thawed to a pleasant drinking temperature. After a short rest he pressed on, trekking down the long, steep sided valley. He had neither seen, nor heard, a soul for days now and was enjoying the solitude. There weren't even any sheep or cattle grazing in this *neck of the woods*.

By late afternoon he was starting to feel a little weary and decided to call it a day. It was around six when he stopped and made camp by a quiet billabong. The GPS indicated he had covered thirty-four track kilometres. Not bad for day one! He made a light meal of beef jerky and finished off the pickle and bread. He had planned no fires so had to sate his high thirst with stream water and lemon concentrate.

About eight, he crawled into his old japara silk sleeping bag and his thoughts returned to the episode in his life that had often left him wondering: Michiko.

8

He remembered the night when he first met her, and how he had let the grog get the better of him. Up to that time, it was the only occasion that he had descended into a state of drunkenness, except for his twentieth birthday party at Kimpo.

After Kenje had arranged for the five of them, plus another girl, Yoko, to meet at the club at eight, he took Jack and Leo a couple of blocks down the street to a small, inexpensive hotel.

'You'll like this place,' he told them. 'Friends of my family run it so I will get you a special price. Their name is Hanieda.'

Downstairs, there was a front desk in a small lobby and an office, tastefully decorated in traditional Japanese style. A cosy bar and adjoining dining room were off to the left of the entrance. The not-unpleasant, piquant aroma of a recently cooked meal permeated the area. When Jack commented on this, Kenje said. 'The food here is very good, my father and uncle often bring us all here for a feast.'

The place probably had about twenty rooms, most of which were on the upper of the two floors. The proprietress spoke no English so Kenje helped them check in. Then he bade them farewell until eight.

The hotel was quaintly attractive and clean and although communication was next to impossible, the Hadiedas, a middle-aged couple, were very friendly. Jack and he had brought a small overnight bag containing minimum personal necessities, in case they ran into an unplanned change in itinerary. Smart move!

After freshening up they went down to the bar, propped on a couple of tall stools and ordered beers from Papa San Hanieda. He had enough English to service their requests for drinks and nuts for the next couple of hours. They had brought a few thousand Yen each and were sitting pretty, as far as cash was concerned.

'So!' Jack started off the conversation. 'You're certainly making a hit with Michiko, I thought you were going to race her off at one stage. Right there in the middle of the afternoon.'

'That obvious, was it? I got the impression Kenje was being a bit protective of her, and I certainly don't want to offend anybody, but I've never felt so drawn to anyone in my whole life.'

'Well you be careful mate, you don't want to get in too deep. Just have fun.' He continued. 'I rather like Sumiko, but I get the feeling she may belong to Kenje.'

'You're probably right on that score. I guess that's why he asked Yoko to come along, like, to be your date,' offered Leo.

'Yeah. Well we'll see how it goes.'

Leo wasn't sure if the beer was stronger than he was used to. But he was feeling a little light-headed by eight when they made their way back to the Guramon.

During the night Leo and Michiko danced and

danced. He was absolutely smitten by her looks and charm. They talked incessantly, except when some of the slower, more romantic tunes were being played. During these they snuggled up and swayed silently to the high quality American music issuing from the bandstand. Watching Kenje and Sumiko dancing, Leo was in no doubt now. They were definitely a number. Jack and Yoko also seemed to be hitting it off really well.

However, about eleven, when Leo and Michiko finally came back from the dance floor, the two of them had disappeared. Kenje took Leo aside and said Jack had told him he had had enough to drink and wanted to call it a night. Jack had asked Kenje to say goodnight to him and say that he'd see him early tomorrow, as they had to travel back to base.

Kenje then told Leo that, because Michiko was his cousin, his family held him personally responsible for her safety and happiness. He demanded of Leo that he treat her with respect and care. Leo attested to the fact that he held them both in the highest regard and assured Kenje he had nothing to fear.

About midnight, Leo was feeling rather the worse for wear. Some hotshot nightclub boys had challenged him to a bout of *skol* drinking. Trouble was – they were downing sake, the rather powerful rice wine. It was more like straight whiskey than wine, and Leo was slowly going under. Michiko was doing her best to look after the foolish young foreigner, but he was fast becoming helpless.

About one o'clock he decided he had better call it quits and get to bed. He said his farewells, telling Michiko and Kenje that Jack and he had to return to Iwakuni on an early ferry in the morning. He told them he *would* come back on his R and R, next month. Michiko walked to the door with him and briefly stepped outside into the deserted street. As they stood in the now darkened doorway, she held his arm and looked up smilingly into his face.

'I've had a wonderful time Leo. It's a pity you have to go back tomorrow.'

Although he felt his speech slurring, he said, 'This has been one of the most enjoyable nights of my life. Please forgive me for letting the sake get the better of me?'

'That doesn't matter,' she said. 'You've handled yourself like a gentleman, and have been quite funny as well.'

As she spoke, she applied a little extra weight to his arm and brought her face closer to his. He bent toward her. Tenderly and softly he kissed her on the lips. She responded delicately. It was the most beautiful kiss he had ever experienced.

She said quietly, 'Please do come back.'

He promised her there was nothing surer. She released her grip and slipped back into the club. He made it back to the hotel without falling down and crept up to his room. Jack's room across the hall was in darkness. He washed, brushed his teeth and collapsed into a drunken sleep on the narrow futon.

Leo woke with a hot feeling at his back, burning eyes

and an extremely sore throat. He sat up and his head was enveloped in strong smelling, choking smoke. He looked over his shoulder and saw a deep red glow in the dark. The rice husk filling of the futon was smouldering. He must have gone to sleep with a lit cigarette.

Hell! He leapt up, hurried down the hall to the bathroom and returned with a pitcher full of water. He didn't want to make a flood, so he slowly poured the water along the line of the smouldering rice husks. Then he opened the window shutters to free the room of the acrid smoke. Satisfied that he had solved the problem, he lay down on what was left of the futon and fell asleep again.

Leo had no idea what the time was when he awoke the second time. He could see it was nearly dawn. His back and shoulder felt hot from the burning episode. Actually, they felt a lot hotter.

'God no!' he exclaimed.

The futon was burning again. He hadn't completely extinguished it. Now he started to panic. What if this was developing into a major fire under the floor? There were no fire extinguishers visible as he raced down the hall, pitcher in hand, trying to be as quiet as possible. He filled the pitcher to the brim, lugged it back to the room and this time gave the futon and the floor a good dousing.

He was now feeling completely sober but his head felt like it was going to explode. Surveying the damage, he saw that the futon was two thirds gone and there was a square yard of black hole in the tatami matting showing badly scorched floorboards underneath. The slow smouldering must have continued for several hours to do so much damage. It was sheer luck that in his drunken stupor he hadn't succumbed to the effects of the smoke and burnt down the whole hotel. The smell of burnt straw and rice husks was overpowering. His nose, throat and lungs were on fire.

He raced across the hall and knocked lightly on the sliding screen door of Jack's room.

'Jack, wake up,' he called softly.

'Go back to bed Leo, it's too early.'

'I must speak to you urgently Jack.'

He suddenly thought, 'Perhaps he's not alone.' Jack opened the door. He was alone and looked fit and not hung-over.

'What's wrong?'

'I think I'm in big trouble, I've burnt the room.'

Jack pulled on his trousers and followed Leo across the hall. When he saw the damage he let out a mild expletive.

Leo said. 'We'll have to get out of here, they'll lynch us.'

'No they won't,' said Jack. 'But if we skip, they'll certainly put the cops onto us and we'll end up in the clink. You'll just have to face the music.'

They quickly bathed and dressed, then went downstairs. Mama San was tidying up the small lounge when Leo approached her.

'Oh hio gazi emuss,' he offered. 'I have bad thing to tell you.'

She didn't understand anything he said, except perhaps his inept greeting. He took her hand and started to pull her to the stairs while pointing up toward his room.

'No! No!' she cried out.

He realised she was completely misreading his intentions. Jack pulled out his Zippo lighter, flicked it alight, pointed to the flame then toward the ceiling and said, 'Fire.'

She understood his message instantly and ran up the stairs with the two young pilots in hot pursuit. Mama San took one look into the room and let out a terrific wail. She began wringing her hands and calling out to others. Half-a-dozen staff and guests were instantly on the scene all chattering excitedly about the situation.

Then Papa San turned up. He quietly surveyed the scene and said, 'Come down, we talk.'

They followed him downstairs to his lounge cum office. He had a kind face and spoke in a calm manner.

'No worry, you pay two thousand Yen, OK?'

Leo and Jack agreed that this was a very considerate offer, but there was no way they could raise that amount between them after the last evening's excesses. It was only about two Pounds Sterling or five Dollars. However, they only had a few hundred Yen left and they needed that for trolley, ferry and taxi fares.

They had some BAFSV and MPC military money,

but no greenbacks. They showed him what they had between them and he indicated he did not want any military money, not that they would use any of that off base. Such dealings were strictly forbidden and punishable by imprisonment.

'You come back?' Papa San asked.

Leo said that he was definitely coming back in one month. Jack looked surprised.

'It's that serious is it? She really got to you?'

'I think so, yes.'

'Well I must say. She is absolutely the most gorgeous girl I ever saw.'

Papa San said, 'You leave watch, you come back, you pay two thousand, I give back watch.'

Leo took off his mother's going away and twentieth birthday present. Although it was only a cheap, non-shockproof, non-waterproof wind-up job, it was the best she could afford. On the large, square back she had it engraved with – 'To my loving son Leo for his 20th birthday. Come home safe. Love Mum.' It was his most treasured possession and probably the only time she had ever called him by his preferred name. He was quite apprehensive about parting with it. Jack sensed Leo's uneasiness and said, 'I'm certain that the old man will keep it for you.'

So he handed over the watch and they shook hands. Leo apologised profusely for the damage he had caused. They had a quick breakfast of noodles, grabbed their gear and made their way via the trolley car and ferry back to base.

Happy memories!

There certainly had been other than happy times during that period of his life though. It was now about nine o'clock so Leo snuggled up in the warmth of his sleeping bag. He *set* his metabolic alarm clock to waken at five, commenced his sleep exercises and was soon in dreamland and back in Korea.

9

He came down on the side of a barren hill making a copybook landing and quickly recovered the silk 'chute, jamming it under some flat rocks. The other three aircraft of his section were now circling him at a couple of thousand feet. They didn't have fuel to stay around for more than about ten or fifteen minutes max, and would have already called in a CAP cover.

Leo crawled into a natural hollow and lay flat so as not to present any skyline exposure to anyone down in the valley. He removed the brightly coloured yellow and red scarves from around his neck and laid them side-by-side to signal to the circling aircraft that he was OK.

His head hurt from the thump on his forehead caused by the imploding canopy. Unlike their USAF brethren with their 'bone-domes', the Australian pilots were only issued WW II type leather helmets. They afforded scant protection. Even so, he had only suffered superficial cuts to his forehead and the bleeding had ceased. He resolved that, when he returned to base, he'd scrounge a 'hard-hat' from the yanks. If he ever did get back to base!

Leo knew he was too far north of the DMZ to be rescued by chopper, and the morning briefing indicated that no navy helicopters were within range of the target area. There was a carrier off the West Coast though. It was probably only forty miles from the mouth of the Chongiu Harbour and about the same distance from the target area. They were on constant standby to provide CAP for any downed South Korean or UN pilots.

The sound of a heavy vehicle rumbled up from the valley below. He had seen a dirt road down there as he descended. It was about a mile away to the east.

Ten long minutes went by with no visual signs of ground activity, then from behind the hill a USN Douglas AD-2 Skyraider roared over the top of him.

'Thank God!' he sighed.

He must have been airborne when 'Daney Red One' put out the call for cover on 'guard' frequency. Blue Section made one last wing-waggling pass and climbed out into the south. Number three would have called 'magpies' by now to indicate that he had minimum fuel.

The Skyraider peeled off his course and made a strafing run across the line of the valley. He was obviously attacking the truck or whatever it was. As the navy pilot let fly with his four, 20mm cannons, Leo grabbed his scarves and scrambled up and over the top of the hill. It was about a two hundred *yard dash and by the time he crashed over the top he was just about out of wind. There was a large stand of trees about four hundred yards down the hill so he headed for it as fast as he could run.*

The shooting over the hill had stopped now and as he lay exhausted under the bushes amongst the trees, he could hear the navy plane looking for him. After a few minutes the pilot obviously decided he could be of no further assistance and buzzed off to the west. He probably reckoned that if he hung around any longer, he might draw unwelcome attention to the downed airman. Leo crouched in the bushes under the scant trees and tried to figure a plan of action. He was feeling very much alone now and wondered if anyone would come to his assistance. Were they just going to leave him for dead?

It was now mid-afternoon and he decided that the best plan would be to lie low and see what happened. The friendly forces knew where he was. The enemy would have a fairly good idea as well. So, if he tried to move before dark it would be highly likely he would be seen and captured. He settled down under the thickest bush he could find and tried to rest. Exhaustion overcame him.

10

Leo awoke from his dream with a start. The sounds of voices and someone crashing through the undergrowth had wakened him. Slowly, he eased the sleeping bag from around his ears. There were two of them; male, Australian accented, and they seemed to be coming straight toward him.

'We're not supposed to be making so much noise,' said one.

'We're the only ones in this sector so I guess it doesn't really matter.'

'OK, but we only have about a kilometre to go now, so let's keep it in patrol mode.'

Leo froze, lest they sense his presence. They passed by him in the dark, just a few metres away. He continued to lie low as they moved away from him. Who could they be? Not regular hikers; it was almost eleven o'clock. They certainly didn't sound military. Their noisy progress gradually faded to the north and he lay there pondering his dreaming. It was so strange. Why did he keep returning there?

He knew that, although some dreams seemed to occupy rather long periods, they were often quite short and probably triggered by a sound, or a movement. Perhaps the noise made by these two had set off a mini-dream that included his episode of hiding on the hillside after being shot down.

After about twenty minutes, he started as he heard distant gunfire. Automatic! Loud shouting followed. If they weren't a couple of rookies on manoeuvres, what the hell was that all about?

After decades of training and exposure to tactical situations, Leo always bedded down only after packing everything ready for a rapid departure. So now, he eased himself out of the sack and put on his boots. Quickly packing his sleeping bag and the couple of loose odds and ends, he made off to the north toward the sounds of the gunfire and shouts.

The clouds were drifting away from the waxing gibbous moon. He could make out a narrow path paralleling the stream. After silently advancing for several hundred metres he saw that the path turned west into a re-entrant. The shooting had stopped but the voices were clearer now. He branched off to the left of the track, carefully moving up the spur-line. After a hundred metres of stealthy movement he calculated that he was now abeam the main source of the voices. Using his small, vision enhancing monocular telescope, he could see in the moonlight, the silhouette and movement of an apparent sentry up the ridgeline about eighty metres away. He eased down the slope a short distance and stopped, secreting himself behind a large gum tree. From here he could make out most of what was being said.

A commandingly deep voice was castigating what Leo estimated to be about a dozen others.

'The exercise is cancelled,' he all but yelled at the top of his voice. 'This was supposed to be a kidnapping, not an ambush assassination.'

He continued, 'You've managed to waste the hostage.'

'Well they fired first,' whined one of the underlings.

'Shut up you snivelling excuse for a soldier. Those

twelve dummies were presented just as briefed, four in each car.'

His voice changed to a lower pitch as he continued with the criticism.

'The subject we hoped to capture was in the back seat of the second car, as you should have expected.'

He moved toward one of the men and grabbed at him, snatching what looked like an AK47 from his grasp.

'The fact is it was Johnson who fired the first shot, not the bodyguards.' He threw his arms in the air and ranted at the top of his voice.

'Then you all just opened up and wiped out everybody.'

Leo scanned the area around them and picked up the subjects of the discussion. About thirty metres up the track in the centre of the re-entrant, he could make out the shapes of three dummy cars. They appeared to be constructed from large packing cases, each with four wheels. They were open at the top and contained plywood shapes resembling seated occupants. One toward the front, right-hand side of each box obviously represented the driver. The three behind would be guards. In the case of the second *car*, the centre figure would be the proposed hostage. These figures were in various states of dilapidation, obviously caused by the shooting.

Someone called out from further up the track.

'Is it safe to come down yet?'

'Yes, get down here for the de-brief,' replied the leader.

A few minutes later two men appeared, rolling up a length of rope. They were obviously the motive power for the dummy car *train*.

He now knew this was not an ADF exercise. These were not professional soldiers. A debrief would not be commenced out here at the exercise site, but back at base. Additionally, he assessed that the weapons were wrong. They sounded like AK-47s and a slower M9 *grease gun*. Something like what may have been used twenty or thirty years ago during elite operations training. This was indeed a strange bunch.

After about ten minutes of generally poor coaching, the leader ordered them to retire. He added an admonishment.

'You will need to do better on the next exercise. That'll be on the day after tomorrow, after you have had a good rest.'

Leo auto-stored his position in the GPS and was just about to crawl away again, when he realised the sentry was moving down the slope to his left. He froze.

'Can I bed down now too?' he called to the leader.

'Yes I suppose so, it's not likely there'd be anyone else out here at this time of night.'

If only he knew!

Was this a gang of civvy gun freaks? Or could it be something more sinister? He knew he'd have to skedaddle back to the hut and return with his 'ahead-of-the-state-of-the-art' surveillance gear. He wished he'd brought the sat-phone so he could report this in, or make some inquiries, or maybe get back-up. Then he remembered the compromised communications and decided to go it alone for the time being.

While the group was making so much noise, he slunk away down the ridge and headed up the valley, back to the south. It was just past midnight so if he could keep up a good pace, he would make it back to the shack by early afternoon. This would allow him time to recover his sleep loss and depart very early to travel back to this place. Then he could scout out the area, estimate the strength of this party and set himself up for some intensive surveillance of their activities.

He made good time and was thankful he had decided to wear dungarees instead of his usual shorts. His legs would have been slashed to shreds during the night-time march back through the dense bush.

The GPS was great. Apart from the odd diversion around impassable obstacles, he was able to maintain a fairly direct track back to his base. So, after the long gruelling trek he arrived at the hut at about 1300 hours.

Leo set about organising his kit for the return to his operational area. He exchanged his rucksack for the purpose-built combat backpack. It looked like a regular haversack. However, this one had pockets designed to hold all of his specialised equipment. The hollow metal frame held a couple of litres of emergency drinking water.

In addition to his normal hiking gear, he packed enough 24-hour ration packs to last for a week. These were much better than the old 'K' rations of yesteryear, but he still preferred to use the old terminology. He loaded the pocket PC with GPS attachment, and a small but powerful pair of binoculars. These had a built in range finder and digital camera. He packed his new, mini amplifying listening device. This had a built-in digital recorder. Then he holstered his trusty Beretta 9mm combat pistol and packed his Night Vision Goggles.

Because his normal communications were almost certainly compromised, he took his personal mini satphone. This was a secret number based on a foreign exchange and had a scrambler. It was virtually untraceable. Then he settled down to get some shut-eye, programming his metabolic clock to give himself twelve hours of sleep. He was well aware of the fact that sleep cannot be stored, but he needed to overcome the level of fatigue he knew he had accrued over the last twenty-four hours.

He thanked his lucky stars those two noisy patrollers had not bumped into him. With that thought running through his mind he drifted off into a deep, dreamridden sleep.

11

As he hid among the trees on the North Korean hillside, Leo had been dozing. He stirred as he heard the soft pad of feet coming his way. Slowly raising his head, he looked toward the approaching sound and saw a young woman, not more than fifty yards away. She was wearing typical Korean peasant dress. On her back she had an 'A' frame, which was loaded with large sticks. The frame was supported by a broad sash across her forehead. He had seen similar women near the base. They were firewood gatherers and spent many hours gleaning the sparse woods for meagre pickings. Judging by the load on this girl's back, she must have been out all day.

He remembered seeing two women like this, standing beside the runway at Kimpo as he took-off one day. As his aircraft approached them, they suddenly dropped their loads and ran across the runway right in front of the pair of Meteors. The aircraft missed them by only a couple of yards.

When he returned from the mission he asked around, to find out why they would have done such a dangerous thing. One of the longer-time squadron members told him this was not an uncommon occurrence in downtown Seoul. The people believed that if a car or truck just missed them, then it would put paid to the demons following them. Leo guessed that a couple of screaming jets would have to knock out at least a year's supply of demons.

It was now late afternoon and the girl, with head down, strained to haul her heavy load up the slope on her way home. She was heading straight for him, quietly humming some sort of tune by which she regulated her shuffling pace. Leo kept as still as a rock, frozen by the fear of getting caught, as much as by any meagre training he had ever received in the principles of camouflage. If she bumped into him or came too close, he would have to grab her and try to keep her silent.

Leo thought, 'I can't do that, I wouldn't want to harm her.' He was very aware that if he accosted a civilian in these *circumstances, they would certainly 'give him the chop' when he was eventually caught.*

'What'll I do?' he asked himself.

His dilemma was soon resolved. When the girl was just five yards from him, she saw him hiding under the bush. She let out a tremendous yell, dropped her load, turned and ran screaming down the hillside, back the way she had come. He heard answering cries coming from below and knew his goose was cooked. He ran in the opposite direction through the wood, stumbling in panic and catching his clothes on low branches. The cover afforded by the trees soon ended and he was faced with a long stretch of open ground. His heart sank as he saw two green uniforms running up the hill toward him with rifles at the ready.

He dived behind the last tree into a shallow depression and drew his Smith and Wesson .38 Special. They saw him and went to ground. Then they commenced firing. Christ! Why hadn't the CAP stayed around to protect him? Where was the cavalry? He knew if he started shooting they would surely kill him.

The rifle fire stopped and a heavily accented voice called out, 'Riff you hans an come out.'

He knew the game was up. He threw his revolver out onto the barren ground. Slowly he stood up, and with his hands raised, walked out into the open.

The two soldiers stood up and while one kept him covered, the other advanced toward him. He was young and dressed in what Leo assessed as Chinese Regular Army uniform. He walked around and behind Leo. Before he knew what had hit him, he was on his knees on the jagged rocky ground, suffering great pain and dizziness from the blow of the rifle butt that had come crashing down on his left shoulder. The soldier grabbed his left wrist, wrenching it behind his back with great force. He felt his arm strain as if to rip itself right out of the shoulder socket.

The pain was excruciating, making him feel instantly sick in the stomach. Before he could even consider reacting, a rope was tightly wrapped around the wrist. He could feel the rough texture burning deeply into his skin. Then his right hand was pulled back and securely tied to the left. He was then roughly frog-marched down the hill toward a truck that had stopped on the roadside three hundred yards away. The burning agony of his left shoulder felt as though his collarbone must be broken. The other soldier recovered Leo's revolver and poking it in his face started a tirade in Chinese. When they reached the vehicle, several other troops emerged.

He was shoved face-first against the tailgate, his legs were kicked apart and he was subjected to a thorough frisking. They took off his 'May West' life jacket and emptied the pockets of his flying suit. When they saw he was wearing jungle green fatigues under the lightweight overall, they untied his hands, removed the suit and handcuffed him.

During this procedure, one of the soldiers grabbed Leo's hand and tried to remove his treasured watch. Leo jerked his hand from the soldier's grasp and was immediately punched hard on the left shoulder. He held back a cry of pain as his arm went limp and the watch was wrenched from his wrist. A blindfold was firmly applied; then a coarse sack, that smelled like it had

53

previously covered a dozen sweaty heads, was pulled over his. His other pockets were cleared, and he was grabbed by several pairs of hands, lifted and thrown into the back of the truck.

He landed with a thump to his head and passed out.

12

Leo woke suddenly. It was five past two. Moonlight was streaming in through the shack window. He had been dreaming again. He rose, quickly showered in cold water and made himself a hearty breakfast to sustain him for the long day ahead. He felt rather vulnerable planning a solo exercise of this nature. One would normally arrange suitable backup, but he did not want to risk further compromise.

He secured the hut, checking the Rover was OK, loaded himself up with his 20 kg pack, and headed off to the north. He followed his original track until he arrived at the head of the last valley where he'd witnessed the strange exercise. It had been a long haul, retracing his previous trek, but he felt little tiredness. The adrenaline was obviously pumping and he realised he had not done anything this exciting for quite a while. Now he diverted to the left and followed the ridgeline until his GPS position placed him directly west of, and above the site.

It was now mid-afternoon. He found a suitable hide and set up his sound-monitoring device. This gear was a tripod mounted probe, which had an extremely narrow detection cone and a powerfully sensitive performance. It enabled the operator to accurately determine the direction of the monitored sounds over a considerable distance. The device had selectable frequency bands. These could be set for various ranges, from deep tones like heavy machinery, up to just beyond human hearing. Even individual insects species could be monitored. With this function, a trained operator could exclude unwanted sounds and thereby improve the quality and range of the reception.

He adjusted the frequency to the range of human voices and searched the area down in the re-entrant where the *exercise* had taken place. After about thirty minutes he picked up several snippets of conversation, but couldn't quite make out what was being said. The direction was slightly to the north of the target area and he assessed that it was farther away.

He decided to move his base to the north, along the ridge on the far side of the re-entrant. After scouting its length he discovered that it ended in a cliff. This was an ideal site from which to conduct surveillance. He set up again and very quickly picked up good quality vocals. He thought it odd that they didn't have someone on watch up here. They certainly were not very professional. Leo settled down to some careful monitoring.

With his binoculars he found a group of medium-sized corrugated iron huts, six in number. They were in a small clearing surrounded by dense but rather low trees. There was some ambulatory traffic, but no vehicular movement. He zoomed in and got a twenty-second video shot of the scene. Then he trained his listening device on each of the visible windows until he found one with voices. The device worked better when the window was closed, because it actually picked up the sounds inside the room by reading the vibrations of the glass. Larger panes would have been better, but he had no trouble listening to what was going on down there.

He immediately recognised the deep voice he had heard on his previous visit to the area. This apparent leader was giving a briefing on some sort of attack they were planning. He was talking about the firing mechanism of an infantry launched artillery rocket. The leader, whom the others called Smith, then went into much detail on the initial aiming of the weapon and the laser guidance. This could be performed by the launcher, or alternatively by a second, remote operator. He explained how this development allowed the gunner to *fire and forget*. He or she was then able to duck for cover after firing. This would prevent a well-equipped adversary from homing in on the source to return fire, knocking out the launcher and disrupting the aim, before the missile reached the target. He then advised the group they would, first thing next morning, proceed up to the cliff for some practice launchings.

He pointed out that this launch site was not as high as Black Mountain, but the practice target was about four kilometres from there. This was close to the correct range of the actual target.

Leo recorded most of this briefing. He realised the

launching site to which Smith was referring, was probably the spot he now occupied.

The session ended and Leo watched as seven men and two women, all dressed in camouflage fatigues, emerged from the hut and dispersed to three of the others. He scanned all the other buildings. From the small trail of smoke emanating from the metal flue of one, and the sounds of pots being banged about, he assessed that a meal was being prepared. The remaining buildings were probably dormitories. It appeared as though he had discovered some sort of terrorist training camp. He wondered if the reference to Black Mountain, referred to Canberra's well-known feature.

He scouted the immediate area and found an ideal spot on higher ground a few hundred metres to the left of his line of vision to the huts. He could camp here and be ready to observe tomorrow morning's activities. He opened a 'K' ration, munched on its contents and waited for darkness. His plan was to sneak down to the camp for a closer look using his Night Vision Goggles.

It had certainly been a busy day so far and looked as though tomorrow would liven up a little more. He was lucky that the weather was fine and the nights weren't too cold yet. Today had been sunny with virtually no breeze. For this he was thankful because it made his surveillance, especially the audio monitoring, much easier.

As dusk descended Leo secreted his kit, crept down the mountainside and positioned himself near the camp. He carefully surveyed the area looking for any telltale signs of watch keeping. There were no dogs, for which he was grateful. These people sounded dangerous, but they didn't have many clues on security. No lookouts posted, no canine presence; not even video or infrared monitoring.

All was quiet, so he donned his NVGs and crawled toward the HQ hut, which he had listened to earlier. He couldn't believe his luck; it was in darkness and wasn't locked. Quietly opening the door, he entered and using his infrared torch proceeded to check out the contents.

There was a large aluminium chart table with maps and papers spread over it. Ten director type, folding chairs were scattered around the table. Against the wall to his right, a small, steel side locker was pushed up against a battered wooden filing cabinet, which was locked. On the locker was a self-contained gas cooker and coffee pot. The floor was of bare composite sheeting, and the whole atmosphere was one of dusty disorder.

On the wall opposite the door, hanging between two draped Nazi flags, was a framed print of a portrait of Adolf Hitler.

Careful not to upset any order of things, Leo thoroughly scanned the papers to find out more about the plan to ambush some dignitary. He found nothing. It was too early, and there was too much activity around the camp to attempt opening the filing cabinet. He studied the maps on the table.

Some of the charts were of the local area, but the one of most interest was a tourist map of Canberra city. There were a few figures and sketches drawn on it and blocks of text. A ring had been drawn around the car park at the foot of the Telstra tower on top of Black Mountain. A bearing line had been drawn from this point, to another ring just off the western side of State Circle. It was marked as a 'Place of Interest', which was numbered 57. He flipped the map over to the directory decode. This was the location of the United States Embassy.

'My God!' he thought, 'They're going to bomb the embassy.'

Next to the circle was an annotation, '1 May 0230K'. Beside this was another note. 'Extraction by helicopter 0250 precisely'. Leo took out his monocular scope, the one with the digital camera attachment. In addition to being useful for general medium range observation, this equipment doubled beautifully as a photocopier. He made a couple of copies of the map with its annotations. Then he took a few shots of the room, including the wall where the picture of *der Fuehrer* was displayed.

He heard a hut door open, and several voices engaging in conversation. Gently opening the door a crack, he peered down the building line. A man and a woman were standing at the open door of a hut, talking to those inside. The male was telling some sort of anti-Semitic joke and they all laughed loudly. They were too close for comfort and the last thing he needed was to be sprung. He waited until they moved on and entered another hut. After ensuring that nothing was disturbed, he slipped out, quietly closing the door behind him.

Silently, he crept over to the bushes at the edge of the clearing and waited to see if there was going to be any more activity. Everyone was indoors now and appeared to be bedding down for the night. He had seen no sign of sentries, but decided not to push his luck by returning to the hut. So he made his way back up the mountain to his campsite. After checking all of his gear, he crawled into the sleeping bag.

It was 2300 hours now and as he lay there, quite wide-awake and gazing up at the stars, his thoughts drifted back to Michiko. He *had* gone back to Matsuyama the next month as promised.

13

Leo recalled spending the first two days of his R and R, shopping in Iwakuni. He bought a special gift for Michiko. It was a rather thin gold chain with a small gold disc mounted so that when flicked or blown on, it would spin. There was a series of small slots, straight and curved, cut through the disc. These made no sense, although they did bear some resemblance to Asian characters. When the disc was spun rapidly the light passing through the slots spelled out in English, 'I love you'. Even though he knew it was sentimentally corny, it appealed to Leo's sense of the romantic and his love of cryptic communication. Although small, the chain and the ring were 24 carat and took a fair percentage of his fortnight's pay. He also purchased small tokens for Kenje, Papa San Hanieda and his wife.

On the Saturday he caught the ferry across the Inland Sea to Shikoku. During the four-hour trip he found the scenery just as beautiful as it had appeared the first time. However, he could not pay much attention to anything except his passionate anticipation of the prospect of seeing Michiko again.

On arrival in Matsuyama he went to the hotel first and was greeted warmly by both proprietors. He remembered their surname, but wasn't sure how he should address them, so he called them Mr and Mrs Hanieda. This seemed to be acceptable. Mr Hanieda was wearing Leo's watch. He took it off and presented it to Leo. It was in perfect condition, and was showing the correct time.

Leo marvelled at how beautifully courteous these people were. There was no mention made of the money owed. He presented them with his gifts, which they were excited to receive. Then he handed over the two thousand Yen. They accepted the money and politely thanked him. All was sweet.

He had travelled in uniform, which was the norm when moving around in Japan, as well as in the war zone. In spite of this, he decided to change into civilian garb for what he planned as a weeklong visit. After shaving and bathing and generally sprucing himself, he walked quickly up the street to the Guramon. It was four o'clock. A group of uni students was present as usual, but neither Michiko nor Kenje was there.

However, he was pleased to see Sumiko, who hurried over to him. She gave him a big smile as she bowed and said, 'Herrow Reo, you rook for Michiko?'

Leo returned her bow, 'Yes I am, Sumiko. How are you?'

She said, 'Oh! I am good. I think she at home, not far, you come.'

Sumiko went back to her friends and apparently told them what was occurring. They all looked over at Leo. Some smiled and waved to him while others put their heads together and whispered. He followed Sumiko out of the club and up the street in the direction away from the hotel.

Apart from the odd comment about the weather, they walked up a long hill in virtual silence. Although there wasn't much vehicular traffic, there were many pedestrians passing in either direction. Most seemed to hurry by with non-expressive faces, intent on going about their business. Sumiko did not ask about Jack, which was OK by Leo. He did not want to have to explain why he hadn't returned. Jack had in fact hitched a ride on a RAF *Hastings* transport plane to Hong Kong for his R and R. Jack had never mentioned the night at the club with Yoko, and Leo assumed he was not interested in seeing her again.

After walking about half a mile they turned into an attractive tree-lined street of elegant, expensive looking houses. Sumiko stopped outside the third one on the left and bade him wait at the outer entrance while she went in to tell Michiko. A few minutes later, Michiko appeared at an inner covered gate and came running down the path to him, her long black silken hair flowing out behind her. She rushed straight into his outstretched arms.

Her upbringing prevented her from kissing in public, so he had to be content with a hug and the feel of her body pressed against his.

'I'm so happy that you came back, I thought you may not,' Michiko whispered.

'Only death would have kept me away,' he replied gently.

Her body shuddered. 'Please do not talk like that, it is bad luck.'

Leo realised he must have broken some sort of taboo so said nothing more. She released herself from his embrace, took his hand and turned to retrace her steps through the beautiful garden toward the house.

The sides of the area were lined with small maple trees that had dark red and black leaves. A meticulously tended lawn spread on either side of the central, curving gravel path, which was edged with a myriad of small brightly coloured flowers. These were giving off a pleasantly, sweet aroma. The path led to the inner gate from which Michiko had appeared. This was set in the centre of a high white stucco wall that had a sort of Spanish look about it. The wall was capped with dark red semi-cylindrical tiles.

He could see Sumiko waiting in the gateway with an older couple. He assumed they were Michiko's parents.

As they approached, Mr Tsushima, who was wearing casual Western clothes, came down the steps.

He stopped and bowed, offered his hand and said, 'Welcome to our house Mr Leo.' Leo returned the bow and shook the hand of this smiling gentleman.

'Thank you sir,' he replied. They walked up to the veranda where Mrs Tsushima, wearing traditional Japanese kimono, obi and wooden sandals, bowed and welcomed him in her own tongue.

Then she said, 'Please come in.'

Leo followed Mrs Tsushima through the large sliding doorway into what appeared to him to be an inner garden. He had never seen such a beautiful entrance to a dwelling. There was an indoor pond to the left of a curving walkway. The path divided, one arm turned left and connected with a narrow, arched bridge over the carp-filled pond. The other bordered a stone garden with raked patterns of stark white pebble chips interspersed with black, interestingly shaped stones and boulders. She took the right fork leading to the narrow front step-up, into the house. Here they all removed their shoes, put on the slippers provided, and made their way into a large anteroom.

As they entered, two servants, an older man with a sparse white beard and a young woman, were standing to one side. As the party approached, the servants bowed. This action was not returned but was acknowledged with a polite nod from Madam Tsushima. They went through into a comfortably furnished sitting room.

At this point Sumiko said something about, '…Kenje,' bowed and took her leave. Then they all sat down on the comfortable lounges. Mrs Tsushima clapped her hands twice, summoning a third servant who entered from a side door and served tea in small handle-less cups.

Leo was starting to relax now; it had all been a bit sudden and unexpected. He hadn't anticipated such grandeur. Mr Tsushima quizzed him about Australia and told him he had met a few Australians in Manila.

After some general small talk, he asked Leo, 'What do you plan to do while you are here?'

Leo was a little embarrassed by this and a little confused. How could he explain to this rather formal family that he thought he had fallen in love with their daughter?

He told Mr Tsushima, 'I hope to spend a week visiting with my new friends here in Matsuyama.'

Leo drew a deep breath then added, 'With your permission sir, I would like to spend some time with Michiko.'

Mr Tsushima thanked Leo for his candour then, after a moment's reflection, said, 'You have my permission go out with my daughter.' He continued. 'However, that permission is strictly on the understanding that you both would need to be chaperoned by my nephew, Kenje, or Sumiko.' He paused, then added, 'And you must not keep her out too late, she is completing a very important part of her studies at this time and even though she is having a short break from lectures, she still has a few projects to complete.'

Leo thanked Mr Tsushima for his trust, and told him he would treat Michiko with the utmost respect and kindness.

Everyone seemed happy with these arrangements.

Michiko sat quietly throughout this exchange but Leo sensed that, by the way she smiled at him; she was certainly pleased with the way he had spoken out openly of his intentions.

Sumiko arrived back accompanied by Kenje, who hurried over to Leo and greeted him with a double handshake, saying, 'How are you my friend. It good to see you again, how is your pal Jack?'

'I'm just fine Kenje and really pleased to see you again. Jack is also well. He decided to go to Hong Kong for his R and R, so he probably won't come here again. He certainly enjoyed our last visit though and asked me to pass on his regards.'

Kenje looked as though he didn't quite understand Leo's last remark, so Michiko explained in Japanese. Everyone smiled and nodded. They all chatted for a while and then Kenje suggested the four of them should go to the nightclub that evening. Michiko and Sumiko agreed happily, and Leo promised to be of better behaviour this time. Kenje and Sumiko laughed. Michiko's reaction was a modest smile. Kenje explained to his uncle how the sake skol kings had trapped Leo. Mr Tsushima smiled and explained to his wife what had eventuated.

'I suppose there was a lesson in that for you?' Mr Tsushima put to Leo.

'Yes sir, there most certainly was. Nothing like that will ever occur again,'

After tea had been taken and some general conversation about world events, Leo bade them all farewell, and said he looked forward to meeting them at the club at seven.

The four of them had a great time at the Guramon that night. Leo gained the impression that the romance between Sumiko and Kenje had blossomed. They spent most of the evening alone, dancing and strolling in the garden. This allowed Leo and Michiko to do much of the same. They talked incessantly and were finding many areas of mutual likes and feelings. Michiko asked Leo if he would like to accompany her to church the next morning, to which Leo replied that he had never been to a Shinto temple before, and would find the experience very interesting. Michiko laughed.

'No, no, I meant *church*. My family is Christian, are you?'

'Yes,' replied Leo. 'I'm a Methodist.'

'Oh!' exclaimed Michiko. 'I don't know anything about Methodists. My family was converted to Catholicism when we were in the Philippines. Are you allowed to go to a Catholic church?'

'We're not supposed to, but we can,' Leo responded.

'I don't think you are allowed to take a non-Catholic into your church though, are you?'

'No, but our local priest takes an open approach. He probably believes he may get some convertees. I have taken quite a few of my Shinto friends along. Have you ever been to mass?'

'No, I never have,' said Leo.

'Well, please come, I have never taken a Protestant before.'

'OK.'

'I must warn you. When we enter, I will go to the font, wet my fingers, cross myself and genuflect.'

'What's that?'

'You know, the quick little kneeling bow.' Then she added. 'I mention this because once when I did that, my following friend tripped right over me.'

'Oh! I'll be careful,' promised Leo.

As they all walked back toward Michiko's house, she explained to Kenje their plans for the morning. Kenje told him he also was Catholic. Sumiko and he were engaged to be married. She was going through the Stations of the Cross as part of her conversion process. They all agreed to meet Leo outside the Church, which was just a few short blocks past the Tsushima residence, at ten thirty the next morning.

When they reached Michiko's place, Kenje and Sumiko said goodnight and continued up the street. Michiko turned to Leo.

'Thank you for a marvellous evening. This has been the most enjoyable night of my life.'

Leo was stunned by this frank admission. He could hardly believe what he was hearing from this most gorgeous girl.

As they moved back into the cover of the overhanging wisteria, he said, 'Oh! Thank you. It has been simply wonderful.'

Leo was at a loss for words, but thought this might be a good time to give her the gift. He took the unwrapped present from his pocket, undid the clasp and gently placed the chain around her neck.

As he leaned forward to reconnect it, she gave a little squeal of delight. Now her face was upturned and her eyes closed. He moved his hands from behind her neck and cupped her beautiful cheeks with them. Then he slowly bent down and gently kissed her on the lips. It became a long, lingering, delicate connection. She had placed her hands around his waist and now drew herself into close contact with him. He felt her body tremble and he experienced a tingling sensation right down his spine. Their lips parted.

Leo moved back slightly and took her hands in his. She opened her eyes, smiled, squeezed his hands, then turned and ran up the path to the house. Leo thought he may have died and gone to heaven. He stood there alone for a few minutes, the heady aroma of the wisteria adding to his feelings of sheer bliss. Then he strolled back to the hotel in a pleasant daze. As he crawled under the covers on the futon, he remembered the last time he had slept in this place. No cigarettes tonight! He soon drifted off to sleep to have pleasant dreams about his newfound love until daybreak.

The next morning Leo awoke early, as was his habit, bathed, shaved and dressed. After a tasty breakfast, prepared by Mama San Hanieda, he decided he couldn't hang around the hotel for two or more hours, or he'd go mad with the anticipation of seeing his darling again. So he walked the length and breadth of the central town district, not really taking in much of what he saw or heard. It did fill in the time though, and he arrived at the church about a quarter past ten.

'It's not very large,' Leo thought. 'More like a chapel.'

As worshippers arrived, they mostly looked askance at him, probably wondering what this young foreigner was doing in their midst. Then he saw Michiko coming up the street, alone. His heart skipped a beat at the sight of her. She was dressed in traditional Kimono. He had expected her parents to be with her, and he didn't want to have to bother making polite, small talk with them. He really wanted to be alone with her, and was glad it would be so, at least until Kenje and Sumiko turned up.

Michiko smiled warmly as she approached him. She looked slightly abashed and Leo thought her cheeks might be showing the slightest hint of a blush. He felt flushed and almost uncomfortable, sure that his Scots complexion, tanned as it was, had also reddened.

She wished him a simple, 'Good morning,' making no attempt to take his hand or touch him in any way. He did realise though, by the look she gave him and the indescribable aura about her, that she was very pleased to see him. Leo understood why the lack of contact was necessary. They *were* in the public domain, and outside the church as well. He did not try to hold her hand, but smiled back at her with equal enthusiasm.

He simply replied, 'Good morning, you look beautiful in that dress.'

'Thank you; I love the necklace – and I saw its message,' she whispered.

She added no other comment, so Leo was left a little up in the air as to whether she accepted, rejected, or indeed, reciprocated the feeling. He was just working up the courage to ask her how she felt about the message, when Kenje and Sumiko arrived.

The Mass was about to start, so after a brief 'Good morning' all round, they went in. Michiko led the way with Leo following as briefed, careful not to trip over her at the font. What she had not told him though, was that when she reached her pew, she would genuflect again. So, momentarily distracted by the surroundings, over the top of her kneeling body, went Leo. Only Kenje's quick grab of Leo's shirt stopped him from going all the way and making a complete fool of himself. Sumiko let out a little giggle. Most of the twenty or so worshippers looked around, with varying levels of disapproval showing on their usually inscrutable faces.

After the service, which to Leo's surprise, was conducted in Latin, they all went to Kenje's place for the midday meal. Kenje's parents were just as pleasant and obliging as Michiko's. Leo was feeling on top of the world, and it appeared to him that all the folks he met genuinely accepted him. Michiko and he frequently held hands, walking and sitting, and this seemed to be naturally received by friends and family alike.

14

Over the next two days, Michiko, Leo and their chaperone friends had a wonderful time. As well as becoming closer to Michiko, Leo was establishing a sound friendship with Kenje and Sumiko. He noticed Kenje always called her Sumi and when he asked if that was a familiar term, they told him people sometimes shortened family names amongst friends and loved ones. The *ko* on the end of a girl's name meant *daughter of*. Some names, like Michiko, were not usually abbreviated in this manner. It largely depended on the fashion of the day.
Sumiko said to Leo, 'I think you are now a good friend to call me Sumi.'

Everyone thought this was a very good idea; so from then on Leo always called her Sumi. He told them Westerners often abbreviated names, but in a less formal manner. He explained how his given name was actually Leonard, but all his friends and family, except for his mother, always called him Leo. His three friends all laughed and said Japanese mothers were like that too.

They visited some of the local sites. These included an ancient Buddhist temple and several Shinto sites. The beauty of the architecture and the polite friendliness of the people fascinated Leo.

On his fourth day there, they took the train to the west along the shoreline of the Inland Sea. At the end of the line was Yawatahama, a delightful coastal town with clean white sand beaches and a pine tree lined foreshore. Out across the water to the west he could see on the horizon, the rugged mountains of Kyushu, the fourth main Island of Japan.

They had come prepared for a swim, Leo having bought some swimming togs and a towel in Matsuyama. After frolicking in the clear, warm water for an hour they sunned themselves for a while. Leo wondered why Anglos described Japanese as *yellow*; they all had much paler, pinker skin than he. In fact, Michiko's skin looked more like ivory.

While they lay next to each other in a rather secluded spot at the back of the beach, Leo said to Michiko, 'You have the most beautiful skin.' He softly stroked her arm as he spoke. She rolled on her side, facing him. As he sat up, she gently ran her hand over his shoulder.

'You have a lovely tan.'

Leo felt an electric tingle all the way down his body. He continued to stroke her arm from wrist to shoulder. Her whole body quivered as she looked around to see if the others were taking any notice of them. Sumi and Kenje were completely engrossed in each other. So as she turned her head back, she looked up into his eyes, fingering the gold necklace.

Speaking softly, she said, 'I love you too.'

Then Leo broke the rules by bending down and lightly kissing her on the lips. She responded passionately for a moment. Then they separated and resumed more appropriate positions before Kenje could spot them.

Leo realised she was feeling guilty about her obvious desire for a more intimate affair. He too, felt pangs of guilt at the thoughts running around in his brain. He fully intended to keep his vow to respect Michiko and his promise to her father. But it was not going to be easy.

As noon approached, they dressed and took lunch at a small sushi bar on the waterfront. Leo had not experienced some of the dishes served. The seaweed and rice rolls and the finely shaved raw salmon were most enjoyable. He wasn't so sure about the squid in black sauce, which didn't taste like soy. He later found out it was made from the squid's ink. Anyway, after a most pleasant repast during which his three new friends all complimented Leo on his mastery of the chopsticks, they made their way back to the railway station.

The sky was becoming overcast and light spots of rain began to fall. During the train ride Leo explained that he was running low on Yen, and his only other money was made up of military vouchers, which he could not use here.

He said, 'Tomorrow, I'll take the morning ferry back to Iwakuni. I will change some money, pick up some fresh clothes and come back the following morning.'

Michiko looked a little downhearted for the rest of the journey. She was obviously getting to love Leo's company by now, and did not want anything to intrude into the relationship at this stage. He knew it would be pointless suggesting that she accompany him. Her parents would never allow her to go. He assured her he would only be gone for the one day.

It was about three o'clock when they arrived in Matsuyama and by now it was showering intermittently. They hurried down the street to Leo's hotel and when they arrived, Michiko said she would like to go in and say hello to the Haniedas. Kenje was not too keen to do so, so he told them Sumi and he would go back to his place and they could all meet at the club later. Leo was surprised that Kenje was allowing them to be alone, but he did not want to question his action.

When Leo and Michiko entered the hotel she said she could see the proprietors later and asked if she could go up to his room and talk. Leo hesitated and suggested it may not be a good idea, especially as he was on his honour to treat her with respect. She said it would be all right, that *nothing* would happen. They climbed the stairs to his room.

Sitting in the two chairs provided, they continued their conversation. Their clothes were quite wet by now and clung to their bodies. Leo stood up, took off his shirt and hung it on the back of his chair. Michiko said she was uncomfortable as well and asked if she could wear his *happy coat* and let her dress dry a little. The thought of this lovely creature half-naked in his bedroom stirred up a relatively high level of excitement in his young breast. He gave her the dressing gown and his *gettahs* and turned his back while she swapped garments.

He thought it was really no big deal. After all they had all been much less dressed on the beach. When he turned back and saw her standing there in the loose coat, her long, shining hair flowing over her shoulders and the inviting smile playing on her lips, his heart skipped a beat. Leo was now torn between his promise to her father plus his own mother's advice about waiting for the right girl, and his more basic instincts. He could see she was of the same mind. They both inwardly realised they were each fervently drawn to the other. Maybe she was the *right* girl. He moved toward her and slowly took her in his arms.

Her eyes closed and their mouths met in a soft but passionate kiss as they held each other very closely. Michiko moved slightly away from him, looking down at the wet patches she felt coming through the dressing gown.

'Your trousers are very wet,' she said.

Blushing slightly, he turned and undid his belt, removed his pants and hung them on the hook on the back of the door. When he turned again, standing there in his boxer shorts, he watched as she moved to a spot next to the futon. She let the dressing gown slowly slip to the floor revealing all of her except that covered by her loose old-fashioned panties. He could not take his eyes off her darkly nippled, beautifully shaped, breasts. He remembered one of his favourite Shakespearean lines from high school.

… Like ivory globes circled with blue, a pair of maiden worlds unconquered.

He had always found that poem, *Lucrece*, erotically exciting. But those feelings were made of boyish fantasy. This was real, and very adult. Yet it almost seemed like a dream, like some strange place he had never visited before.

He moved back to her, took her in his arms and they kissed again, her hardened nipples pressing against his chest. The stirring in his loins was almost painful and he was embarrassed by the thought that she would feel his increasing tumescence. Michiko moved back a little. She had a strange look on her face. It was somewhere between serious and quizzical? She took his hands in hers and they both lowered to a kneeling position, facing each other on the futon.

'Leo,' she said, 'I am frightened, I have never been with a man, and I have vowed to wait until I marry.'

Her whole body was trembling now. She added in an almost inaudible whisper, 'But I want you so very much.'

'Sweet darling,' Leo said, 'I love you so much and I

respect your vow. I too am a virgin. Everything will be fine.'

'Oh Leo, I love you truly and I am - so - happy. Can we lie down for a little while?'

Slowly they sank onto the futon and lay facing each other in a tight embrace. Leo was now in full erection. He reached down and moved his penis into the inviting space between her closed, slender thighs. They were both now in an extreme state of sensual excitation. Only the thin material of their undergarments separated them from a more electric contact.

As Leo moved his body ever more tightly against hers, his member, acting as if it had a mind of its own, navigated a path between the folds of cloth until it found direct contact with her hot, moist vulva. She gasped as his glans slid slowly past her swollen labia without entering her. He could feel her erect clitoris rubbing against the top of his sword of love. As he moved slowly forward then back, she moved in contra.

His mind was flying somewhere above the silver clouds. His vision was blurred with a hundred rainbows and his breathing was shallow and rapid as if in the throes of hypoxia.

Michiko was now quietly moaning as she stroked his head and the small of his back. Her vocalizing became deeper. They were moving more quickly now. She gently bit his ear. Then, as if by some magical signal, he had his most powerful orgasm ever; and Michiko had her first.

They lay there for a few moments, his penis gently

rubbing the entrance to her unexplored, vestal sheath. Then, as his erection subsided, he rolled her gently onto her back, slid down and softly kissed her breasts, playing his tongue over her nipples and around the aureoles. She sighed and gave a little giggle. He laid his head between her breasts and they both drifted off into an après love slumber, tightly clasping each other.

When they awoke it was after five thirty. They were both experiencing mixed emotions of joy and guilt and Michiko was very quiet. They *cleaned up* as best they could without leaving the room, dressed, and crept furtively downstairs. Michiko did not now want to see the Haniedas. They went out into the street without meeting anyone. The rain had ceased and Leo walked her back to her house, arranging to call by at seven thirty to escort her to the club.

That night the four of them had another great time at the Guramon, chatting, laughing and dancing. Leo had introduced them to Jitter Bugging and they were all becoming quite adept. As the evening came to a close, Michiko became a little pensive. She said she would like to come on the trolley with him the next morning and see him off on the ferry. Kenje said he thought that would be OK with her parents. He would not be able to chaperone them as he had another engagement in the morning. However, Sumi was free and she agreed to accompany Michiko to see Leo off.

They all walked back to Michiko's house where Kenje and Sumi said good-night and left the two of them to say theirs. Once they were alone, Michiko told him this had been the most wonderful day of her life, but she felt guilty about what had happened at the hotel. She would have to tell the priest at her next confession. Leo said he was sorry if he had done wrong, but felt that they had nothing to be ashamed of. It all seemed perfectly natural to him, and it was a true expression of their love for each other. He said he was certain they had not sinned.

'Sin might be enjoyable, but it could not be so beautiful.'

'That sounds very wise for one as young as you.' She continued, 'I will think about it before confessing. Perhaps confessing something so beautiful would change it into a sin.'

They kissed goodnight and arranged for the girls to come to his hotel at eight thirty in the morning to accompany him to the ferry.

The next morning Leo was waiting in the lobby, all ready to go when they arrived. This was the first time Michiko had seen him in uniform, and she told him she was very impressed and how handsome he looked. She admired his silver wings and touched the sergeant's stripes on his sleeve. They walked to the trolley car terminal and trundled off to the ferry pier. Michiko was in very low spirits, and when Leo asked her what was wrong, she started to cry and said, 'You are not coming back, Leo.'

Leo responded in shocked surprise, 'Of course I am sweet lady. You know I have promised to. I just have to change some money back at the base.'

'Maybe they won't let you come back,' she said.

Leo could not figure out what had caused this sudden despondency; perhaps she thought he did not now respect her after yesterday's experience.

'Surely not,' he thought. They had both been so happy when they parted last night. Sumi was a little surprised at Michiko's manner and tried to console her.

They arrived at the ferry and found that it was just about to leave, so he had to hurriedly buy his ticket and say goodbye. He held her close and kissed her wet cheek. She looked so sad. He went up onto the stern deck and waved as the boat pulled away from the dock.

She cried out, 'Please come back?'

He called back, 'I will, I will.'

Now she really started to cry as she waved forlornly. Sumi had her arm around Michiko's shoulder and trying to keep a smile on her lips, also waved as the ferry got underway. He watched and waved back until he could no longer make them out. Then he found a seat and sadly made the four-hour return journey to Iwakuni.

When he checked in through the guard gate on arrival at the Base, the USN SP said, 'Sergeant Kirkland, there's an urgent message here for you; you are to report immediately to the Orderly Officer.'

'Thanks!' said Leo. He went straight to the OO's office.

He was greeted with, 'Where have you been Sergeant? Your squadron operations office has had an APB out on you for the last two days.'

'I'm on R and R sir,' replied Leo. 'I wasn't instructed that I had to report in.'

No, that's correct, you weren't,' said the OO. 'But I have some bad news. Two of your guys collided over the target a couple of days ago and both of them went in. Your R and R is cancelled and you are required to return to Kimpo via the earliest available means.'

Leo's heart sank. He wondered which two colleagues he had lost. Also, he could not comprehend how Michiko had known he would not be returning the next day as he had promised.

There was no way to get a message to her. She had no phone; he didn't know how to use the Japanese telegram system; and there were no military means available. He had to take the early courier service back to Kimpo the next morning. He was devastated.

He wrote from Korea to her house address but received no reply. He then wrote to her, care of the Guramon, with the same result. Then he was shot down. When he was repatriated, almost nine months later, he was not permitted to go off base and was whisked off, straight back to Australia.

Yes, as it turned out, this was the sad ending to the most exciting episode in his life. But it was probably best for all in the long run. He was far too young, and so was she. On his meagre air force pay, he would not be able to keep her in the manner to which she was accustomed. Inter-racial marriages were frowned upon. Even though Michiko was Christian, there was still the fact that she was Catholic and he was Protestant. It was not destined to be.

However, he would never forget the sight of her standing on the pier, crying her heart out and waving – and he would never understand how she knew he would not return, or why she never answered his letters.

Leo felt sad and alone as he curled up in his sleeping bag. He set his mental alarm for five o'clock and was soon sound asleep.

The dream returned.

15

As he came to Leo realised he had been propped up between two soldiers on the bench seat in the back of the truck. The one on his left was jabbing at him, tugging at his RAAF shoulder insignia and jeering in a high-pitched voice, 'Raff, raff, riffraff.'

They were travelling over an extremely rough road now and every bump jarred his very being. One of his captors pulled the sack off his head and forced a bottle against his lips. He tilted his head back and swallowed what tasted like brackish water.

Leo recalled that during his escape and evasion training, he had been taught that the best time to escape was immediately after being captured.

He quickly assessed his situation. His collarbone was extremely painful and he had a terrible headache. He forced himself to disregard these woes and tried to be objective. With his head tilted back he could see momentarily beneath the blindfold. He could tell from the sun's position, out to the right; that they were heading in a northerly direction. This meant they were travelling deeper into enemy territory. His hands were still cuffed behind his back and there were two or three more troops sitting opposite him. There was no chance of making a break for it under the present circumstances. He finished drinking and the sack was dragged back over his head and tied under his chin. The journey seemed interminable.

After what he estimated to be about three more hours since he regained consciousness, the truck stopped, the tailgate dropped and he was pushed out onto rocky ground. They bundled him down a rough track and through a door, marched him a few paces and left him standing. After several minutes the sack was pulled from his head and the blindfold removed. He was positioned in front of a wooden table, behind which sat two Chinese officers. At one end of the table was a young, rather plain-looking woman with a pencil and notepad and opposite her was an older Korean-looking man in white civilian clothes. He thought of the figures running from the target area.

'So! What have we here?' said the more senior officer in well-structured English.

'A young Australian pilot who has just murdered some innocent citizens of The Democratic People's Republic of Korea. I know from your identification tags that your name is Kirkland

L G; your service number is A97353, your blood type is A2 and that you purport to be a Methodist. What is your rank?'

Leo hesitated, his rank was Sergeant Pilot, but he quickly remembered being briefed that if a non-commissioned pilot went down behind enemy lines, he would be commissioned immediately. This was in the belief that officers would not be subjected to harsh treatment.

'Pilot Officer,' he replied.

'You are to address me as 'Sir'. That's the same as Second Lieutenant isn't it?'

'Yes, Sir,' Leo replied.

'Well, I see no rank insignia.'

Before Leo could respond the officer said sneeringly, 'I can see by the 'A' in your number, which I believe stands for 'Airman', and the un-faded mark on your sleeve where your stripes have been removed that this must have been a recent promotion, or else you are lying.'

'Which is it?' he snapped.

'We were told by the CO that if we were shot down, we would be commissioned the same day sir.'

'How convenient,' the officer contemptuously rejoined. 'You're not good enough to be an officer until you become of no further use to your air force. If you think this will bring you special treatment, you are wrong. We treat everybody equally in The Democratic People's Republic.'

He then gave an order to the guards who again blind-folded him, placed the sack over his head and frog marched him out of the room.

He was taken across open ground, then down what felt

and sounded like stone steps. He counted fourteen. He was pushed roughly through an opening, and a heavy sounding steel door was slammed behind him. A key turned in the lock and all became silent. Leo gingerly felt his way around what was a very small stone room. He was still handcuffed and blindfolded with the sack over his head. He couldn't even tell if there was any light, so it was quite difficult to ascertain just what his situation was.

The place was only four paces square and he could find no bed or other furniture. He sat down on the floor. Because he was rather lithe and athletic, he was able to work his wrists down to his heels and get his hands in front of him. This was accomplished with great difficulty. Then he worked the sack and blindfold off. There were no windows, except for a small barred opening near the ceiling opposite the door. Meagre twilight filtered through it. The dirty little hole was completely empty.

He needed a 'pee' badly so he had to do it in the corner of the already foul-smelling cell. Then he sat down, huddled in a corner and drifted off into a fatigued, tormented sleep.

16

Leo woke to the sound of a Kookaburra laughing and saw it was almost five o'clock. He climbed out of his sleeping bag into the chilly April air. He was still fully clothed, except for his boots, which he quickly put on. He packed up his sleeping bag, broke out another 'K' ration and ate.

After securing as much of his gear as he could, he

set up his listening device and scanned the area around the camp. There were the usual early morning sounds, voices, running water, rattling of pans, doors opening and closing. Targeting the HQ hut, he could hear the deep-voiced leader, Smith, briefing his group.

'Well!' he thought, 'They don't appear too professional, but they can certainly get off to an early start.'

The general gist of his instructions was that they would be firing three rockets with dummy warheads at a rock feature on an outcrop northeast of the camp. He reconfirmed that they would launch the practice attack from the cliff to the west. Leo scanned the proposed target area with his range-finding binoculars. He could make out what appeared to be the object described in the briefing. It was a large exposed rock on a low cliff-face down the valley, about four thousand metres from his position. The cliff, on which he now stood, *must* be the launch site.

All rose and left the hut. With Smith, were the same crew of nine he'd seen earlier. However, three others had joined the group this morning. They all moved to the hut from where the kitchen noises emanated. Obviously, this was their mess.

After about half an hour, they came out, laughing and jostling each other. They all disbursed to separate huts and after about another fifteen minutes, emerged and assembled in front of a smaller building at the end of the row. One of them went around the end of the building and returned driving a large 4WD pickup. The group then carried four long boxes and some smaller packages from the hut and loaded them into the vehicle. Then all climbed on board and the truck drove off down a track leading to the south, toward the ridgeline from which he had conducted his first surveillance. Leo wondered if he might have chosen the wrong place to view their activities. He decided to wait it out and continued to track the vehicle with his sound device as they were now out of sight.

After another half hour, the sound of the vehicle, in low gear, began to increase in volume. He caught an odd glimpse of it from time to time as it crawled in a westerly direction up the ridge to his south. He tracked it aurally now as it continued to the west, then appeared to turn north and slowly come closer. After another twenty minutes it came into sight, moving toward the cliff edge. This *was* the spot he had suspected they would use as a launching site. He didn't have a particularly clear view of the activities, but with the odd sighting through the trees and the magic listening device, he could assess exactly what they were doing. Smith was describing how to set up the rocket in its launch tube and how to balance it on the right shoulder with the assistance of a monopod. The second person acted as a steadying agent for the launcher, something like a camera crew *grip*.

The third person, the apparent controller and principle aimer, wore a shoulder-mounted aiming device. This was apparently gyro-stabilised. It had two forward-extending handles that enabled the wearer to maintain an accurate aim. Once the missile was launched, all he had to do was visually place the aiming circle or cross-hairs near it, click to capture, then shift the aim to, and hold it on, the target. The weapon then automatically *flew down the wire*, which was in fact a laser beam directed from the aiming device, until it hit the point of aim. It would work equally well with a moving target.

This was certainly much more up-to-date weaponry than that used during his initial encounter with them. They had obviously completed a few dry-run sessions ex-situ and were eager to let fly.

As the squad proceeded to set up the first launch, Leo crept closer until, with the assistance of his binoculars, he had a good view of the proceedings. They had already been briefed on the weapon having a dummy warhead, simulating the weapon's high explosive one. Leo was a little confused as to just what the weapon was. He was familiar with TOW and *Javelin* anti-tank weapons. He had read as well, about later developments. For example, the Lockheed *Predator*, but this one was different. It looked more like a Hughes *Stinger* SAM, not really suitable against a ground target. They fired the first missile and it travelled true to the rocky target. Everyone cheered as the rocket found its mark, the impact knocking a few chunks of rock off the outcrop and shattering the dummy warhead. The second and third teams had their turns with similar results.

Smith then ordered the standby team to prepare the *spare* weapon. They were briefed to perform one extra action in the launching procedure. That was, to flip the cover off the safety switch and throw it to the ARM position before firing. This was to be a live shot. They were all excited at the prospect of seeing the real thing. The weapon was launched with its warhead armed. When it hit the target, even Leo was awed by the power of the fiery explosion, which shattered the huge rock into a thousand pieces.

After all the congratulatory yells and backslapping were over, Smith ordered them to pack-up and they moved back to their camp. Leo had seen enough. These madmen were really going to do it! They were going to blow-up the United States Embassy in Canberra.

He debated whether or not to take unilateral action to stymie their plans. No – he was outnumbered and there were too many variables to contend with. He *would* need backup. He was sorely tempted to contact the office by phone, but because of the earlier glitch, this was problematic. Maybe this group was responsible for the intrusion into the agency's communications. Given their observed expertise so far, he doubted this would be the case, but he couldn't take the risk. He would hurry back to the hut and drive in to make his report. It was over two weeks to the planned attack date, so one more day shouldn't matter. He packed his gear and set off for his shack. It was now well after noon, so it meant another trek through the night.

Leo pushed himself through the afternoon as hard as he could. He had momentarily thought to shed some of his gear in the interests of speed, but quickly decided against this. It went against all the tenets of his training. One can never be sure what may be needed later; and discarded equipment may fall into the wrong hands.

By about 2300 hours Leo was completely exhausted. He knew that if he didn't get some sleep he wouldn't be capable of safely driving back to HQ to turn in his report. There were only about four kilometres of uphill slogging to go; but he *must* sleep. He laid out his sleeping bag, took off his boots, climbed in and fell rapidly into a deep sleep.

17

Leo woke with a start. Faint light was coming in through the barred opening. He could hear marching feet and Chinese commands outside. It sounded like a squad drilling. He looked around the room and noticed part of the stone wall next to his head was crumbling. There was a small hole that seemed to go through to the next cell. Leo heard a faint groan.

He called softly, 'Who's there?'

A British-sounding voice said, 'Who are you?

'My name is Kirkland and I'm an Australian pilot.' Leo responded.

'A piece of advice Kirkland, don't tell anyone anything about yourself. You can't tell who they are or whose side they're on. And no matter what the Chinese offer you, or threaten you with, make it strictly name, rank and serial number.'

He continued, 'There is a new technique in interrogation being used here; it's like they're trying to twist your brain. I will tell you that I have been bucking their system by not co-operating. They have broken both of my thumbs and beaten me badly.'

'So why do you persist?' Leo asked.

After a long pause his fellow prisoner answered.

'Because, before they put me here in solitary, I saw the effect of this treatment on some of our American brethren. To put a name to it, they appear to have had their brains washed. They have come over to the Communist's way of thinking and some of them sound like traitors.

Leo heard the outside door to the passage open.

'Shush,' said his neighbour. 'They're coming for one of us.'

Leo hurriedly pulled the still tied blindfold on, replaced the sack and just managed to work his feet forward over the handcuffs before the door opened. His body ached all over and he was shivering with cold and fear.

'Get up! Get up!' yelled a high-pitched, jarring voice. Leo recognised his tormentor from the truck journey. He tried to force his buttocks between his arms. It didn't work. He had to roll on his side to accomplish the feat.

As he strained to get his cuffed hands up his back, his captor kicked him viciously in the rear and yelled, 'Have you been trying to escape riffraff? You are in big trouble.'

The kick and the extra effort on Leo's part, forced his cuffed hands over his rump and up his back. He gingerly climbed to his feet. He was led outside with a noose around his neck, and forced to jog along a rough gravel path. With the guard savagely tugging on the rope, he stumbled and fell several times. Each time he fell they pulled hard on the rope until he regained his feet. The pain and humiliation were almost overwhelming. After about ten minutes of this brutal treatment, he was forced through another door.

The sack and blindfold were pulled from him and he found himself in another office, before another table manned by another set of military and civilian personnel. This lot looked even more vicious than his first interrogators. However, he recognised the leader as the same sneering Chinese officer who had conducted his first questioning.

'Mister Kirkland, we meet again. Let me introduce myself, I am Captain Wang of The Army of the Democratic People's Republic of China.' He put his fists on the table, sat up straight-backed and continued in a sneering tone.

'I will explain some of the rules and polices which we, in PW Camp Number One, apply to the foreign criminal invaders of the UN.'

His voice changed to a high pitched staccato.

'Rule Number One - Prisoners must co-operate at all times. Rule Number Two - Any attempt to escape will be met by death to the perpetrators. Rule Number Three - All prisoners must learn the ten principles and repeat them when ordered to do so.'

He continued in an almost patronising fashion. 'Let me assure you; we understand why one as young as you can not be expected to know much about the realities of life, or the forces which come together to mould a society such as ours. Therefore, let me explain our policy of the 'lenient treatment'. If you co-operate with us you will be given extra privileges. If you do not, your stay here will be most uncomfortable.'

'Do you understand?'

'Yes, sir,' said Leo.

'Very well!' retorted his interrogator.

'Let us start your education. What is the first principle of Communism?'

'I don't know,' Leo answered.

'Ignorant capitalist pig. The first principle points out that, "There are two classes, the proletariat and the bourgeoisie". The second principle confirms that, "All history is a record of class struggle".'

'Yes sir,' said Leo. 'I will try to remember that.'

'You will do more than try, you miserable excuse for a human being,' rejoined Wang.

'If you do not learn by heart, the ten principles, you will be severely dealt with.'

'Now,' he continued. 'Where were you based and how long had you been there?'

Leo recalled his briefing on induction into the squadron. He had been told that if captured, he should not risk torture by not answering questions. Any classified information he had, would be well known to the Chinese and he should not worry about talking.

However, the recent advice from his next cell neighbour was fresh in his mind. He could well imagine from the attitudes of the interrogators so far that, if he talked too much, he could fall into the trap they were probably setting to catch him in. He decided not to answer any more questions.

'Well? Are you not sure what your unit is?'

Leo remained silent.

'I demand an answer, pig,' yelled his tormentor.

Leo responded, 'I am Pilot Officer L Kirkland of the Royal Australian Air Force, my serial number is O97353.'

'Oh! Very clever Mister Kirkland, you think we will accept your adhering to the Geneva Convention. I already told you what to expect here. However, it is early days and you will soon learn what is best for you.' He gave a gruff command to the guards.

The blindfold and sack went over his head and the rope was placed around his neck. He was pulled out of the room, out of the building and across the rough ground. They stopped. He was turned, pushed back against what felt like a pole and the rope was wrapped around and around him until he was tightly bound. They left.

The morning dragged on. His legs were aching from the static position and the pooled blood in his feet made them feel as if they would explode. He wriggled, trying to loosen the rope, but he was too tightly bound

He remembered his mother saying that his father had told her about standing on parade for long periods of non-movement. He told her that his trick for overcoming the problem was to wiggle his toes to encourage circulation. Leo tried this, and slumped a little to allow the ropes to take some of the weight off his legs.

The hot sun stifled him under the black hood and several times he almost passed out. He could hear the soldiers drilling nearby again. Every now and then they would march past, jeering and pelting him with handfuls of gravel.

After what must have been nine or ten hours, the guards

came back, untied him and marched him back to the cellblock. He was shoved into a cell, the handcuffs and sack were removed and the guards left, locking the cell and passage doors behind them. Leo took off the blindfold. He was in a different place. This cell had three solid walls with bars on the passage side.

There had once been a window in the back wall but this was now bricked-up. Faint light was coming from the end of the passage where they had entered. Pressing his face against the bars, he could just manage to see that there was a small skylight over the passage door. This allowed scant afternoon light to filter into his cell. He couldn't hear any sounds to indicate if there were any other captives nearby. He decided not to try to find out.

A waste bucket sat in one corner of the cell with a roll of soaking wet toilet paper on the floor next to it. In the other walled corner, on a rough wooden stand, was a pail of murky water, presumably for washing. There was a small table with a bottle of drinking water. Bolted to the side wall was an iron cot with a woven wire base. There was neither a mattress nor bedclothes.

Leo was overcome by dizziness and a dreadful thirst. He sat on the cot and gulped down some water. Having not eaten for two days, he was feeling very weak and unhappy. He smelled the water in the pail; it had a mild soapy aroma. He reached in and retrieved a soggy cake of plain soap. As much as this whole set-up horrified him, he could at least have a wash. He soaped his face, neck, arms and upper body, rinsed off and part-dried himself with the blindfold. Then he towelled off with his shirt. The door at the end of the passage opened and two guards come in. One was carrying a small bowl, which he shoved under the barred door. Leo moved toward it.

'Get back! Get back!' screamed the guard.

'When we come, you stand at wall.'

After they had left, Leo picked up the bowl. It contained a pile of overcooked rice with what looked like a few vegetable scraps. There was no spoon or fork. Leo sat down on the cot and fingered the welcome food into his mouth. It smelled fishy and tasted rancid. When he had finished the meagre rations, he rinsed his teeth with the bottled water and drank some of it. He was feeling a little brighter now.

Darkness had descended and there was no lighting in the cell or passageway. Leo was exhausted. He was thankful the August night was mild as he curled up on the wire base of the cot and drifted off into an exhausted sleep.

18

Leo first heard the faint, familiar sound while he was still asleep. It interrupted his dreaming. Opening his eyes and seeing the trees and bushes in the first-light gloom; he gradually became aware of his surroundings. Then he recognised the distant sound as it increased in volume. It was the *wocker, wocker* of a *Huey*, Bell UH-1. This was the type of helicopter he had flown in Vietnam.

Was he now dreaming of *that* war? No! He was wide-awake! The sound was coming from the south, farther up the valley toward his hut.

Climbing out of his sleeping bag, he jerked around as he heard a muffled explosion. The resonance of the helicopter blades deepened as the Huey obviously entered a tight turn. As he hurriedly shoved his sleeping bag into the backpack, he heard the rotor-speed decrease and the engine shut down. It had landed. What on earth was happening up there?

Leo grabbed his binoculars and listening device, quickly strapped on his Beretta holster and hid the rest of his gear. He took off up the steep side of the valley toward his hut. He figured it would take thirty to forty minutes to cover the four *clicks*. This place was very familiar to Leo; he had scouted out the whole area as he laid two caches to be available for any unexpected happening. This was shaping up to be just one of those occasions.

After about twenty minutes, he had worked his way up the slope to the ridgeline extending above his hut. He heard a second, more powerful explosion.

'What in hell's name is going on?' he thought. His climb brought him near *cache A*. So he decided to spend ten minutes opening it and getting out his camouflage suit.

This was no ordinary outfit. Not only did it provide excellent day and night concealment, it had two new, top-secret features. The first was the chameleon function, which the boffins had developed a few years earlier. Light sensors on the back and front of the suit and on the sides of the hood, drove the system. They provided power for the microcomputers embedded in the neck, and read the colours of the immediate neighbourhood as well. The computer interpreted these signals and converted them into colour-changing micro-currents in the suit's surface on the sides opposite the sensors. The effect was to cause the suit to mimic its surroundings, making the wearer practically invisible in many environments from desert, through savannah to forest and jungle.

The second function was nearly as smart. The suit was designed to contain about ninety eight percent of the body's infrared (IR) radiation, converting it to low-frequency heat. Much of this heat was converted into low voltage current and used to charge the back-up power cells. Any residue was diffused gradually into the surrounding air. The rate of dissipation could be controlled to regulate internal warmth. So it doubled as a survival suit. The outfit rendered the wearer completely invisible to satellite and airborne IR detection equipment and made the wearer virtually impossible to discover at closer ranges with ground-level devices.

He zipped closed the loose back section, designed to cover his pack, and donned the suit, leaving open the mask front. Then he hurried up the ridge to a point directly above the shack. Now he moved down the slope with more stealth until he was no more than one hundred metres from his objective. Leo settled down and took out his listening device. He had not brought the tripod, so had to steady it on the side of a sapling while he scanned the area. Tuning in on the speech range, he picked up several voices and initially, was having difficulty in making out what was being said. Then, a momentary shiver ran down his spine as he recognised the Director's voice.

'I think we're just about done here. If no-one has reported this in the next two weeks, you can come up on the premise that we haven't heard from him, and you can discover the dreadful tragedy.'

'OK,' another familiar voice answered.

'But I don't want to discuss it now. I know we had to do it, but I'm pretty upset seeing him like that.

It was Harry!

'God!' Leo muttered, 'What have they done?'

There were a few more instructions given, and then he heard the chopper winding up. As it lifted, Leo caught a glimpse of it through the trees. He followed it with his binoculars and identified it was an *H* model in army colours, but it had no tail number or any other identifying markings. Then it was gone!

No sound came from the surrounding bush. It was as if the world had stopped. Leo began shivering uncontrollably. What had happened down there? He felt as though he needed a good slug of bourbon. He closed his facemask and waited for half an hour, concealed on the hillside, in case they came back unexpectedly. The birds began moving and chirping again as he worked his way down to the hut.

As it came into view, Leo was stunned by the utter devastation. It was mostly burnt to a cinder. He cautiously approached the northern side, making sure he disturbed nothing. He detected the unforgettable smell of burning flesh emanating from the smouldering ruination that had been his pride and joy. The shivering started again as his mind raced to imagine what horror he might find. Inside the wall nearest him, or what was left of it, was where his cot was positioned.

He looked through a gap in the boards and there, curled in a foetal position was a badly charred body. Who had it been? Were they attempting to fake his demise? Now he was really shaking and felt overwhelmed by a strong feeling of nausea. The stench was terrible.

Leo slowly moved around the outside of the ruin, careful not to rearrange anything, assessing the damage. To his trained eye it looked as though the initial explosion had been caused by a rocket propelled grenade fired through the window. It must have been a type designed to produce great heat and flash, vaporising its casing and producing no shrapnel. Most of the glass was blown outward from the internal explosion.

However, under the window frame there were sufficient remains to show that initially, the missile had shattered one pane inwards on entry. An attempt had been made to carefully place the pieces outside, but some slivers had been missed. He supposed the perpetrator figured on the intensity of the devastation fooling all but a very thorough forensic investigator.

Leo continued around the hut and found the remains of his Rover. It was completely useless. It was burnt out but the tank had not exploded. However, the gas bottle had. This explained the second bang and why the Range

Rover had been destroyed. He found it difficult to imagine how his whole establishment had burned down to a smouldering wreck in much less than an hour. Then he realised the architects of the heinous act had faked the completeness of the conflagration by using some sort of blowtorch or flame-thrower to exacerbate the damage.

Going around to the front again, he used his binoculars to make a closer study of the interior. He looked over at the body and there, beneath the cot, was his Canadian Club whisky bottle and three beer cans. All were empty and singed by the fire. His visitor had really celebrated his find. But his ensuing comatose state had assisted in his demise. At least he would not have suffered.

They had obviously made some sort of alteration to the plumbing from the gas bottle to simulate a leak, and then used the blowtorch to make this look like the source of the first explosion and ensuing burn. He would dearly love to retrieve some goodies from the cellar but could not afford to upset the forensic status of the scene.

As Leo tried to come to terms with this sudden and frightening event, he heard a low whimpering sound coming from the northern side of the building. He moved silently to the corner and sneaked a look. The source of the pitiful sound was a smallish, scruffy border collie cross. It was sitting on its haunches near the cot and its grizzly occupant. It was in a very upset state and when it sensed Leo's presence it trotted off to a tee tree bush near the forest's edge and sat at attention. Leo could see that the dog appeared to be guarding something under the bush. He still had his binoculars in his hand so he zoomed in on the object and saw what appeared to be a swagman's *bluey*.

Now the presence of the body was explained. This unlucky person must have come upon the hut, broken in and settled in for the night, leaving his swag and canine friend outside. Leo's initial reaction was one of deep sorrow for this fellow and his mutt. What a quirk of fate that he should have decided to squat in Leo's domain on the very night he, Leo, was apparently marked for assassination.

Why? Why did they take this action? He couldn't imagine what events had occurred for them to execute such a drastic deed. Especially Harry.

Leo realised he had been given a reprieve and a ready-made cover. At least until a PM was carried out on the body. However, if he left the dog here until someone came upon the scene, then his cover would be blown earlier. This was because the perpetrators knew he didn't own a dog and they would soon put two and two together. He could waste the dog and hide its body, or try to take it away from here. This would be fairly difficult but certainly more humane. He decided on the latter course.

He approached the dog slowly with cajoling noises. The animal seemed to be mesmerised by the camouflage suit and was probably in a state of doggie shock from the last two hours of excitement. Leo was able to approach it, give it a pat, and fashion a leash with a piece of rope from the swag. He picked up the roll, making sure no evidence was overlooked and with the dog in tow, headed back down the valley to where he had hidden his pack.

He needed time to think this whole thing through. He had to get his act together quickly if he was going to survive. His prime concern up until now was to stop the terrorist attack. Now it was going to be much more difficult and certainly more dangerous.

Was there a link? He could not see how this would be at all possible. None of the *terrorists* had an inkling he had been in their area. This must have something to do with the drug connection. Were they in some sort of conspiracy with the dealers and thought he might spring them? It seemed as though the whole world had gone mad.

Firstly, there was the virtually inexplicable plan of those Nazi terrorists to bomb the embassy. He wondered just what their motivation could be. Additionally, he was now faced with this out-and-out shameful attempt on his life. He was starting to question his ability to cope with it all.

19

It was late morning and the weather was slowly deteriorating. Low cloud was increasing and a light drizzle had commenced. Leo was feeling rather hungry and he was sure the poor mutt was similarly disposed. In spite of this, he decided to get himself organised and further away from the area before he could think about sustenance.

He replenished his water bottles from the creek; then climbed up to *cache A* again to retrieve some necessary articles.

There was a money belt which contained twenty thousand dollars in untraceable US and Australian currency and two passports with associated papers for changing his identity. He took out the two pairs of fake Victorian number plates, one for a car and the other, for a motorcycle. He placed these, with the accompanying registration certificates, in a hidden pocket next to the frame of his backpack. There were some emergency ration packs and 9mm ammo. He packed all of this, emptying the cache.

Leo started thinking about the unlucky soul who had taken his place in the hut. Who was he? How should he handle notification? And what was he going to do with the dog? He unrolled the swag, looking for some form of ID. There was nothing, no old letters, and no printed matter of any description. There were some rather grubby clothes, an old billycan, cutlery, a couple of cans of well out of date beans and some other personal paraphernalia. Leo realised that, short of reporting the matter to the police, there was nothing he could do to resolve this problem. But there was no way he could go to the authorities at this time. He wrapped the swag securely in the protective plastic package, placed it in the cache and closed it.

Then he proceeded to *cache B*, which was up over the ridge about four kilometres to the northwest of the hut. In this cache he had another twenty thousand dollars.

He took it out. He removed the Uzi machine pistol and more 9mm ammunition. He wished he could recover the MP 5N sub-machine gun from the hut's cellar, because of its greater range and accuracy. Like the Uzi, it used the same 9mm round as the Beretta. However, he could not afford to upset the crime scene and anyway, the Uzi was much easier to conceal. He took the spare warm sweater and pushed it under the straps of his pack.

Leo closed the cache then set out to the northwest at a steady forced march for the next four hours to place a safe distance between himself and the nightmare scene behind him. It was late afternoon when he finally pitched his hooch and settled himself and the dog out of the rain, which was becoming quite heavy. By now they were both starving, so he broke out two *K* rations. He fed and watered the dog, and himself, and settled down to work out a plan of action.

20

Firstly, how was he going to stop the attack on the embassy from being carried out? Secondly, whom could he trust? Thirdly, how was he going to handle the problem of the Director and his own partner killing him? Or so they thought. Normally he would have acted through his own agency, with regard to the terrorist matter. But now he would have to go direct to the American authorities; they had the greatest motivation to act quickly.

He knew he could trust his old buddy from earlier covert actions – James W Harrison, Colonel, USMC. He was just the person. Jim was the Chief US Defense Liaison Officer in the Australian Defence Forces HQ in Canberra. He would believe Leo's information, act on it and maintain secrecy. However, if he contacted the Colonel directly, given the levels of screening at the upper echelons of the military and intelligence forces, his cover would probably be blown.

Apart from a couple of ex-colleagues who probably couldn't be of much help at the moment, there was only one other person whom he could trust completely. She was an operative in the Royal Australian Navy's codes office, who, in her spare time happened to be his beloved daughter, Janine. He could use her as a safe go-between. She would be able to approach Harrison with ease and security. He was after all, her surrogate *Uncle Jim*. They had all been close friends during her younger years. Then, both families had shared many happy hours during an earlier stint of Jim's on exchange with the RAN in Canberra. Jim and his wife Helen had no children and they showered their young *niece* with much love and affection. In fact it was her association with Jim that had encouraged her to get a job at Navy Office as a civilian cryptographer.

Now came the big decision. Could he risk involving his daughter in this perilous situation? He had made it a strict rule to always protect her from any connection with his work. She had no knowledge of his job. To break this self-made promise now may place her life in jeopardy.

He decided he had no other course of action available to him, and realised her circumstances were already potentially dangerous. When the Director found out they had not killed him, he would go after her to either grill her as to his whereabouts, or worse, use her in some sort of hostage role.

He set about writing and encrypting a message to her. It took him about half an hour to compose an explicit but concise message for Harrison. Then about another half an hour to encrypt it in the secret double code, which he and Janine had used in her youth. He was sure she would remember it and be able to do the job well.

Using his secret sat-phone he called her private mobile number. It was switched off. Then he called her at home. Janine answered the call with, 'Hello.'

The very familiar voice just said, 'Go mobile and scramble. No names.'

Then he hung up.

Though a little startled, she pulled out the special mobile her Dad had given her a few years earlier and turned it on. Then she selected the scrambler function, realising she had never used it before, and waited.

When it rang, she answered it saying, 'Hi!' She checked herself before calling him *Dad*. 'How are you? I've been trying to call you for weeks, I have some exciting news for you.'

'Hello sweetheart, I'm well. Sorry I haven't called you for some time, I have been extremely busy. I'm afraid your news will have to wait until I see you. What I am about to tell you will come with some big surprises and a few shocks. For safety and security reasons I cannot talk for long, so listen very carefully.'

'OK!' she exclaimed.

'Firstly, what I am going to tell you is *Most Secret*. You and I are in extreme danger so you must follow my instructions to the letter.'

'Heavens Dad!' She bit her lip at letting the name slip. 'What's going –?'

'I'm sorry to cut you off honey but just listen. I'll explain more fully in a fax, and when I see you.'

'Eh OK.' She sounded non-plussed.

Leo briefed her. He said firmly, 'In the old parlance, *this is not an exercise*. I have worked in Security Intelligence for many years.'

Janine gasped.

He continued. 'I am at present in a most dangerous predicament involving terrorists and an extreme case of internal evil in my agency that, I believe, is not related to the terrorists. Two operatives think they have killed me, so at present I am completely covert.'

Janine felt her pulse starting to race, but uttered no sound.

He went on, 'If, in the near future, you are told, or hear news indicating I died in an accident; accept it as fact, and act as you would if it were true. When *they* find out I am still around and a threat to them, they will come after you. You and your uncle are the only people whom I can trust at the moment. As soon as I hang up, I want you to pack a rucksack with minimal gear to last about three weeks. You have to go to him, taking a circuitous departure route to ensure you are not followed. Check in somewhere out of the way. You have to leave as soon as possible, and immediately after you receive the fax, which I will send as soon as you are ready to go; and I mean, within the next half hour at most.'

'I understand.'

'Do you remember *ankle/arm*?'

'I think so – yes I can remember.'

'Have you ever given it to anyone else?'

'No, it's always been exclusively ours.'

'Wonderful! I know this is going to be hard to come to grips with in the short term. I'm fairly sure you have not been into covert ops before. But you would have received some rudimentary training in your current job. Just remember the basic rules you were given. And I know I don't have to ask you to trust my judgement completely.'

'You certainly do not!'

'You have my personal sat-phone number?'

'Yes.'

'Good! Organise for your mail to be collected and tell your boss you need to take a couple of weeks family emergency leave. Talk to no one else. *No one!* As soon as you are ready to leave, set the date on your fax back two days. That is, earlier. Call my number, let it ring three times and hang up. Then wait for a two-page fax. As soon as you have the fax, do not wait to read it, take it with you and decipher it when you get to there. It will give you further instructions. Reset the date on the fax and leave with no delay, in case your phone/fax is being monitored. Now read that back.'

She reiterated the salient points and Leo was satisfied she understood. She was one smart cookie.

'That's great honey. I love you. See you soon, bye!'

'Love you too, bye'

21

Janine hung up and wondered what her dad had done to get into such a dangerous situation. It all certainly sounded weird. His call tended to explain some of the unknowns about what his job was. A secret service agent!

'My God!' she said aloud.

She had been involved in national security for the last twenty years, and had never an inkling that he was in the same business. Why was someone trying to kill him and why was she in danger? Why did she have to get out of town? He certainly was insistent and she knew from her long association with him that he would not have been so if it were not for good reason.

She went into the bedroom, pulled out her old rucksack and started to pack gear for a three-week sojourn as he had instructed. She then phoned her boss at home and told him that, because of serious family problems she had to take three weeks compassionate leave; immediately.

He asked no questions and made no comment, except to say that, if she needed any help, she was to call him. Then she rang the apartment manager and asked her to please collect her mail for the next three weeks. She was quite used to Janine leaving at short notice so this posed no problem.

Now she was ready to depart. Janine set the phone/fax date back two days. She pre-selected *scramble* on her mobile and dialled his private sat-phone, waited for three rings, then hung up. She deleted the number from the call register and waited. Two minutes later her fax rang and the two-page message came through. As she expected, the content was a matrix of numerals. Although he had not elucidated, she knew this message must be extremely important and there must be a serious security connection.

Janine shoved the pages into her handbag and reset the date on the fax.

'What was that all about?' she wondered. Then she grabbed her pack and hurried down to her car.

In line with his instructions, she initially departed to the north from her Balgowlah apartment and made a couple of stops and reversals of direction to ensure she was not being followed. Then she headed down Freeway 31 toward Canberra to see *Uncle Jim*. To maintain the apparent need for secrecy, she decided not to go right into the Capital. So she found a small out-of-town motel near Queanbeyan.

After settling in she pulled out the fax pages, a pad

and pencil and prepared to de-cipher their contents. It had been many years since she had used the *ankle/arm* code devised by her dad. Apparently they were still the only two beings on the planet who knew it. She still marvelled at its simplicity and its lack of need for a direct or devised key. She made a cup of coffee, laid the message on the bed and set about turning it into a readable text.

2161328181	3232328132	3293818181	6143328191
3243325352	3232623253	8193323281	3232936221
8153326232	5381813253	6232328181	3261323293
3262623261	8181328161	8153216232	8143323243
8153743232	3232438153	8161328181	3262618161
8132325332	9362216262	3253216281	9362626181
2143618181	3232532143	2161328181	8132534332
2181743232	8121323262	3232433261	8181324381
4332818162	6232818193	3281623243	6243436121
7481328121	4332326232	3281815332	3281618132
6262816181	4332933232	4332216232	8121433281
8143323281	3261416221	6174746142	8191612162
2143329332	8143323253	2132325381	8132538181
3132329332	6281936181	2162328132	6232813241
4343326232	8143323293	8153325331	8181938181
3253433232	4332816132	3253618181	3232937432
3281328232	5381433232	3243626281	6143213253
2132329362	3221623262	6181624332	8181742143
3293815332	5321323262	8161213232	3232438193
2162733261	8181936232	6181813281	6181936232
3232324352	3232214332	4332326132	3281537432
8181626132	8181623293	8132626252	8143324381

4332324132	9362628193	2143325332	8181218161
2132326161	8121324332	3293626161	8143818181
4381433281	9381533281	8121329381	4332535232
3232324332	3243213293	3281813281	4332328181
8181325381	4332323281	8153329332	8162628153
3232816181	3232328132	8193329381	3243323253
8153329332	6221328161	3262323232	4381938153
3262328132	3281323232	8132613232	3232438174
3293323281	3261326262	6181813281	4343815232
8153325381	4332818153	7461439191	6163437421
4363433221	6343746163	9161814221	6363433293
2162213261	8162433281	6243214362	6132818132
8151323232	8181813293	2132323262	6232818132
8132323361	8182323281	4332626232	3232438193
3232434332	8174813293	6262618181	3281434381
6262819332	9381433293	6221819332	5381324332
3232748132	9352326181	4321327121	3281534332
4381213274	8132933232	2143733232	8181325232
3253618174	8132933262	2143328132	4381938153
3261618181	4332816261	4332328181	3262328143
3232324362	6281617481	3293326232	9381433232
8132819332	5381328143	3293814381	5332813262
6132329381	9343814332	3253818181	7432814332
4332626132	8152328193	6163744361	6391616361
8261838163	6162812181	3293328121	6261818132
4332328121	3232337332	3281433232	9321326132
4381323281	4332336232	7432328181	3281432143
3281438181	3252324343	3293814332	6281616262
6281329381	3343328232	3262618181	8181742143

```
3281626281    2181818161    4381813281    9332813232
8132428262    6221433232    6262628143    3281323261
6181823281    9332813262    6132323381    3381323293
3281326262    6232813262    3241328132    6262813281
8133616343    6374616361    8121329343    3262623281
2162323362    4362614343    3293214332    3243622132
6181818132    8132623293    3281616332    5174436163
8174329332    6132813262    3233622151    8181612132
3181636232    8181816181    8132326243    8181324362
3262618181    8132328132    8193325321    3281323281
2143216221    4381618153    2162214332    9332814332
3292613232    3274813253    9181328181    3232328131
3271433232    8181326262    8192438132    8121325281
6221617432    7181328143
```

After about half an hour she had made the first level transposition. It was then a simple matter to decode the second level. As the message unravelled, she experienced a sense of spine-tingling anticipation and an overwhelming awe as to the consequences of what she was getting into.

The message read;

JANINE MOST SECRET IN EXTREME DANGER DO NOT PASS THIS TO ANYONE EXCEPT COLONEL JAMES W HARRISON USMC AT ADF HQ VALIDATION CODE IS PALADIN 9X7341 PLEASE REMEMBER TO PARAPHRASE TEXT MESSAGE ONE HAVE DISCOVERED PROBABLE TERRORIST PLOT DO NOT DISCUSS WITH MY AGENCY SUSPECT LEAK OR WORSE YOU MUST TAKE DECISIVE AND

IMMEDIATE ACTION INTENSE TERRORIST TRAINING IS BEING CONDUCTED AT 33 18 42 S 150 16 18 E PROBABLY ANTI AMERICAN NEO FASCIST I HAVE CONDUCTED EXTENSIVE COVERT SURVEILLANCE OVER LAST TWO DAYS AND DISCOVERED INTENDED TARGET US EMBASSY ACT 05010230K WEAPONS ARE LASER GUIDED HAND LAUNCHED ROCKETS FROM BLACK MOUNTAIN 4 CLICKS NW OF TARGET NEAR CAR PARK AT 0230K ESCAPE BY HELI FROM AREA 0250 BEWARE X1 OR X9 AM ON RUN FROM INTERNAL PLOT PLEASE GIVE JANIZE SANCTUARY X7 END

Janine felt completely flabbergasted. It had all been so rushed. She hadn't even been able to tell him about the interesting phone call from Sumiko Tsushima.

About two weeks earlier she had answered the phone and a female voice had said, 'Hello, my name is Tsushima Sumiko, are you Ms J Kirkland?'

'Yes,' Janine answered. 'My name is Janine.'

She remembered the story her father had told her of the lost love of his youth. Her name had been Tsushima. She particularly remembered the name because, during her philosophy studies at Uni, she had read Tsushima Shuji, whose pseudonym was Dazai Osamu, a well-known Japanese journalist of the '30s and '40s. Her Dad had mentioned that Michiko's family was related to him.

'Please excuse my asking, but I have made many

enquiries, trying to find the relatives of a Mr Leo Kirkland, and was wondering if you knew of him?'

Janine felt a tingle of excitement as she answered, 'Leo Kirkland is my father.'

There was an audible gasp, followed by a long pause, and then the lady on the phone asked, 'Was he in Japan in 1952?'

Janine thought for a moment, then answered, 'Yes, he was.'

'Then he is still alive?'

'Yes he certainly is. Are you a relative of, I think her name was Michiko?'

'Yes I am,' said Sumiko, after another long pause. 'Could I meet with you and your father soon? I live in Canberra?'

Janine told her, 'My father's out of town and I've been unable reach him at this time'. She continued, 'When I *can* contact him, I will call you back and we can arrange to meet.'

She had written down the Canberra number and had been trying to reach Leo ever since.

When Leo hung up after sending the message to his daughter, it was nineteen thirty. He went over the events of the last twelve or so hours. It seemed more like twelve days. Everything had changed so dramatically in such a short time. He had long ago given up praying, but made a silent entreaty to whatever good force may exist in the universe, to please look over and protect his sweet offspring.

As far as dealing with the third problem; his so-called colleagues, Leo assessed that there was nothing more he could do now until morning. He checked the dog's lead and secured it to his wrist. Then he climbed into his sleeping bag. With the patter of the rain on his stretched poncho, he soon drifted off into a deep sleep.

He knew his dream would return.

22

The blaring military march music almost split his head open. Instantly awake, Leo leaped off the cot forcing the heels of his hands into his ears. It must have been more than a hundred decibels. The powerful speaker was almost invisible behind a tough metal screen in the ceiling. God! He could feel the sound waves bouncing off the back of his eyeballs. This persisted for about half an hour.

Then it was shut off, just as suddenly as it had started. The silence was unreal. Had they burst his eardrums or had he been rendered nerve deaf? No! Because then the voice, the loud, sneering voice, which he would come to know well and learn to hate, started.

'The first principle – there are two classes, the proletariat and the bourgeoisie.'

'The second principle – all history is a record of class struggle.'

'The third principle – ....'

'Good grief!' thought Leo. 'How long will this go on for?'

It continued for about fifteen minutes. The ten principles of communism, repeated over and over again.

Then the tack changed and a soft, 'Tokyo Rose' type voice with a cajoling tone started praising The Democratic People's Republic. She continued with gushing accolades for the boundless wisdom of Kim Il-Sung and his purity of thought. She spoke of the great admiration in which his guide and mentor, Chairman Mao was held and of the power of the Communist Party. She compared the wonderful beauty of these truths with the criminality of that puppet of the Americans, Dr. Syngman Rhee in the decadent, capitalist controlled South.

After about another half an hour the monologue ceased. A high-pitched 'feed-back' whistle replaced it. This was not as loud and was almost bearable compared with the preceding aural invasion.

The door at the end of the passageway opened and he heard two voices, maybe Korean, but he wasn't sure. The Chinese seemed to be running the show in this place, but this dialogue was different. Leo could hear what sounded like tin plates being slid across the stone floor. This resolved his speculation as to whether or not there were other prisoners in the building. He had decided not to attempt any contact, in light of what the British prisoner had told him. Two guards came into view in the gloomy morning light. One had a medium sized metal bowl in his hand and he pushed this under the bars of Leo's cell. They said nothing to him. While this was taking place, Leo stood against the opposite wall as he had been instructed to do.

As soon as the guards left he moved to the bowl and picked it up. It was about three quarters full of soggy, bright purple rice. Leo was not going to be phased by this. He just closed his eyes and fingered it into his mouth. It had virtually no flavour but felt good in his belly.

After eating the stale food he rinsed his mouth with water from the bottle and drank it. Then he washed as best he could, using the blindfold as a sponge and wringing it out to dry himself.

It started again; first the loud march music. This was followed by the dreaded voice reciting the ten principles. Then it was 'her' turn, what's her name? Was it 'Peking Lil'? Her latest trick was an attempt to convince him there was a better life under communism. After all, weren't all men equal? Leo believed they started out that way, at least as far as rights were concerned. But he doubted very much that they continued to be so. He wondered what Lil, or whatever her name was, thought about the equality of women. Leo thought that, in spite of the rhetoric, it didn't appear to him that they were treated equally in any society, including a communist one.

The door to the passage opened and Leo heard a couple of grunts as if someone was straining to lift or drag something. Then two guards appeared in front of his cell, dragging a prisoner by the arms. He was of brown complexion and unconscious. He wore no shoes and his feet were covered in blood. They ordered Leo to the back wall, opened the cell door and threw in their hapless victim. The cell door was slammed shut and they left.

Leo studied his new cellmate. To Leo, he appeared to be of Arab appearance. He was quite good looking, with a drooping moustache and maybe a two-month old beard. He started to come around, blinking and letting out an almost inaudible moan. Leo helped him up to a stooping position, guided him to the cot and sat him on it.

He mumbled something in a foreign tongue.

'... eh deh reem.'

Leo understood this as, 'Thanks'

The man took a swig from the water bottle Leo offered, and handed it back. He looked at Leo.

'You American or British?' he asked.

'I'm Australian,' Leo replied, almost biting his tongue as he remembered the advice from the British prisoner.

'I am Corporal Abdul Akkisla of the Turkish Brigade. I was captured during the battle at Kunuri and have been a prisoner for more than one and a half years. How long have you been here?'

Leo assessed that this man was not only genuine, but very strong. He explained his circumstances, then said, 'I didn't know the Turkish Army was here.

'I didn't know the Australian Air Force was here,' Abdul replied.

He beckoned to Leo. As he came closer, Abdul grabbed him by the shoulders, and pulled his head down next to his own. He smelled terrible. Before Leo could react, Abdul whispered, 'Excuse me sir, they may have microphone in here, don't say anything.'

Leo nodded his understanding and Abdul went on.

'They may try to make you talk by threatening to torture me. Say nothing sir, they cannot hurt me any more now, don't let them get inside your head.'

Leo nodded again. Abdul released him and recommenced normal conversation, explaining that the food and facilities were dreadful, especially as the weather would soon be turning cold.

They spent the rest of the day locked up. The only contact with their captors was the one-way, regular intrusion of the blaring music, the recitation of the ten principles and the snide propaganda. During these periods of loud music and boring discourse, Abdul and Leo took the opportunity talk. They guessed that if there was a hidden mike, it couldn't compete with the din.

When Abdul continued to address him as 'sir', Leo asked him to call him by his first name, especially as they were both in this dreadful situation together.

'If we do not observe a strict military code, then the enemy will win in their efforts to break us,' Abdul said.

He told Leo about his last companion, Cemal, who was a Private in his artillery unit. They were captured together and had remained in this place for all of their internment. Cemal was a devout Mohammedan. He had fashioned for himself a fez and prayer mat, located the direction of Mecca, and five times each day prayed to Allah.

They had both maintained their division of rank, even to the extent of conducting their own morning parade and inspection. The Chinese and Korean guards made Cemal's existence particularly painful with additional torture and ridicule about his religious activities. He had never wavered under their tyranny and always maintained strict military and religious discipline.

One day, while they were in the exercise yard, Cemal had laid out his mat, kneeled facing the west and commenced his prayer ritual. As he placed his forehead on the ground, a Chinese officer came up behind him and delivered such a powerful kick in the rump, that Cemal flew head first along the ground. His forehead scraped through the gravel, which tore away all the skin. With neither complaint nor hesitation, he forced himself to get up and resume his original position. He placed his bleeding head on the ground again and spread his arms forward.

As he knelt there in supplication before his God, and in defiance of his Devils, the officer walked around in front of him, drew his pistol and shot him in the back of the head.

Leo felt an overpowering nausea. He turned and vomited into the toilet pail. Abdul apologised for upsetting him, then explained that he, Leo, must understand what an evil place this was. Cemal would rather have met his maker than give in to these infidels.

He told Leo, 'These disgusting animals, cannot frighten me. Their actions have strengthened my determination to remain my own person in the face of any harsh conditions. I will not surrender'

He said that he was not a fundamentalist Moslem. But he would wage a personal Jihad against that particular officer when the opportunity presented itself.

He said 'By Allah's hand that will happen. I must avenge my loyal friend. I will pursue that murderer to the ends of the earth if necessary, and kill him.

To Leo, this sounded just like the Old Testament's 'Eye for an eye ...'. It went against his Christian upbringing but *he fully understood the emotions and forces involved here. In his heart he agreed with Abdul's commitment. This murderer should have to pay for his heinous crime and there was no system in this evil place that could ensure a just outcome. Leo asked if he knew which officer it was.*

'Captain Wang,' Abdul replied.

Around dusk the passage door opened, two guards came in and distributed bowls of boiled rice. These meagre helpings had been so over-cooked that they more closely resembled jelly. As they stood against the back wall with one guard training an AK47 on them, the other opened the door and shoved in a grubby futon and two tattered blankets. They clanged the door shut and left.

After they had eaten, Leo and Abdul prepared for bed, Abdul elected to sleep on the wire based cot.

As Leo thankfully curled up on the futon, he vividly recalled the last time he had used such a bed. They both drifted off. Abdul, who was well conditioned to the circumstances, slept deeply. Leo's slumber was much more restless. He stirred several times and lay awake for hours as his mind played back over the story of Cemal and the despicable Captain Wang.

23

In the depth of his dreaming Leo heard a low whimpering sound, which woke him. He peered out of his hooch. The rain had cleared. He could see the dog curled up at his feet and feel the warmth of its body through the sleeping bag. The dog must have been dreaming too. As he eased himself out of bed, the dog woke, and wagging its tail, licked at Leo's hand. He had really taken to his newfound master. Or was he just begging for some food? What was he going to do with this potential burden?

Leo broke camp and shared a ration pack with the mutt in the pre-dawn twilight. As the sun came up he moved off, dog in tow, toward the town of Cullen Bullen. He chose Cullen Bullen because it appeared to be the nearest place, likely provide both sustenance and transportation.

After a long hard slog, they arrived at the top of the escarpment overlooking the town at dusk. Leo decided not to attempt the steep descent in the dark. He replenished their sapped strength with the inevitable, and now boring, K rations, and settled down for the night.

Next morning, Leo rose before first light and struck camp. They each devoured a chocolate muesli bar, then launched down a steep re-entrant that cut a deep cleft into the cliff face. About nine o'clock they reached the town and made their way up the highway to the *Royal* hotel. Inviting aromas of breakfast cooking bade Leo to go in and eat. He was certainly sick of the ration packs. He took the rope off the dog's collar and told him to *stay*. The well-trained animal sat there as Leo went into the bar and sat on a stool at the window bench near the entrance.

The blonde waitress came over and Leo ordered the five dollar fifty breakfast off the chalkboard; black coffee, bacon, eggs and toast. The coffee was just OK, but when he tucked into his meal it was all delicious! As he took the first sip of his second cup of coffee and looked at the dog sitting patiently there in front of the hotel, Leo thought he might take something out for it to eat.

Then, as he watched, a woman came up to the dog, which jumped up excitedly in obvious recognition. She patted and hugged it, then looked toward the hotel entrance. Leo almost panicked as she walked straight to the door, a big smile on her face, and came in looking expectantly around the room.

When she didn't recognise anybody, she said, 'Did anyone see the man who came with that dog out there?'

The man behind the bar looked straight at Leo and he realised he would have to own up. He hadn't decided which of the fake identities he would adopt yet. On the spur of the moment he chose to become the American tourist. He'd hardly spoken to the waitress so he didn't think she would pick up his change in speech.

Putting on his well-practised Mid-western accent, he said, 'I brought the dog Ma'am, I found him a couple of days ago, wandering in the forest.'

'Oh!' she exclaimed. 'He belongs to my father.'

Leo worked hard at concealing his emotions. How should he handle this situation? He realised she was entitled to an explanation about her father's demise, but he could not tell her here and now about the events of the last few days. He hated to do it, but would have to lie to her.

Before he could say anything, she said, 'I'm surprised that Barney, that's the dog's name, would leave my father. They were inseparable. Where did you find him?'

'About ten miles north of here.' Leo lied. He hoped it didn't show.

'I'm becoming very worried now,' she said. 'Something must have happened to him. Would you be kind enough to come with me to report him missing? He's not really a hobo, but acts like one and likes to go walk-about from time to time. But Barney always accompanies him.'

Leo had to think very quickly now.

He said, 'I would really like to finish my meal first, I've been out in the bush for some time and I'm famished. I can't add much to what I've told you. The dog must have become separated from your father and gotten lost. Why don't you take Barney and I'll go to the police station on my way out of town.'

Before she could answer, Leo asked firmly, 'What's your name – and your father's?'

She replied, 'Helen Dorevitch, and my father's name is Eric Jones.'

'OK!' he said, maintaining the upper hand. 'You go and report your concerns. I'll drop in on the cops later on.'

The woman left quietly, leaving Leo feeling like a heel. He silently pledged to redress this situation at the earliest opportunity.

He finished his coffee and paid the barman, who didn't look too impressed with Leo. Then he asked if he could rent a room for a couple of hours to shower and change. The barman said he could accommodate the request and it would cost twenty dollars. Leo accepted the deal. He took his pack to the room where he rearranged his gear, showered and changed into a clean shirt and dungarees. He decided to retain his now well-developed beard.

Leaving by the rear entrance he walked up the road to the only service station, which still sported two of the old kerb-side pumps. There was a sign in the window –

HONDA CT125 TRAIL BIKE FOR SALE

He went into the garage and the attendant approached him, with a friendly greeting.

'Hello, I'm Sean, can I help you?'

'Hello Sean. My name is Anderson, I'm an American tourist; I've been hiking and touring round the countryside up here. I came in on a bus but I've decided to get my own wheels to give me a little flexibility. I saw your sign in the window. Could you give me the low-down on the bike?'

He listened to the man's sales pitch. This included the fact that the bike had an almost completely silent engine and exhaust. Sean explained that this would allow him to explore the bush tracks without disturbing the wildlife.

'I'll take it,' said Leo.

The salesman requested his passport and driver's licence, then asked what the method of payment would be. Leo gave him the false documents, which were in the name of Alan Anderson. The American *Driver License* was endorsed for motorcycle as well as automobile.

'I'll pay cash, in greenbacks.'

Sean looked duly impressed, especially as there had been no haggling over the price. They completed the transfer of ownership, and finalised the deal. This included a helmet and a worn pair of leather gloves. Leo adjusted the helmet to fit, and secured his pack on the pillion rack.

He set off on his way to Sydney to start sorting out his problems with the Director and Harry. There was no way he was going to front up at the police station. Mrs Dorevitch had probably reported her concerns to the police by now. So they'd probably be looking for him in the not too distant future.

Twenty kilometres south, he pulled off onto a side-track and changed the number plates. He swapped the registration certificate and driver's licence in his wallet and became Gordon Johnston, Australian citizen, a farmer from Victoria. In order to confound any possible attempt to relate him to the Cullen Bullen incident, he changed his clothes again, cut off his beard with scissors and smooth shaved with his battery-powered shaver.

Leo reached the western suburb of Parramatta a little after noon. He was too exhausted to make any command decisions so he had a quick sandwich, checked into a cheap motel and went to bed.

Falling asleep almost instantly, he returned to his dream world, Korean saga.

24

Leo woke from his dreamless but fitful sleep as the first rays of the sun shone through the skylight over the passage door. Abdul was already awake, sitting on the edge of the wire cot. He did not look happy. His feet looked awful; with bloody scabs forming on the tops of his toes where he had been dragged, face down over God knows what surfaces, or distance.

As he came to his senses, Leo bade him good morning and asked Abdul if he would like him to try to bathe his feet. Abdul looked somewhat surprised at this offer, and indicated that he would dearly welcome such treatment.

Just then, the passageway door opened and two new guards entered, accompanied by a prisoner who was lugging two pails of water. As they approached their cell, Abdul and Leo obediently stood against the back wall while they opened the cell door. The 'trusty' prisoner placed both pails, which looked as though they contained a soggy cake of soap each, inside the door. Then he recovered the waste bucket and the pail of used water. He took them out while one of the guards kept them covered with an AK47. He returned shortly with the waste bucket. It had been emptied but neither washed nor rinsed. He went outside again and brought in two bowls of rice, which had been dyed a brilliant green this time. Each had a slice of stale, plain bread on top.

Leo asked the trusty if it would be possible to get some bandages and antiseptic for Abdul's feet. The prisoner looked at the feet, winced and replied with an American accent, that he would see what he could do. The three of them left, and after washing their hands Leo and Abdul partook of their meagre bounty.

After about fifteen minutes, one guard and the trusty returned with another bucket of water, slightly warmed, a cake of what looked like antiseptic soap and some roller bandage. He added another bottle of drinking water and two small rice cakes. Things were really starting to look up.

'This is beginning to look like the Waldorf,' said Leo wryly

Abdul cautioned him, saying, 'It will not last for long. Most times when they do small acts of kindness, it's just to give you a false sense of security.'

This obviously had the effect of making the next session of ill-treatment even more intolerable.

Leo arranged the pail of soapy water next to Abdul and set about attending to his wounded feet. He was surprised that, even though Abdul was only a couple of inches shorter than his own six-foot frame, his feet were at least a couple of sizes smaller. Using the blindfold, which he had managed to wash out the previous night, he lathered up the lye soap and gently bathed Abdul's feet. The soles, as well as the tops, had been badly injured.

'Thank you sir,' said Abdul. 'This is something like Jesus' washing of his disciples' feet.'

Leo looked surprised and said, 'I didn't know Moslems knew anything about Jesus.'

'Oh yes! We recognise Jesus as a prophet, second only to Mohammed himself. We just do not believe he is the Son of God.'

While Leo carefully dried and bandaged Abdul's feet, they entered into a long and meaningful discussion about their respective religions. When the feet had been duly attended to, Leo asked if Abdul thought that his, Leo's, boots would fit him.

Abdul looked a little embarrassed.

'No sir, I cannot take your shoes, that is too much.'

Leo insisted, 'You must wear them, unless they are too tight over those bandages, at least until your feet start to heal, then you can return them.'

'It would not be right for a corporal to take an officer's shoes!' exclaimed Abdul.

'Well, if you are going to treat me like an officer,' said Leo with a firmness in his voice, 'Then I had better start acting like one.' He continued, 'If an opportunity to escape arose, it would be your duty to take it. With your feet in their present state, you wouldn't be able to. So, as your superior officer, I'm making it an order.'

'Very well sir, thank you; but it will only be until my feet heal a little.'

With that all agreed, Leo carefully placed his boots on Abdul's tender, bandaged feet and loosely laced them.

Leo and Abdul spent the next two months together, sharing the cell and many confidences. They restricted their conversations to the periods of loud music and propaganda, or when they were in the exercise yard or on work detail.

They were jointly and severally tortured frequently. On one occasion, they were taken, cowled and handcuffed as always, to another place. When Leo's sack was removed, he was shown Abdul. He was bareheaded, gagged and bound to a chair. He had been placed inside what looked like a bottomless, corrugated steel water tank that was lying on its side. They were in a large, stone room with a concrete floor. Next to the drum-like tank stood a large brute of a man, who looked as if he was about to wield a heavy sledgehammer against its side. Two of the hated interrogators were also present, and all three wore crude ear protectors. The sack was placed back over Leo's head and the interrogation began.

When Leo refused to answer, the brute brought the hammer down onto the tank with an enormous blow. Even though he had the sack over his head, Leo felt as though it had burst his eardrums. Surely it was a trick.

He thought, 'They couldn't do that to someone who was inside the tank with no ear protection. They must have removed Abdul from the tank and were trying to trick him into talking. Otherwise, why had they head-sacked him again?'

They continued to question him, and when he refused to reply down came the hammer again. He heard a muffled moan. Leo remained silent, and the hammer fell yet again and then a fourth time.

Then the sack was whipped off his head. There sat Abdul, still in the tank, with tears of pain streaming down his face. Leo felt a rage stirring in him, he wanted to grab the hammer and lay into these animals until they were pulp.

Leo growled. 'What do you want to know?'

Abdul made a muffled 'No' sound under the gag and

violently threw his head up and back several times. Their eyes met and Leo knew this brave man did not want him to succumb to this diabolical pressure. Leo looked stubbornly at his captors and saw they had the message. One of them nodded to the brute and he swung the hammer into the tank one more time, despite Leo's lurching forward and banging his shoulder into the man's ribs. The brute slowly put down the hammer, turned and sent Leo flying across the room with a mighty backhand blow.

The interrogators knew they would get no further with this pair at this time, so they were roughly returned to their cell.

When they had a chance to discuss this event later on, Leo said, 'I wonder why they don't separate us, not that I want them to. But I thought they would have figured out by now, that we are working together to beat their game by remaining friends and helping each other.'

Abdul said, 'I like to hear you say we are friends. I feel exactly the same way. I never thought I could have such feeling for a white Christian. But I realise we are not so different in our deeper thoughts. I think these people have been robbed of any finer feelings by their brutal leaders and do not understand our – What is the word? Solidarity?'

'Yes,' replied Leo. 'That's the word.'

Even though Leo's officer status brought him no special treatment, he did suffer one rank related, ironic and potentially dangerous episode.

One morning just before dawn, he was hauled, head

in sack and handcuffed, out of the cell along the passage in the direction, opposite to the main entrance. They went out another door and Leo was forced to sit on a chair. His hands were un-cuffed, placed on the table in front of him and what felt like a knife and fork were placed in them. Then the sack was whipped off and he found himself sitting in an outside, stone walled courtyard. In front of him was a plate with two cold and greasy fried eggs, two rashers of bacon and a slice of mouldy toast.

He caught a glimpse of what looked like a glass of milk, before a brilliant flash of light surprised him. He looked up to see a man standing on the wall. He had just photographed him. Before he could react in any way, the sack was whipped over his head and he was whisked back to his cell. He was non-plussed by this act, and didn't think to mention it to Abdul.

Several days later, while Leo was walking around the exercise yard, six British Army prisoners ganged around him, forcing him into a corner.

One of them said, in a sneering Cockney voice, 'Here's our little 'Blue Orchid' squealer, cop this!'

He let fly with a punch to Leo's abdomen, causing him to double over. Blows then rained on him from the rest of the group with additional jeers.

'Here's some 'Lenient Treatment' for you.'

'Cop this Aussie commie.'

He was forced to the ground. After delivering him several hefty kicks, they threw some crumpled sheets of paper on the ground and left. As he picked them up, Abdul came to him, lifted him in his arms and carried him back to their cell.

While Abdul checked him over for injuries, Leo unravelled the papers. The first one was headed – *CAMP No 1 NEWS*. This was followed by a large photograph of himself, sitting at a table obviously about to tuck-in to a tasty breakfast. The caption underneath read,

'Pilot Officer L Kirkland, RAAF, receiving the Lenient Treatment for co-operation'.

There followed an article extolling the virtues of one who co-operates and pointing out how the readers too, could be better looked after if only they would join hands with the Democratic People. They must see that this was the best, the only course to take.

Leo explained the circumstances of the photograph to Abdul, who looked down at the 'news' sheet and commented on what a diabolical act that was.

Abdul and Leo tried to convince the disbelieving prisoners as to the facts for a long time. It wasn't until a similar incident occurred, affecting one of the British army officers, that they were finally believed. The damage had already been cemented in place though, and their captors had added another permanent wound to the psyche of many of the prisoners.

25

After deciphering the message, Janine carefully para-phrased it, making it impossible to match with the original should it fall into the wrong hands. She made sure she missed no salient points. She burnt her original deciphering pages in the hand-basin, washing the ashes away. Then she rang Jim Harrison at his home.

'Hello, Colonel Harrison,' was the efficient military answer.

'Hi! Uncle Jim,' she responded. He had always been that to her, ever since she first met him as a young child.

'Janine, honey, what a pleasant surprise, how are you?'

'I'm fine, how about you and Auntie?'

'We couldn't be better, how's your Dad? Haven't heard from him in ages.'

Well, I'd like to talk to you about him. Could we meet for lunch tomorrow?'

'Hey! You're in town! Sure, where would you like to go?'

'Can I pick you up outside your office at twelve? I'll be driving a red Hyundai sports.' He detected a note of urgency behind the gay tone of her voice.

'OK, I'll see you at noon.'

She again deleted the number from the call register in case her phone fell into the wrong hands.

Janine pulled up in front of his Russell Offices

building on time, and he was waiting on the steps. When he climbed into the passenger seat, she leaned over, gave him a peck on the cheek and drove off. She took him to a small al fresco place out in Watson.

He noticed the circuitous route and the diversionary stop on the way. She looked a little tense and said nothing as they drove. Janine selected an outside table, away from the other diners, making sure they could not be overviewed or overheard.

'So what's going on honey?' asked Jim.

Janine leaned her face against her elbow-supported hand to hide her lips from any possible surveillance, and said in a serious tone, 'Dad's in bad trouble, he sent me a coded message, which he asked me to pass on to you only. He said that it was Most Secret.'

'Did he give you a validation code?' asked Jim, also disguising his speech.

'Yes.'

'What was it?'

Janine reeled off the code from memory. 'Paladin 9X7341.'

Jim pulled a small Palm Pilot from his pocket. He logged into it and entered a string of characters.

He waited a moment and said, 'This is extremely serious Janine.' He looked around casually and cased their circumstances. When he was satisfied they couldn't be overheard, he continued, 'That's a cipher for a serious threat to national security.

'I can assure you, that's exactly what it is and it involves a planned threat to your embassy here,' Janine replied.

'You'd better give me the whole story.'

So she told him all she knew. She referred to her few cryptic, abbreviated notes to ensure she missed nothing. He entered some of the details into his Palm Pilot, such as the coordinates of the terrorist camp, the weaponry, times and details of the attack on the embassy.

Then he asked for more details about the attempt to kill Leo. She told him about the attempted assassination and how he had to be aware of a conspiracy involving X1 and X9. She asked Jim what this meant.

Jim replied, 'As Leo said, this is all classified information, and I'm only telling you more because your dad is involved. I take it you realise he is employed in security intelligence?'

'Yes, but I only found out when he called me yesterday.'

'And you know what MO9 is?'

'Yes. I think it's an ASIS office.'

'Well, that's near enough. MO10 or MOX is a deeper level. X1 is the Director of the agency and X9 would be one of Leo's peers. He is X7.'

'Yes, that's how he signed off on the message.'

Jim responded, 'Sometimes I think his designation should be X Double O 7.'

Janine smiled at his little joke and said, 'In his message he asked for you to give me sanctuary.'

Jim assured Janine he would take care of the terrorist

threat, and that she should immediately move in with Helen and him in their apartment in the embassy enclosure. She would be safe there from any attempt to take or harm her. This seemed like a good idea to Janine, provided Jim's assurance about foiling the terrorists was realised. Otherwise, she would really be in the line of fire.

After she had given him all of the information, Jim felt concerned.

'There's something missing.'

'How do you mean?'

'Apart from the X names, were there any proper nouns; people's names, or code names in the original message?'

'Yes, he addressed me by my first name and he called you James W Harrison – Oh! And he had the initials for the Australian Capital Territory.'

'Were any of those names repeated?'

'Yes, he wrote my name twice but the second time it was misspelled. I checked it twice but he definitely had a 'z' instead of the second 'n'.'

'Just what I wanted to hear! You two have your own little secret codes, but Leo and I have used that validation trick in the past, the misspelling the second instance of a name. It proves to me, beyond doubt, that the message is definitely from him and not a ploy by some other agency—or by you for that matter'

'Good grief! Heaven forbid!' she exclaimed.

'I never realised just how secretive and careful you field guys have to be in this SI business.'

Jim took her hand in his and with a most intensely appreciative look on his face said, 'Girl you have just done a terrific job here. I'm very proud of you, and I sure know your dad is. Don't you worry too much about him. He can look after himself, and we'll look after you.'

Janine drove him back to his office. Then she collected her gear from the motel and went to stay with Helen, who had been pre-warned by Jim from the café.

26

Harold Thwaites rushed into the Director's office. He was in a highly agitated state and nervously blurted out, 'He's been found; it was just on the news. A couple of hiker's stumbled onto the site and reported the burnt out hut to the police. They have found the body and are trying to establish its identity. What action do you want taken?'

'Did they give the location?'

'Yes, they said that it was in the Wollemi National Park.'

'Better brief a couple of agents. Tell them that we think it may be Kirkland and get up there. I'll contact the police commissioner and explain that we'll be taking over the investigation. Take Howard and Lorenzo.'

Harry left and the Director called the State Police Commissioner. The commissioner explained that the body was already with the coroner's office and if he wanted to gain control, then he would need an order from the Federal Court. The Director hung up; he was livid. He hoped Thwaites would be able to ensure that no evidence, which may be detrimental to their plot, was uncovered. Now, he would just have to hope they had been thorough enough to fool the coroner.

Harry and his two colleagues helicoptered into the site late in the morning. The state police had been notified they were coming. It had been explained that their office had been seconded to assist in the investigation, because the victim may have been a secret service agent.

This information had already been leaked to the media and the police had not been able to completely prevent their attendance. However, they had limited the number to half a dozen and had confiscated all camera equipment. As they disembarked, the trio, heavily disguised with large dark glasses and moustaches, were surrounded by this paparazzi troop. Then the questions started.

'What is your name please?' one young lady asked Harry.

'I'm sorry people, but for reasons of national security, we cannot answer any questions. I expect the government to make an announcement when more is known about what happened here.'

He continued, 'Now I must ask you all to leave the area. This is a crime scene and we cannot afford to have it contaminated.'

Another asked, 'Is it true the victim could be some sort of spy?'

'No it isn't, and I insist now that you all leave, or I will have to ask the police to intervene.'

With that the reporters packed up and moved a few hundred metres down the track and camped, waiting for further developments.

While Harry's companions carefully looked around the scene, he approached the detective in charge.

'Hello, my name's Thwaites, how is your investigation going?'

'Hi! I'm Detective Inspector Bellman, how do you do? We are doing OK so far. The fireys have been through the place with a fine-tooth comb. They reckon the burn was too extensive to be the gas bottle, which exploded. Also, something has been thrown or fired into the hut through the window.'

Harry swore under his breath, 'F...! I knew we should have cleaned up that glass evidence.'

'You'll be interested in this,' said the detective. He led Harry through the ruination to the centre of the hut. They had rolled back the scorched rug and exposed the cleverly concealed trap door leading to Leo's cellar. The door was open and the policeman beckoned Harry to follow him down the narrow steps, which he lit with a powerful torch.

'This guy had a mini arsenal down here. If he wasn't just a gun freak, or a terrorist, he was certainly well prepared for some serious eventuality.'

Harry studied the cellar and its contents and marvelled at Leo's ingenuity.

'Also,' Bellman continued, 'We've had a missing person report from a woman in Cullen Bullen, about thirty five Ks from here, to the northwest. She filed the report on her father, yesterday. She said she had found her father's dog sitting outside the hotel. When she couldn't see her father around she asked the people in the hotel if any of them had seen who brought the dog.'

Harry really started to take notice now as Bellman related how the woman then told him that an oddly acting American had come forward and told her he had found the dog wandering north of the town, and had adopted him.

Bellman continued, 'She did not believe him and when he left town, without calling in on the police as he had promised to do, she became very suspicious. When she heard about this on the news this morning, she fronted up at the police station and expressed her concerns that her father may have been the victim.'

Harry couldn't believe what he was hearing. They may have really blown it. The *American* could very well be Leo. Harry realised that, if he had in fact escaped and was out there, then they would be in real trouble. They must act quickly.

He separated himself from the group and called the Director. He knew the Director's instructions relating to a communication breach was just a ruse to fool Leo, so he had no qualms about making electronic contact. The Director took it all in and immediately saw a solution to the problem, if they had in fact killed the wrong man.

'Look,' he said, 'You brief Howard to get right down to the coroner's office and find out which one it is. He is to advise me ASAP.' After a slight pause, he continued,

'If it's Leo, we'll leave well enough alone on the accident theory for now. If it's the other, we'll cook up a story of a conspiracy, perpetrated by Kirkland, to commit the murder. If necessary, we can revert to plan B where we use the fake evidence we arranged at the pub to incriminate him in the drug deal.'

'But that would mean giving up our part of the action,' whined Harry.

'Stop griping,' replied the Director. 'It'd be a small price to pay to get us off the hook. We can make it appear like he was faking his own demise to cover up his misuse of power, and crimes committed by him, to allow him to escape prosecution.' Another pause. Then he added, 'We can make him a fugitive.'

Harry thought, 'Is there no end to this man's cunning?'

'OK! I'll get right onto it,' he said. Then he added, 'The police are already following the strong lead relating to the missing person. So he's quite likely to be the body we assumed was Leo. He must have been an acquaintance, or maybe a squatter.'

The Director swore. He already suspected Leo was onto their drug connection. That's why they took the action to waste him. If he were alive and free to pursue them, then he would be a formidable adversary.

Harry left Lorenzo to continue the oversight of the

police investigation and flew out of the devastated site. He dropped off Howard to pursue the forensic element and hastened to the Director's office. When he arrived, he found that his boss had already obtained a search warrant for Janine Kirkland's apartment.

The Director said, 'Before we go, get onto the *NSA* contact who organised the *Echelon* scan of the area. Get the rest of the IR tapes covering the period. Let's see, up to what time did you check to see if he stayed in there?'

'Yeah, well, until just after midnight,' Harry replied.

'OK, get the tape covering from midnight to two hours after the attack, I want the whole period reviewed, from an hour before we saw Leo, or whoever it was, going into the hut at seven, until two hours after the attack, so we can see if there was any other movement.'

Harry made a couple of calls to set it all up and they left for Janine's place, accompanied by a couple of highly trained investigators. The Director told them Leo was suspected of misfeasance, and Janine may be involved in a conspiracy with her father. They sped off to the Balgowlah address.

On arriving, they firstly questioned the apartment manager about Janine's whereabouts and the general pattern of her comings and goings. The manager was a little wary of them at first. But when they explained how the investigation related to matters of national security, she was more forthcoming.

She told them Janine had left quite hurriedly a few days earlier with a rucksack. When asked, she gave them

Janine's car registration number and description. Then she let them into the apartment and retreated to her office. Harry called the office, checked on the car details and arranged an APB on the car and Janine. He gave strict instructions that if found, she was not to be approached, but placed under surveillance until they could take over.

They went through the place with a fine-tooth comb and initially found little of great interest. Then, after putting together some of the papers they had found, they were surprised to discover that some of the material indicated a connection with security intelligence. It appeared as though she might work for some element within the SI organisation. The Director had no prior knowledge of this and told Harry it may put a new twist to the situation. If she were an operative, then it may make it easier to build a believable conspiracy case against Leo.

He asked the electronics investigator to check the phone records and examine the fax machine for evidence. This highly trained technical expert made a few calls to mysterious numbers, performed some complicated keystroke rituals on the fax, then unplugged it and carted it off to his lab.

Harry and the Director completed their search and headed back to the office. The Director checked the SI database and made a surprising discovery. Janine Eliza Kirkland was indeed employed within their field of interest. She worked at Naval Intelligence, in the cryptography section.

27

Leo woke from his dream-filled sleep and rolled out of the comfortable motel bed. It was already after seven thirty. He hadn't had such a good, sound sleep in what seemed like a month. He was getting used to the recurrence of his Korean experience by now, but still wondered why it kept returning.

He showered and shaved; nicely in time to collect the breakfast tray the proprietor slid through the small opening next to the door. As he started eating, the eight o'clock television news commenced. The headlines showed a low-level helicopter shot of the burnt-out wreckage of his hut. The commentator was describing how a body had been found in there and the police were investigating possible suspicious circumstances.

She said there were rumours ASIO may be involved and there may be some sort of spy connection. She added that no one in authority would make any comment at this time. But the newsroom would keep the public informed as new information became available.

Leo wondered how much the Director knew. If the conspirators thought their plot had succeeded; the news indicating nothing to the contrary, then he was safe for the time being. He realised though, that he must assume the worst-case scenario and plan on the assumption they knew he had survived their assassination attempt.

He decided he would have to take extreme, possibly unlawful, measures to catch them. He assessed from his earlier concerns that they must be involved with the drug ring their office was investigating. The incident at the pub where his cover was apparently blown; when the proprietor slipped him the Mickey Finn, must have been a blind. They had concocted the whole thing to throw him off the case before he woke up to their scheme.

This explained why the Director had sent him on furlough after the blown surveillance exercise at the pub. Of course, it also gave a reason for the attempted assassination.

That was his starting place! The publican, what was his name? Heinrich, Ernst Heinrich! He had a score to settle with that bastard anyway. So far, his investigation had shown this man to be directly responsible for the acquisition of heroin and other drugs, and of the distribution to high-school children. The Director and Harry's involvement in this atrocious trade was intolerable. It was no holds barred now. He had to put an end to this evil as quickly as possible, before they could get him or Janine.

In addition, he may be needed by Jim to help neutralise the terrorists.

Leo packed his gear, paid the bill and left. He rode to a hideout he had established as a safe house many years ago. It was in an otherwise deserted warehouse down on the Balmain waterfront. He had leased the space from a former colleague and converted it into a crude apartment-cum-fortress with a couple of well-secreted escape routes. The centre section was soundproofed and several hidden IR TV cameras protected the whole area.

Unlike the hut, no one knew of its existence except the owner, who was now retired and a highly trusted friend. Leo had used this as a base for several solo covert operations during the *cold-war* days. Since the collapse of the Soviet Union it had just been his personal hideaway. He used from time to time when he wanted to get away from it all, or go on one of his three day binges. As he moved in and made himself comfortable, he remembered some of those black days, the DTs and the demons.

He realised that for several weeks now, he had neither taken a drink, nor suffered the pangs of desire that always accompanied previous attempts to straighten out his problem. His place on the wheel of fortune had turned to a favourable position. He swore he would make it remain there and never again allow it to rotate to the nadir.

He promised himself that as soon as all these nasty situations were resolved, he would retire. The prospect of spending some quality time with his daughter again was a most attractive one. Maybe, just maybe, there was a pot of gold at the end of the rainbow. Perhaps he should try to find it at last. He didn't even bother to empty the whisky and beer down the drain. He knew now that he had beaten the problem and would not be tempted by their presence.

Leo decided he needed vital information from Heinrich, so he set about planning his surveillance and probable apprehension of this drug dealer. He placed the motorcycle in the small ground-floor room. This had an external door to enable a rapid departure, should he need one. He walked up to the main road and caught a taxi to a car rental agency where he hired a mini-van. Then he drove this back to his base, changed the plates and added some disguising stick-ons. After loading his eavesdropping equipment, he had some lunch and settled down to have a nap before launching on his night excursion to deal with Heinrich.

He quickly nodded off and returned to his Korean dream world.

28

Leo and Abdul had shared the same cell for the next five months, enduring all sorts of ill-treatment and degradation. Cemal's murderer, Wang, constantly tormented them. He took great pleasure from taunting Abdul about his religious beliefs. He gained mocking pleasure whenever he drew attention to the facts of Cemal's demise. He often pointed out how they could both follow in his footsteps if he so desired.

One day in the middle of winter, Wang and about six others, came for Leo. Two of them were tough looking females. They blindfolded him, sacked his head and hauled him off to another room. He was pushed roughly into the corner of two stone walls. It was near freezing and when he was told to strip off his clothes he hesitated. They cursed at him, shoved him face down on the floor, pulled his sweater and shirt off over his head, along with the sack, and removed his shoes and socks. All the time, Wang made sneering remarks and jabbed at his body and head with the long 'waddy' stick he always carried. Then he was rolled on his back and his trousers were removed.

They dumped him back on his face and after Wang had applied a couple of stinging blows to his buttocks, he was hauled to his feet and shoved back in the corner.

Leo was left standing in his underpants whilst his tormentors muttered in Chinese. He began to shiver violently, which elicited laughter and taunting remarks from the group. Then, through the blindfold he realised they had turned on some very bright lighting. Gradually, his body started to warm and his shivering ceased. After about a quarter of an hour, he started to feel uncomfortably hot in the face and upper torso. His feet, and his hands which were now handcuffed behind his back, were freezing.

Suddenly, the blindfold was whipped off and his eyeballs felt seared by two pairs of large, incandescent globes set on standards. These had been placed in front of him, each slightly to one side and only eighteen inches from his face.

As his eyes became accustomed to the glare he could just make out the silhouette shapes of his captors, standing at the back of the room.

'Now, Mister Kirkland,' sneered Wang. 'Let us have a little enlightenment from you. What is the first principle?'

Leo remained silent. Suddenly, he was hit in the face with great force by a bucketful of freezing water. He gasped as the chill ran through his partially heated body.

'Come, come Mister Kirkland,' the hateful voice bellowed. 'Let us not draw this out. What is the first principle?'

Leo mumbled, 'There are two classes, the proletariat and the bourgeoisie.'

'Very good. Which are you?

Leo waited a moment, then said, 'I am a pilot in the Royal Australian Air Force.'

Almost instantly, he was hit full in the chest with another pail of freezing water. Some of the splash-back hit one of the large globes, which exploded, showering his face and body with shattered glass. His lids had closed automatically, so none of glass went into his eyes. However, he could feel the stinging sensation where some slivers had superficially penetrated his skin. He also sensed some large pieces lying on and around his bare feet. He remained stock still, maintaining his bearing, with a defiant look on his face.

Wang was not a bit perturbed by this apparent accident and continued with his interrogation.

'I am fast losing patience with you Mister Kirkland. If you do not cooperate, you will be placed in a most invidious situation. Now, pull down your underpants.'

This was the first time they had wanted him completely naked and he was particularly embarrassed by the thought of stripping in front of the women. He stood still. A dark shape moved toward him behind one set of lights. A boot crunched on the broken glass. Then a hand reached for his jocks and ripped them off.

'Ugh!' exclaimed Wang. 'Uncircumcised, filthy, what a miserable excuse for a male organ.'

Leo glanced down at his cold, shrunken member and felt a huge wave of humiliation break over his whole body. One of *the females came forward and stood next to him. She started stroking his belly and thighs. Leo tried to turn away from her but was firmly grabbed by two of the guards and held facing the room.*

As the woman slowly started to stroke his penis, some of the males started to cheer and make taunting remarks. Leo had turned his face away from the woman and closed his eyes. Now he was suffering total degradation. He could not believe what was happening. He was starting to get an erection. More cheers ensued.

Then, when his penis had reached about half rigidity, without any warning, it was stuck a heavy downward blow. He cried out in extreme pain and opened his eyes to see Wang standing in front of him, his dreaded nightstick, raised above his head as if to strike again. The audience was now laughing in full derision of their victim.

Leo fainted.

He came to while being dragged on his belly along the corridor to his cell. He was still naked. The whole front of his body was being scraped along the stone floor and he was shivering with cold and shock. They hurled him unceremoniously into the cell as Abdul stood helplessly against the back wall.

As soon as the guards departed, Abdul placed the futon on the wire mattress, picked up his friend and placed him gently on the bed. He had felt the slivers of glass scratch his arm as he lifted Leo and wondered what diabolical treatment the evil gang had dished out this time.

As Abdul picked out the broken glass and bathed his friend's tortured body, he remembered well their first meeting and how Leo had looked after him in his time of need. They were now bonded in a deep friendship, which he knew would help them both endure this outrageous scourge. Leo looked up into his companion's eyes and saw the compassion expressed there.

Abdul said, 'What have they done to you this time my friend?'

Leo described his ordeal and thanked Abdul for his care.

'You are a very brave young man, sir,' said Abdul. He continued, 'I know that between us, we will beat these infidels.'

Leo said, 'Abdul, if it wasn't for your strength and encouragement, I don't think I could have survived this long. But I now know how it is and I agree with you. They can only beat us by killing us.'

Abdul covered Leo with three of the four blankets they had in their cell and Leo soon drifted off into an exhausted sleep. Abdul sat on the end of the cot, curled up in the remaining blanket, and grabbed snatches of sleep as best he could, while watching over his friend.

29

Janine was now safely ensconced in the Harrison apartment at the US embassy. When the news about the discovery of the body of a possible spy splashed across the TV screen, Janine was shocked. Even though Leo had warned her of this possible outcome, she wondered if the circumstances may have changed and that maybe he really was gone. It *was* exactly as he had described. So she would have to accept the situation for the time being.

She felt that, although Leo had instructed her to tell no one except Jim, she had to confide in Helen as well. If they mentioned Leo, it might be too much of a shock. So for the sake of Helen's peace of mind and so she could understand Janine's own position, she swore Helen to secrecy and told her about the plot. She explained that if Leo's identity was revealed in relation to the death, they must act as if it were real. This would require the pretence of grief and if necessary, being involved in a fake memorial, or maybe even, a burial service.

Helen handled this new information well. She was quite used to sudden changes, and the occurrence of strange events. She shared a confidence with Janine, telling her that Jim had told her he was working on foiling a terrorist attack uncovered by Leo, but knew nothing of the details.

The Colonel had been extremely busy for a couple of days, apparently following up on the terrorists. He had told Janine nothing more about the bomb plot, or what action was being taken to foil it. She took this opportunity to refresh her friendship with *Auntie* Helen. They had always been close, but Janine had not had an opportunity to spend time with the Harrisons for a few years.

Although the circumstances were far from desirable, this was a good occasion to renew their friendship. The two of them spent some happy hours reliving old times, swapping recipes and generally enjoying each other's company.

Helen told Janine, 'I'm a bit worried about Jim's safety with this terrorist thing. He hasn't, to my knowledge, been involved in anything dangerous for years, and he may have lost his touch dealing with bad boys.'

'I shouldn't worry too much on Jim's account,' Janine responded. 'He seems to be squarely on the ball with this one.'

Janine started thinking of the call she had received from Sumiko Tsushima. She must have been the friend of Michiko, whom her father had mentioned on several occasions. She recalled that Sumiko was engaged to marry Michiko's cousin. This would explain why she had the same name.

She wondered why she was in Australia and why she seemed so interested in locating her father. Janine surmised that it must be to renew old acquaintance. She certainly had sounded nice on the phone and Janine was keen to meet her.

One morning, she found the number Sumiko had given her and called. An operator answered, saying, 'Good morning, this is the Embassy of Japan, how may I help you?'

Janine was surprised that she had reached the Japanese embassy. She identified herself and asked to speak to Tsushima Sumiko. The connection was made and

Sumiko answered. She was extremely pleasant, sounding most anxious to talk with Janine.

She asked, 'Could we meet somewhere and talk.'

Janine said, 'Yes, that would be good. Let me think for a moment.'

She comprehended the possible risk in going out but brushed the thought aside and arranged to meet Sumiko in an hour at the same cafe where she had taken Jim.

Without explaining whom she was meeting, she told her *aunt* of her plan to go out. Helen questioned the wisdom of being seen in public, given the possible risks, which Janine herself had explained. Janine said she couldn't believe that her father's enemies could have followed her here and figured it was probably OK.

She felt a compulsion to meet Sumiko and allowed the feeling to cloud her better judgment.

30

Back at their office, Harry and the Director waited for the reports to come in. There would be one from Lorenzo at the *scene*, one from Howard, who was checking the Coroner's office, and the police APB on Janine.

As they were discussing their options, Lorenzo called in. He told them about the local police turning up at the scene. The woman from Cullen Bullen, who had placed the missing person report on her father, accompanied them. She had her father's dog with her. The leashed dog had gone directly to the burnt out area and the cot on which the body had been found. It whined terribly, and then led them to a bush about fifty metres from the shack. It sniffed around as though it knew the area. The onlookers detected no signs of any evidence.

Then the dog took the police racing down the hill to the north, about a kilometre, and started scratching at a spot under a large tree. Here they discovered a cache, which when opened contained a swagman's *bluey*. Back at the scene the lady tearfully identified it as her father's gear. There was no doubt. The body was his. They felt sure the coroner's report would confirm this.

The Director immediately arranged for the issue of an APB on Leo, to be arrested on charges of murder and conspiracy. Naturally on this issue, the state police were in charge and the pair of real conspirators felt they had left enough in the way of clues and information for the police to proceed with the investigation.

They were more circumspect in relation to Janine. They wanted her as an extra insurance against nailing Kirkland. So when the police surveillance contact informed them about her car being located at the US embassy in Canberra, the Director advised him that this was a national security matter. He, in conjunction with the *feds*, would now handle the case. The police contact said that, because the subject was now in the ACT, the Federal Police had already taken over the stakeout, and gave him the mobile contact number. The Director then phoned the surveillance operative and requested that

Janine be kept under surveillance until they could take over the next day.

He told the officers, 'She is not to be approached in any way, because we want her to lead us to bigger fish.'

As the two of them prepared to set off for the Capital, their chief cryptologist came in with the results of deciphering the message the technicians had managed to recover from the memory circuits of Janine's fax machine. He told them the electronics guys had placed the receipt of the fax on the 12th. This was two days before their attempted assassination. So the schemers assessed that Leo would not have known about their plot.

The Director was anxious to learn the contents of the message. The cipher expert explained that initially, after an intensive brainstorming exercise, they had figured the initial decode of digital text. However, this only gave them a set of gobbledegook letters that they had found impossible to decode.

The Director was furious. He raved at Harry and the technician, 'Why can't this whole section of so-called experts break a code devised by a *non-expert*?'

Harry and the tech looked a little non-plussed by this outburst and neither answered. The Director commanded them to keep at it until they achieved a result.

He and Harry headed for the Capital.

31

Even though Janine rationalised it would be safe to venture out, she still took a circuitous route to the cafe. On entering, she saw an attractive Asian lady sitting in a booth looking expectantly in her direction. As she approached, she marvelled at how young this woman looked. She was expecting someone from around her father's time. This person looked more her own age.

'Probably a daughter or niece of Sumiko,' she thought. She had the palest Asian skin Janine had ever seen and beautiful, almond shaped eyes.

Sumiko stood to greet her with a traditional bow, to which Janine responded in similar fashion. Then Sumiko offered her hand in a Western style handshake.

She said in perfect English, 'Hello Janine, I am so happy to have found you.'

Janine was a little surprised at the warmth of the greeting, especially from a stranger, and an Asian as well. As they sat down on opposite sides of the small booth table, the waitress came over and took their coffee orders.

Then they started what would be one of the most exciting conversations in Janine's whole experience. Sumiko told her she was part of the Japanese diplomatic corps and had been based at the Canberra embassy for five months. Janine was completely intrigued by this woman. She felt an instant affinity with her, and even sensed there was something, somehow familiar about her. She was most impressed by her direct manner and her western style of speech.

Janine told Sumiko about her early life, her mother's death, and of the wonderful relationship she enjoyed with her father. She asked Sumiko about her life and what relationship she had to Michiko. Sumi told how Michiko had followed her father into the diplomatic service. Because she was female, she was not able to attain the level of ambassador, or even that of consul in those days. However, she had enjoyed a long and distinguished career in the service of her country.

She told Janine how Michiko's father had intercepted Leo's letters from Korea, preventing her from finding out the circumstances of Leo's non-return. It wasn't until after her father's death many years later, that her mother gave her the letters. She also gave her the one from Leo's friend Jack. This told of his being shot down over North Korea and his probable death. She was devastated by this news and had always believed that, because he did not ever contact her, he must have died. Sumiko, on the other hand, said she had always thought there was a chance he may have survived. So, ever since she had been in Australia, she had been trying to trace him. She must have phoned around one hundred Kirklands nationally.

It now became clear to Janine why her father had always wondered why Michiko had not answered his letters. She asked Sumiko whatever became of Michiko. Sumiko hesitated, and then continued with her story. She asked Janine if her father had told her that he and

Michiko had been lovers. Janine was surprised at the personal nature of this question. However, she felt a strong bond of trust forming with this delightful person.

So she told how her father had described his relationship with Michiko as a beautiful and innocent experience. He also told her that, apart from his unconsummated love affair with Michiko, he had never been with any woman other than her mother. She firmly believed him and had always felt proud of the fact. Sumiko expressed how she found great warmth in the story, and Janine sensed that she experienced some real joy in hearing it.

Sumiko then became very serious. She said, 'What I am about to tell you Janine, will come as a big surprise to you.'

Janine felt an exciting, tingling sensation right down her spine.

'What is happening here?' she thought.

Sumiko said, 'Michiko is my mother. She named me after her best friend who married my uncle, Kenje. They were both killed in a car accident on their honeymoon just before I was born.'

Janine let out a shocked sigh. She was now starting to get apprehensive about the outcome of this story. The chronology was getting all mixed up. Or was it coming together?

'My mother told me about the only time that she had ever been with a man. Even though they had not had complete intercourse, she had become pregnant. She told

163

me that she bore me out of wedlock, which was a most difficult cross to bear in Japan in those days.'

She paused momentarily as Janine looked into her eyes with a growing sense of anticipation.

'It was even more so, her being part of a catholic family. She has never married and raised me as a single mother.'

Sumiko reached across the table and took both of Janine's hands in hers. Janine felt an overwhelming sensation of comprehension.

They looked deeply into each other's eyes and said in unison one questioning, the other informing. 'We are sisters.'

Then they both burst out crying.

The nearby customers looked around at these two women who were obviously experiencing a deep emotional moment. The two, who were completely oblivious to their surroundings, gushed forth with story and response for the next hour.

Sumiko told of the good and bad times during her childhood. They were mainly good. Both of her grandparents had been wonderful to her and had supported Michiko through troubled times. Sumiko too, had never married, devoting all of her energies to caring for her mother and, like her mother and grandfather, enjoying a full career in the diplomatic service. Janine asked where her mother was now.

'She is retired now' said Sumiko. 'Grandmother died several years ago, so she lives with me, at the embassy.'

Janine became quite excited at this news. She asked if Sumiko had told her mother what she had discovered about Leo.

'Yes,' she replied. 'Mother is most excited at the prospect of meeting him again. I know she is still in love with him. But where is he?'

Hesitant to tell Sumiko too much about the current situation, Janine spoke cautiously.

'He is still out of contact and I have not been able to tell him yet, about hearing from you.'

Sumiko showed a little disappointment, but appeared satisfied with this answer, and they continued their tête-à-tête.

Janine told how she had not married. She had long ago decided the reason was probably that, even though he had developed an alcohol problem, no prospective suitors had matched up to Leo. She knew it was a ridiculous concept, to judge their attributes against her own father, but that had been the case. Sumiko asked if Leo still suffered from the drinking problem and Janine told her she wasn't sure, but thought he had probably beaten it.

There was now a strong bond forming between them and they both were excited at the prospect of informing their father of this newfound joy. Sumiko asked Janine to please call her Sumi, as she preferred to be called by her friends and family. She told Janine she would like to introduce her to her mother.

'I have already told her about discovering Leo's daughter, and she is very keen to get to know you.' Sumi had also told her mother of their meeting plans. She asked if Janine would like to drive her back to the Japanese Embassy, as a DC limousine had dropped her off. Janine thought this was a great idea. So Sumi phoned the driver and told him a friend would be bringing her back to the embassy in about half an hour, and asked him to advise her mother.

Janine decided not to phone Helen and tell her of their plans. She did not want to discuss her new discoveries until after Leo had been enlightened. They paid for their coffee and headed for Janine's car.

32

Leo awoke from his nap about 1700 hours and had a quick energy snack before setting off to check out Heinrich. He was rather apprehensive about the action he was contemplating. He had limited constabulary powers. To illegally arrest or capture someone, and then to deny them their personal freedom, went against all of his principles. This policy was particularly compelling now, in light of the recently revisited experiences suffered during his incarceration as a POW.

Leo felt as though he needed a good slug of whisky. Well, actually, he didn't. He now knew he had beaten that devil. He hadn't touched the stuff for about a month and knew he was, now, clean. It had only been a kind of crutch to help him overcome some fears he hadn't really understood.

Many years ago, he had achieved an understanding of post-traumatic syndrome and the need some people have for counselling. He had always felt he was not one of those weaker individuals. He was above any of that sissy stuff. However, with hindsight, he *had* suffered nightmares for years after his return from Korea. The Vietnam experience had also taken a great toll on his psyche and was certainly a major factor in the failure of his marriage. He probably had needed help then, but didn't know it. It certainly wasn't offered by the powers that were, in those days.

He now knew that a person had to be able to find his own strengths and recognise his own weaknesses, to survive this world's tests and traumas. He identified strongly with the lines of an old Billie Holiday song that goes, 'God bless the child that's got his own … .'

Leo arrived at the hotel a little after seven. He checked the area to ensure no other surveillance was being undertaken. Then he parked the van near the lane at the back of the hotel. There was a high corrugated iron fence with chained and padlocked double gates. Next to these, was a small access gate with a yale-type lock. Leo peered through the cracks and established that there was no one there in the darkened backyard. He quickly picked the lock, quietly opened the small gate and slipped inside. The unattractive area contained a stack of wooden crates to the left of the one, outward-opening door. To the right of the door, was an untidy array of steel beer barrels. He gently tapped a couple of these. They we empty. Leo exited through the small gate, snibbing the lock open and pulling it closed behind him. He moved the van to a position next to the small gate and unlocked its rear door, ready for quick access. He took his binoculars and listening device, crossed the road, and the ditch, in front of the hotel, secreted himself in the bushes and settled down to watching and listening.

After about half an hour he heard Heinrich's voice emanating from the bar area. From the other sounds, he assessed that business was quiet. There were probably four other voices, including the barman. After about another half-hour, Heinrich told the barman he was going out the back to sort out the empty barrels.

This was the chance Leo had been waiting for. He made his way around to the rear of the hotel and quickly slipped through the gate. Pushing it closed behind him, he moved to a position next to the hinge side of the left-hand opening door. None too soon!

As he unsheathed the hypodermic syringe, which contained a quick-acting anaesthetic, the door opened and Heinrich appeared. Leo leaped at him from behind, grasping his head at mouth level in a powerful headlock with his left arm. He shoved the needle into the right side of his victim's neck, discharged its contents and hung on tightly as Heinrich threshed about. It only took three seconds for him to become a limp sack in Leo's grip.

He dropped his captive, closed the rear door then capped and secured the syringe. Next, he shouldered the unconscious man and carried him out, dumping him in the back of the van. He relocked the gate; his rubber gloves ensuring no fingerprints or DNA were left behind. Then he drove back to his safe-house.

Once inside, he unloaded Heinrich who was still unconscious. Leo checked his vital signs then carried him up to the spare room. He had cleared this of everything, except a not-too-comfortable chair that he had placed in the centre of the floor with its back to the door. He bound Heinrich to the chair with his hands handcuffed behind him, gagged him with tape and blindfolded him. He left him to recover from his anaesthesia. Leo figured this would take about one more hour.

It was now just after 2100 hours, so he decided to take a catnap. It was going to be a long night. He soon drifted off into a dreamful sleep.

33

It was now June 1953. Abdul and Leo had survived the harsh North Korean winter and the dreadful actions of their captors. There seemed to no limit to their devilish imaginations.

A rather cruel, non-contact torture was the 'denied water' treatment. This commenced by being held in solitary for two, or sometimes three days with no water. Then the prisoner was tied to a chair, hands secured behind, while a trickle of water was poured from a pipe in front of his face. As the captive strained forward in vain effort to suck in some of the precious fluid, the pipe was moved away, just out of reach. This torment was sometimes carried out for hours on end, or until the pitiful soul fainted from exhaustion.

These evil deeds, the beatings and the incessant brain washing had not taken a great toll on the pair's spirits. This was mainly because they took care of each other.

The 'dung pit' treatment was their most despicable experience. One of them would be tied up, dumped in the six-foot deep trench and subjected to the humiliation of being urinated and defecated on by the guards. If one of them had to spend, perhaps three days in there without food or water, the other would clean him up, then nurture and revivify him.

They continued to follow Abdul's regime of strict military discipline when in the presence of others. This amused, yet confounded their captors who could not quite fathom them out. They had long since decided it was prudent to learn the ten principles and recite them when demanded. This saved them many beatings and helped convince these Communist fanatics that they were winning them over. Though neither of them ever cooperated enough to warrant 'the lenient treatment'.

One morning at daybreak, four Korean guards came to their cell. They both automatically took their places, against the back wall. The guards entered and cuffed their hands in front of them. Then they were blindfolded and the inevitable sacks placed over their heads. Nothing was said. They were bundled outside and herded across the gravel yard where Leo was forced up into a truck. Here he was seated, facing forward, on one of several wooden planks fixed across the tray.

In his blind and bound state, it was difficult climbing across the planks, and when seated there was barely enough legroom behind the row in front. From the body contacts and the sounds around him, Leo figured there were more than a dozen other occupants.

He had just made himself as comfortable as possible when the familiar voice of the dreaded Wang said quietly, 'You are now being taken to camp number three, you must not talk and must not try to move.' He continued, 'Any attempt to escape will be met with death.'

They departed and headed along a reasonably smooth road. It was quite warm in the back of the topless vehicle and Leo assessed from the feel of the sun on his bare arms and the left side of his body, that they were travelling generally in a southerly direction.

After about three hours, Leo heard the approaching roar of piston-engine aircraft, diving toward them. Then, the rat-tat-tat of machine guns. The sound of bullets striking metal and flesh, intermingled with the screams of those taking hits, threw everything into turmoil. Leo recognised the sounds of the aircraft. These were 'Mustangs', North American F51 fighters. He had flown this type during his fighter conversion training. They must have been ROKAF. The South Koreans, who had the largest number of attack aircraft, even outnumbering the USAF, were the only units still operating these magnificent WW II aircraft.

Perhaps the truck he was in was part of a convoy, because it was unlikely any allied squadron would attack a single vehicle. The truck swerved to the right throwing him against the person next to him and then down onto the truck-bed. A limp and obviously bleeding body fell on top of him as he tried to hold on to the plank seat from below. The truck lurched over the edge of the road and careered down a steep slope. Then it veered to the left and rolled over onto its right side, coming to a scraping stop.

Leo was stunned and hurting, but he felt intact. A few people were groaning around him. After a couple of minutes he had recovered his senses enough to rip the sack off his head and pull the blindfold down from his eyes. He was covered in blood. There were bodies everywhere, a mixture of UN prisoners and Korean or Chinese guards. Leo quickly looked around him to assess his situation.

Abdul was nowhere to be seen; perhaps he had been placed in another vehicle or had been thrown out as they plunged into the gully. The truck had come to rest at the bottom of a small draw, which had a narrow creek running through it. It was sheltered beneath some relatively dense trees.

He was amazed to find he hadn't been hit. Because of all the blood and the pain of being banged about, he could not tell if he had suffered any other injuries. He could hear other vehicles speeding off, with the planes in hot pursuit, continuing the machine-gun attack. Leo hoped they didn't contain any more prisoners. This was more than enough damage by friendly fire.

His initial observation was that the back of the driver's

side of the cabin had been penetrated by up to ten 50-calibre rounds. The driver would be dead. There appeared to be six guards. None of these seemed to be alive. He counted eight other prisoners, six appeared lifeless and the other two were moving and groaning. He could not believe how lucky he had been.

As he eased himself out of the back of the truck, he heard some heavy grunts and saw someone attempting to climb up past the small window in the back of the driver's cabin. It was Wang. He must have been in the passenger seat and would have had to extricate himself from under the driver's body. Leo went to ground next to the body of one of the guards and feigned death.

Out of the corner of his eye he watched Wang pull himself up and out of the driver's window, which was now the highest point of the vehicle, then climb down to the ground. His uniform was covered with blood. However, apart from some slight bleeding about his head, he appeared to be unhurt. He stood at the front end of the truck and looked around at the carnage. As he took it all in, he let out a string of harsh sounding Chinese words that Leo assumed were expletives.

He started to move amongst the variously sprawled bodies. When he came to the first, writhing prisoner, who had obviously been hit by the attacking aircraft, he drew his service pistol and without hesitation, shot him in the head. The second conscious prisoner, whom Leo recognised as one of the English officers, tried to raise himself on one elbow and called out.

'Don't shoot!'

Wang turned toward him and raised his weapon. Leo leapt to his feet and lunged, screaming at the monster. Before he could make contact, Wang fired, dispatching this second captive as well. He then turned the gun on Leo, slowly and carefully aiming between his eyes. Wang had the most cruelly evil look on his face.

'I'm really going to enjoy this,' he sneered. 'Goodbye Mr Kirkland.'

In that instant, there was a horrific cry from around the front of the truck. Abdul appeared, leaping at Wang's back like a screaming leopard, his arms raised high above his head. Before Wang could fire, or react to the attack, Abdul's hands passed down either side of his head and pulled the chain of the handcuffs up under his chin. As Abdul wrenched the chain into the hated throat, Leo dived at their tormentor's knees in a rugby tackle. This applied even greater pressure to the stranglehold.

It was all over in a split second. Wang had paid the price for his evil and Abdul had avenged the murder of his friend Cemal. He had also saved Leo's life one more time.

Now they acted quickly and in unison. Abdul went through Wang's pockets, searching for the handcuff keys, while Leo checked first the prisoners, then the guards, for signs of life. He found none. The friendly fire, the despicably murderous acts of Wang, and his own execution, had left Abdul and Leo as the only survivors.

Judging by the rapid departure of the other vehicles, it was unlikely that this incident would be discovered in the short term. So they calmly organised themselves. Firstly, they undid each other's handcuffs. Then they washed as best they could in the creek. Next, they kitted themselves with military boots, fatigues, jackets and caps from the dress of their guards. Most of these garments were badly bloodied, so they did their best to rinse off as much of the grime and gore as they could in the stream. It was a grizzly experience, for Leo especially.

His combat experience was the remote kind, gained from the cockpit of a speeding jet, supplemented by training in simulated hand-to-hand fighting and the use of firearms against lifeless targets. Even the harsh treatment, to which he had been subjected since his capture, did not inure him to this ghastly situation. Although Abdul was a toughened Turk, his artillery background did not fully equip him to cope with such an event either.

They cut and tore off any insignia from the uniforms, so they wouldn't be taken as spies, should they be recaptured. Abdul armed himself with an AK47, a bandolier of extra magazines and a bayonet, while Leo took a .45 automatic pistol from a badly shot-up Korean guard. He recognised it as US Army issue, probably taken from a captured or killed American. He recovered some extra clips of suitable ammunition from the gruesome body.

They found a couple of packs of the Chinese equivalent to 'K' rations and three water bottles. Hurrying, they headed off in a westerly direction toward the coast. Despite their poor treatment over many months, they were both physically and mentally fit. Once they had separated themselves from the horrific scene, Leo's spirits rose to the challenges of survival and evading re-capture.

They trekked for several hours, managing to keep up a fairly stiff pace with Abdul taking the lead.

As they passed through an area of scrubby trees, Abdul suddenly lurched forward and fell prone on the ground. He did not cry out and as Leo caught up he saw that his friend was not moving. Blood was seeping through the lower right side of the back of his shirt.

'He must have been shot,' thought Leo, although he had heard no report.

Leo quickly turned his friend on his left side and established that he was still breathing. He placed his ear against Abdul's chest and detected a weak, slow heartbeat. He pulled up his shirt and found the source of the bleeding. Abdul had obviously sustained a small, but deep shrapnel wound during the attack. He had kept this to himself, plugging the wound with a piece of cloth. He must have been haemorrhaging internally ever since.

Leo tried to bandage the wound, which strangely was not producing much blood. As he completed his first aid, Abdul stirred and groaned. He tried to speak, but only a sigh passed his lips. When he started to shiver violently Leo raised his head and cradled him in his arms. He was at a loss as to what action he should take to help.

Abdul looked up into Leo's eyes and in a whispering, croaking voice said, 'I'm sorry my friend, but I think I'm going.'

His skin had turned to a sallow, almost grey colour and his pulse was beginning to race. Leo clutched him closer and started rocking back and forth.

Then, as Leo softly moaned, 'No, no, please hold on?' Abdul closed his eyes and drifted off into a quiet death.

Leo continued gently rocking his lost companion and wept freely. He felt an overwhelming, fearful disbelief, that having come through all of those trials and horrors with strength and courage, it could end like this. Just when it seemed as though they might reach freedom at last.

34

Leo awoke from his sad dream. Tears had streamed over his nose and down his cheek during his sleep and he felt rotten. Remembering the loss of his friend in such a vivid dream had wrung him out. It was almost ten o'clock, and he calculated that the publican would be coming around from his knockout dose soon. He lay there, remembering the final episode of his Korean experience.

After holding Abdul's body for what seemed like an eternity, he had put him down, then dug a hole with the bayonet and buried the AK47, and some other gear that Abdul had brought with him. He lifted his lost friend's body onto his shoulders and carried him up over a rise, looking for a more appropriate place to bury him. Over the top of the hill, he came upon a small clearing with soft turf and several large boulders at its edge. It was bordered by low conifers and looked a peaceful spot. He assessed that it faced almost due west, the general direction of Mecca. Leo chose this place to lay his companion's body to rest. He set about digging as deep a grave as possible in the sandy soil.

After several hours he had managed to make a hole about three or four feet deep and six feet long. For one last time, Leo gazed at the strong face he had come to love as that of a brother. He looked at peace.

Carefully, he cut the nylon cord beneath Abdul's top dog tag and removed the second one, leaving the first around that strong neck. This was in the hope that someday, someone who cared would discover his remains, and ensure that they were disposed of properly.

He gently kissed Abdul's forehead, wrapped his head in his shirttail to keep the dirt off his face and placed him carefully in the hole. He knew no Muslim prayers, but remembered the words of the twenty-third psalm and thought them appropriate. He softly recited that beautiful piece.

'The LORD is my shepherd; I shall not want.

He maketh me to lie down in green pastures: he leadeth me beside the still waters.

He restoreth my soul: he leadeth me in the paths of righteousness for his name's sake.

Yea, though I walk through the valley of the shadow of death, I will fear no evil: for thou art with me; thy rod and thy staff they comfort me.

Thou preparest a table before me in the presence of mine enemies: thou aniontest my head with oil; my cup runneth over.

Surely goodness and mercy shall follow me all the days of my life: and I will dwell in the house of the LORD forever.'

He carefully covered the body, packing the soil firmly around it. Next, he rolled some of the boulders over the place and packed smaller rocks around them to mark the grave, and to give it some protection from predators.

He broke off a branch from a softwood tree on the edge of the clearing and carefully removed the bark. After sharpening the point of the bayonet on a rock, he inscribed the branch as deeply as possible. The inscription read:

CPL ABDUL AKKISLA TURKISH ARMY
UN SOLDIER JUN 53 RIP

Leo jammed the branch upright between the boulders. He mapped the position with a pencil and pad he had found in a dead guard's pocket. He drew profiles of three topographical features around the spot with estimated bearings to triangulate the site. Finally, before he left the place, he made a personal vow.

If he survived and was ever able to, he would visit Abdul's home village and tell his people of their time together, and what a wonderful human being this great Turk was. He would also give them the dog tag, which he now tied securely to his own for safekeeping. The sun was low in the sky as he bade his friend a last farewell and set off to the west. Rain clouds began streaming in from the northwest.

He slogged on over hill and dale into the night. The land here was fairly undulating and barren. Apart from stumbling several times over rough patches, he made good progress for several hours. The rain started, lightly at first, but gradually it increased as he climbed yet another hill. As he came over the crest, he could see in the valley ahead, the lights of what looked like a village.

Immediately in front of him he could make out the lines of a small hut. It showed no lights and appeared to be derelict. He crept around it and estimated it was no more than fifteen feet by eight, and about as high. It had no windows and on the western side was a small door, about five feet by two feet.

'Must be a shepherd's shelter,' he thought. He slowly pushed open the unlatched door. It was pitch black inside and the earthen floor felt as though it was covered in dry straw or grass. It smelled musty but not really unpleasant.

As Leo now lay awake in his comfortable bed, he remembered that back then, he had been so absolutely exhausted he could have slept on a bed of nails. The straw-covered earthen floor was delightfully inviting and it was quite warm in there. He just took off his pack and, using it for a pillow, straightaway fell into a deep, uninterrupted sleep.

He slept until the light of dawn started filtering through the cracks around the door. He was instantly wide-awake and listened closely for any sounds outside.

Hearing none, he slowly pulled open the door. The daylight streamed in as he looked back into the hut.

A cold shiver ran down his spine as he saw, standing against the rear wall, two caskets. In each was a bandage-wrapped body, one taller than the other. He felt ill as he realised he had spent the night in the company of two mummies. There was something almost Egyptian about the two *sarcophagi*. His whole body reacted with an electric tingling and he felt as though he was about to throw up.

Grabbing his backpack, he lurched out into the burgeoning day, oblivious to the possibility of being seen. Luckily no one was out there. He stumbled forward and found himself in the midst of about twenty dome-shaped mounds. These were around four feet high, grass covered and punctured by rabbit warrens. They were gravesites. He was in the middle of the village cemetery. The two in the rough mausoleum must have been a village chief and his wife, forever overlooking their earthly domain.

Leo remembered seeing mounds like these among the trees beside the road between the Kimpo air force base and Seoul. Someone had explained that Korean people bury their dead in a sitting position, usually facing their home, and build a mound over them. He had made the trip into Seoul only once and he remembered it well because of a rather unusual occurrence.

On one of his off-duty days, the squadron entertainments officer had arranged for a busload of members to go for a swim in a downtown pool that the British

Commonwealth Forces had taken over. When they arrived there they found the pool in a dreadfully polluted state. The water was a dark green colour and the scant furniture around the pool was badly in need of a good coat of paint. Jack and he had decided they couldn't be bothered wasting time by just sunbathing like the others in such dilapidated surroundings, so they went looking for somewhere to eat.

They found a small cafe not far from the pool and went in. The menu was all in Korean, although an Arabic number identified each dish. They decided number fourteen was the go and pointed to it to order from the waitress.

When their meal arrived it was a sort of chop suey with noodles and pieces of meat. These tasted like pork. The flavour was sweet and sour and it was served quite hot. This was washed down with some weak, Chinese style tea. They were feeling rather satisfied when the little old gentleman at the next table spoke to them.

'You American boys?' he asked.

'No,' answered Jack. 'We're Australians.'

'Ah so, Goshu boys, you rike Korea food?'

'It was OK,' Leo answered.

'You know what you ate?'

They were hesitant to answer, fearing they would be told something they may not wish to hear. He continued without prompt.

'That favourite Korea food, stirr-born baby.'

Both men laughed at the absurd suggestion. Obviously, he was making fun of them. But the old papa san did not appear to see any joke and maintained his inscrutable expression.

Jack said to Leo, 'It tasted like young pork. Do you think he means unborn piglet or calf? I have heard a rumour like that, but it still sounds pretty revolting.'

Leo responded, saying, 'I have no idea, but it does kind of take the edge off the meal.'

They paid the bill and left. Neither would ever know whether the old man had taken a rise out of them; or that perhaps they may have in fact eaten something outside their normal dietary range.

Leo recalled that after the graveyard event, he had managed to evade recapture for several weeks, surviving on the meagre Korean military food and a couple of snakes he had caught. Gradually, he had made his way toward the West Coast where he planned to steal a boat. His idea had been to attempt to make it out to the naval vessels to be picked up, hopefully by Australian or other friendly forces.

However, luck had not been on his side, and he was finally found sleeping in a disused barn, and returned to custody right about the time the armistice was being signed in Panmunjom.

His treatment was much better this time around. He suffered no recrimination for his escape, because the prisoner exchange programme was under way. He had figured that his North Korean and Chinese captors, probably wanted to use any act of apparent good treatment of prisoners to strengthen their position in the armistice negotiations. After a further three weeks he was repatriated.

He could not go back to North Korea to attend properly to Abdul's remains. With the continuing confrontation between North and South, he knew he never would. He had passed on the details of Abdul's grave, as well as he was able, to the authorities. These included his roughly sketched map.

He never did keep his personal vow to visit Abdul's village and this often bothered him. Maybe one day, he would.

Anyway, more important things were at hand; like his planned interrogation of Heinrich. He rose, washed his face and headed for the room where Heinrich was probably awake by now.

35

Jim Harrison had ordered a high-level reconnaissance and satellite scan of Leo's report area. These had indeed revealed the huts as described, but there was no human or vehicular movement. Colonel Harrison's superior officer was half inclined to dismiss this as either a hoax, or the ravings of a demented mind. However, from bitter past experience, he knew that to ignore information like this was not acceptable. It was just not worth the risk.

So the Brigadier gave Jim carte blanche approval to take whatever action necessary, to foil any attempt to attack the embassy. Jim arranged for a small party of the Australian Army Anti-terrorist Force (East) to be lifted into the area by helicopter to assess the situation, and requested their leader to report their findings to him. The on-site investigation had revealed that the location was completely sterile of any evidence, except that approximately twenty or more people, and four vehicles had busily occupied it. This activity had occurred up to as late as three days ago. Then they had moved on. The vehicles had departed to the north. However, when the trail reached a sealed road, the party lost track of them. It did appear as though they had headed west from where they joined the road.

Now, all stops were out to find and neutralise them.

36

Harry and the Director took over the surveillance of Janine at 1100 hours. The local man had followed her to a small cafe in a northern suburb of the Capital. He told them she had been in there, meeting with another female, for about an hour.

He pointed her out and handed over the watch to

them. Harry identified her using a photograph from her apartment. Neither recognised the other woman.

They watched the two, who were engrossed in animated natter, for another half an hour. Then the women rose from their booth, paid the cashier and left the cafe. Janine's companion was of Asian appearance, of indiscernible origin. They appeared to be good friends. They walked a block to Janine's car and she drove off in the direction of the CBD. The Director ordered Harry to follow in standard fashion, two cars behind, and told him that as soon as she dropped off her companion, they would take Janine into custody.

Janine proceeded through the city and across Commonwealth Avenue Bridge. As she approached the end of the avenue, she took the State Circle exit.

'My God!' exclaimed the Director, 'She's heading back to the embassy. Once she gets inside we'll have one dickens of a job taking her. Force her over next to the park.' Harry started to overtake. There was virtually no traffic as they joined the Circle.

Harry asked, 'What about the companion?'

The Director snapped, 'We'll have to take her as well now. Do it!'

Harry pulled up alongside the little red car and with an expert manoeuvre, forced Janine against the kerb. Janine instantly knew she had blown it. She should have taken notice of Helen; and her own reason, and not ventured out. She swung the wheel hard over to the left and jumped the kerb, careering across the grass into the park.

Sumiko screamed out, 'What's happening?'

Janine answered, 'I'm sorry Sumi, please forgive me, I have placed us in a dangerous situation. These evil people are after Leo and they are trying to capture me.'

Harry was instantly on her tail and his much more powerful vehicle was easily forcing her deeper into the deserted park. Sumi was now completely terrorised as Harry forced them into a line of large bushes. As her car came to a sudden stop, Janine pushed the button, locking the doors and yelled out, 'Get on the floor!'

She commenced blasting on the horn, making the Morse code for SOS; three short, three long and three short.

Harry and the Director leapt out with pistols drawn and rushed to either side of her car. The Director flashed his ID and yelled, 'Police; open the doors and leave the car with your hands on top of your head, both of you.'

Janine said quietly, 'We will have to obey them; don't give any inkling that you know of Leo. Say we met at a US embassy party and arranged to meet for coffee.' She unlocked the doors and they both exited the car as instructed. Sumi was crying in stark terror.

She sobbed, 'My name is Tsushima Sumiko, I am an officer of the Japanese Embassy. I know nothing about this, and I claim diplomatic immunity.'

'Shut-up bitch,' snarled the Director. 'If you are an associate of this person, then you are under suspicion of breaching Australian national security. Your diplomatic immunity is cancelled.' He continued, 'Both of you, lie face down on the grass and place your hands on the backs of your heads.' '*Move*,' he yelled. Both obeyed without further hesitation.

Harry had come prepared for the capture with cuffs, ankle shackles, tape and blankets. After making a quick check to ensure there were no witnesses, he removed two sets of gear from the boot. He cuffed their hands behind and shackled them, then taped their mouths and eyes and placed sacks over their heads.

After wrapping each in a blanket so they couldn't kick or struggle, he placed them both in the boot of the Director's car. The Director drove off, with Harry following in Janine's car. The whole episode had taken about three minutes, and as far as they could tell, no one had observed them.

They drove back across the bridge to the city where Harry deposited Janine's car in the police compound. He explained how it had been found abandoned after she had evaded their tail. He told them that he and the Director were following leads to re-establish their lost contact.

Then they took the girls to a Safe House, designated SH-6, in the Molonglo hills behind Queanbeyan.

37

It was around ten thirty when Leo prepared for his interrogation of Heinrich. He quietly entered the sound-proofed room. His captive was squirming in the chair trying to get free. He had involuntarily urinated and sat in the mess. Leo was torn between compassion for this person, who must have been very confused and frightened, and cold hate for the despicable trafficker of deadly drugs to the young.

He suddenly grabbed the end of the mouth tape and ripped it from Heinrich's face. The painful scream brought back bad memories. Leo said nothing.

'Who are you? What do you want?' whimpered Heinrich.

Leo remained silent, allowing his captive to frighten himself further. After a minute of silence Leo raised his hand and boxed Heinrich's right ear, hard. He knew from past experience that although this would do no damage, it was most painful. The blindfold, and the totally bewildering effect of not knowing what to expect next, would go a long way to breaking down any resistance to interrogation.

He really hated to do this and it certainly brought back vivid images of his own treatment as a POW. But he was getting desperate now. He must find the Director as soon as possible.

'God knows what additional evil that bastard will

cook up against me!' he thought. 'I must bring him to task before he finds Janine.'

Heinrich whined, 'I don't know what you want, who are you? I have done noth –.'

'Shut up!' said Leo, in a deep and threatening manner. He was disguising his voice with an American accent.

'You will say nothing except to answer my questions. What do you know about Harry Thwaites?'

After a slight pause Heinrich answered.

'He is from some police department, I think.'

'What else?'

'What's in this for me if I talk?'

'To start with; your life. If you cooperate, I will recommend that your assistance be considered during any possible proceedings against you.'

Heinrich obviously had no resistance to this sort of pressure and he began to spill the beans. Leo turned on his recording equipment, spelled out the time and date and identified Heinrich as the informant. He reserved identifying himself for the time being.

Leo said, 'Before you say anything more I must advise you that I have just started recording this conversation. I caution you that you are not obliged to say anything, and whatever you do say is being recorded and may be given in evidence. Are you prepared to continue without representation?'

'OK.'

'Just repeat that you understand you are not obliged

to say anything and you do not need a lawyer at this interview.'

'I understand that I'm not obliged to say anything and no, I don't want a lawyer.'

'I'll now ask you again, what do you know about Harry Thwaites?'

'As I told you, I think he belongs to some police department.'

'What else?'

'He and his boss sprung me and they promised me I would not be prosecuted if I cut them in on the deal.'

'What deal is that?'

'The importing of a couple of million dollars worth of crack cocaine and heroin.'

'Who is Thwaites' boss?'

'I don't know his name. Thwaites did call him the Director once, and I saw him one time in a car when he dropped Thwaites off at the hotel.'

'Could you identify him?'

'I think so, provided he didn't know. I would want protection.'

'I understand you spiked the drink of one of Thwaites' colleagues. What was that about?'

'Well, Thwaites said this bloke wasn't in on the deal and there was a chance he might expose us.'

'Who was he?'

'I don't know, one of *them* I guess, I think they might have done away with him.'

'Did they say that's what they were going to do?'

'No, not directly. But Thwaites was very concerned that if they kept up the surveillance, which was s'posed to be a blind, then this guy would put two and two together and blow the whistle on us. Then we'd all go to jail. He said something about the Director neutralising him.'

'Do you realise that if in fact they did kill him, or even attempt or conspire to do such a thing, then you would become an accessory before the fact; a very serious offence?'

'No, I didn't. I don't think I want to say any more now, until I see a lawyer.'

Leo's sat-phone rang, so he quickly suspended the interview at ten forty five and rushed out to answer it, closing the door behind him.

'It must be Janine,' he thought. Without checking the screen, he picked up the phone and quietly answered.

'Yes.'

'Leo, this is Jim, luckily Janine gave me your number. We are on scrambler. Firstly, intelligence has intercepted comms that indicate the attack has been moved to an earlier date, but we have that in hand. I don't want you to be involved, because a much more serious situation has arisen.'

'What's that?' asked Leo.

'Janine has disappeared.'

'What! How did this happen?'

'I don't know; except that she went out this morning, against Helen's advice, to have coffee with a friend. She didn't say how long she'd be, but she has not returned.

Helen was loath to ring the police under the present circumstances and I just got in. Helen's in one hell of a state. She blames herself.'

'My God!' Leo exclaimed. 'I feared this might happen. The silly little beggar's probably been apprehended by X1.'

'Helen overheard Janine ask for somebody named; what sounded to her like ,"something-shima Sumiko".'

Leo gasped.

Jim continued, 'The phone hadn't been used since she made the call, so I hit redial and got the Japanese embassy.'

Leo felt the hairs on the back of his neck stand up. To think he had been revisiting all those memories of long ago so vividly over the past few weeks, and to now learn that Janine was in touch with Sumi. It was almost too much to comprehend. That must have been the urgent news she had wanted to give him.

Leo said, 'Well I know who that person is, but I don't think she would have any direct bearing on her disappearance. It would have been a compelling reason for her to risk going out, though.'

Jim went on. 'I asked to speak to Sumiko, explaining that I didn't know her surname. I was immediately put through to their security office. They asked many questions to establish my identity, and I told them that I was concerned about someone missing from our embassy. They told me that Sumiko Tsushima, a staffer, was also missing. I'm on my way over there now; we've got the AFP on the job as well. They must have taken this Sumiko as well.'

'Look Jim, I have apprehended one of their accomplices and am interrogating him. He may be able to shed some light on this, but I doubt it.'

'OK!' said Jim. 'I'm truly sorry about this development, we should have been more diligent.'

'Nonsense!' Leo replied. 'You have both been great. You tell Helen it's not her fault at all. It's me they want, so I don't think Janine is in immediate danger. You fix the other problem, I can look out for my people.'

'Thanks Leo. Good luck, to us all and if you need back-up, use this secure line to call me. You have the number?'

'Yes, Jim, see you.'

'You be careful, 'bye.'

Leo hung up. His head was spinning.

He thought, 'Sumi had obviously married Kenje. I wonder if she has news of Michiko.' This was mind-boggling.

He couldn't ponder over this now though. He had to figure out how to rescue his daughter, probably Sumi as well, and wrap up these evil ones ASAP.

Leo decided to release his prisoner and get down to the capital as soon as possible. There was no way open, in the short term, to hand Heinrich over to the authorities. He figured that the police would most certainly be looking for him because the Director would have an APB out on him, on God knows what trumped-up changes. He would put nothing past that despicable cur now.

He returned to the room and tried to get information on the whereabouts of the Director and Thwaites. Heinrich knew nothing. He was obviously just a pawn in this game, but may be useful as a witness later on.

He retaped Heinrich's mouth then told him he was to be released for the time being, and that he should remain in Sydney.

In a forceful voice, Leo said, 'If you attempt to abscond, you will be dealt with severely and any bargaining advantage will be forfeited. Do you understand?'

'Yes,' mumbled Heinrich through the gag, nodding his head violently.

'Expect to be brought in for a confidential interview sometime in the next two weeks,' said Leo. Then he injected him with another dose of the knockout drug.

'This is for all of those young kids who stick your drugs into *their* bodies, Ernst, and make you rich,' thought Leo.

He had forgotten neither the Mickey Finn, nor his complicity in the *neutralise Kirkland* plot. So he wasn't careful shoving the needle into that ugly neck. He had increased the dose too and hoped that it gave this nasty piece of work, a horrible hangover.

38

Jim Harrison hung up on his call to Leo. He was not feeling particularly happy. His beloved *niece* was obviously in a critical state of danger, as was her father, and both Helen and he felt partly responsible. Perhaps he should have been more proactive in warning Janine of the potentiality for danger, and made more secure arrangements. Anyway, he would have to rely on Leo to solve that problem for now.

It appeared, from the most recent communications intercepts that the attack would come in the next couple of days. Security Intelligence had not been able to trace the origins of the calls, but they were certain the attack attempt was imminent. At this stage, there was no concrete evidence to establish just how the culprits intended to conduct the assault. They had nothing more to go on than Leo's sketchy information.

Jim, in company with the SAS Colonel in charge of the operation, had done a recon of the area. They discovered that the car park was on the northern side of the Black Mountain tower and had no clear view of the embassy. So it would not be a suitable launch site. The viewing area at the top of the tower would, of course, be ideal. But the out-of-hours lock-up security was so good as to preclude its use.

However, the large platform at the base of the tower had an ideal aspect on the southern side giving a line-of-sight path direct to the embassy. Through their binoculars they could even see *Old Glory* fluttering in the breeze. This deck contained service equipment for the tower and was a proscribed area. At the planned attack time the whole complex would be unmanned, so they would have no trouble utilising it.

As is often typical of Aussie security awareness, the area, although proscribed, was accessible over a one metre high railing. It didn't even have video surveillance.

Those authorities involved in handling the case of the suspected attack were adamant the general public should not be allowed to become aware of the situation. They did not want to start a panic, or initiate unilateral action by any other agency. This was one of those occasions when assessing the *need-to-know* priorities was a nightmare.

There certainly was a contingency plan to evacuate the embassy and the surrounding properties at short notice. Now, because the threat was imminent, all military and civilian personnel had been sworn to secrecy. Those who wished to leave, or were non-essential, had already moved out. The remainder had been placed on a half-hour evacuation schedule. The AFP, also under strict secrecy, was on immediate standby to close off streets and to ensure that the exodus was complete.

The press had been completely excluded from any intelligence relating to the plot. The investigative journalists and their editors suspected something was afoot. However, there existed a codeword of which the top reporters and news editors were well aware. When issued, as it had been yesterday, they knew it signalled an impending, serious threat to national security. All understood that if they kept mum and a publishable story broke, then they would be thoroughly briefed. They were well aware that, apart from being dangerous, any leaks would be serious breaches of the federal emergency legislation, generating hefty penalties.

For the past two nights the police had set up a checkpoint, in the guise of a *booze bus*, on the only access road to the tower. Outside, the officers were conducting random breathalyser checks, but were not pulling anyone into the van. Inside the van was a squad of heavily armed special response police ready for a rapid reaction to any threat along the road. Unmarked units were patrolling the surrounding roads on the lookout for any suspicious activity and extra satellite surveillance was in train.

The SAS had deployed three, five-man sections to patrol the walking tracks around the mountain. There was also a platoon lying perdu around the car park at the tower. All watched and waited.

39

Smith gathered his teams about him. For the past week they had been dispersed, waiting patiently for the big day. Since learning that the training camp had been found, he was worried about discovery. He therefore summoned them early, to their holding camp; a hideout in the

Kosciusko National Park. This was several kilometres south of Brindabella and about an hour's drive from Black Mountain.

He had four three-person crews, each armed with a missile and a remote aiming device. Individuals carried a sidearm for self-protection, should they be detected, and each crew had one sub-machine gun. All appeared to be psychologically primed to die if necessary to achieve the aim.

They were a mixed bunch with varied reasons for being on board. Smith couldn't be sure whether each individual was so prepared on the basis of personal fanaticism or by feelings of self-immortality. He didn't really care though. What he was sure of was that for whatever reasons, they were all phobic anti-Americans.

The core members of the group were the eight stalwart members of his Nazi phalanx. Except for one Irish man and a tough Southern European female, they were Australian-born, Anglo-Saxon males. Some of these probably had police records, or even police backgrounds. He didn't want to know anything about those aspects of their personal history. Even though they had been associated for about two years, he didn't have a deep knowledge of any of them. They were a secretive lot, as was he, each with his or her own personal agenda. And he preferred to keep it like that.

Then there were two Muslim extremists who had come from the Middle East via Indonesia. Both were of Iranian origin. They had alternated domicile between their home country and Saudi Arabia, plying their terrorist skills and attitudes wherever a cause, and possibly the remuneration, took them.

The last pair was an Australian man and wife team. He was a disgruntled ex-military type and she, a weapons freak. These last four were a fairly motley lot. First impressions were deceiving though. He had trained them to a point where he considered they were all up to the job. He had chosen them carefully over several months and had been exercising them for several more. He was sure that with all of his thorough preparation, they would achieve the aim and knock out the embassy. In forming the teams, he had separated the Middle-Eastern men, but kept the couple together.

All had been over the plot on many occasions. They had driven around the site to familiarise themselves with the layout. Apart from actually trekking on the mountain, they had conducted several full-dress rehearsals. They had thoroughly checked out the area around the tower for launch sites, aiming bearings and helicopter landing sites. Now it was the time for final briefing – Sunday evening.

The teams would be transported in a van and a truck to four points around the Black Mountain Nature Reserve, where the walking tracks commenced. No use was to be made of the access road to the tower. Initially, he had planned to block the road with a bogus roadwork crew. Apart from the plan being too resource intensive, he figured it might have drawn unwanted attention from the authorities. So he scrapped the idea.

The first team, Team One, would be dropped at the most northern access to the nature reserve on Belconnen Way. He would make the drop himself driving the white van. This team had the longest trek. He had allowed them three hours to make it to the summit and to set up for zero hour. Their drop-off would be at 2330 hours.

He would deliver Team Two next, to the western entry about halfway down Caswell Drive. Then he would proceed to the west side of Capital Hill to observe the attack. Teams one and two were to meet at the tower and after securing the area, set up their launch site from the southern side of the service deck at the base of the tower. This was the primary attack point.

The deputy leader driving a military type covered truck would transport Team Three to the eastern entry on Frith Road. He would then place Team Four at the southwestern entry point on Rani Road. They had the shortest trek to their assigned location.

To provide maximum use of their redundancy and ensure success, teams three and four would make their way to the secondary attack point. This was the barbecue area lookout, near the *Touch and See Nature Trail*, about five hundred metres south of the tower. Smith knew one rocket would do the job. If all four teams made it to their attack points, and he could see no reason why they shouldn't, then they would make four deliveries. He had no desire to find any secondary targets, and had no concern for collateral damage.

Earlier in the morning he had dispatched a bogus power company crew to place an IR strobe light on a pole in line with the target. This would assist in identifying the aiming point.

Once on the ground, the teams were to maintain strict no-phone procedures. They had no radios. Smith did not want any possible surveillance pick-ups. Between 0250 and 0300, the helicopter would pick up teams one and two from the tower car park and then lift the other six from the BBQ area. They would be flown back to the hideout where he and the deputy leader would join them for a Champagne breakfast at dawn.

40

After they arrived at their safe-house, the Director and Thwaites carried the bundled-up women inside. Still shackled and handcuffed they were placed on chairs; the sacks were removed from their heads and their mouths un-taped. Then their interrogation began. They had been placed in separate rooms, Thwaites questioning Sumiko whilst the Director examined Janine.

'Miss Kirkland, would you please confirm that you work for Naval Intelligence?'

'I'll tell you nothing.'

'Miss Kirkland, do you know who I am?'

'I have absolutely no idea,' Janine lied.

'Let me enlighten you as to a few facts and circumstances. I am the Director of a high level section of our SI organisation. *You,* have no need to know more than that. *I,* know quite well where you are employed, so let's cut to the chase. Why are you in Canberra?'

'I'm here purely on personal business.'

'Who is your friend?'

'She's a person I met at a local party and we arranged to go out for coffee. I know very little about her.'

Then Janine threw in a red herring.

'Is she the reason you have arrested us?'

'You are not under arrest, and I'll ask the questions.'

'Are you having a lesbian affair with the Nip?'

Janine was initially shocked by this suggestion, but quickly assessed that this was his intention.

'Why haven't you cautioned me?' she replied coolly.

'Look Kirkland! I'll take no nonsense from you. You will answer my questions without this shillyshallying, or pay the consequences. Your father, who works for me, is in serious trouble. Not only is he involved in a serious breach of national security, he is guilty of murdering an innocent passer-by to fake his own demise.'

Janine was astounded by the evil accusations.

'I do not believe a word of what you say. I am sure you are the perpetrator of any crime involved and you are trying to frame him.'

'I'm warning you. Shut your mouth. Where is he?'

'I don't know where he is and if I did, I wouldn't tell you.'

The Director ripped the tape from her eyes, pulling hairs from her head, eyebrows and lashes. Janine screamed in pain.

Meanwhile, Thwaites had already removed the tape from Sumiko's eyes, albeit without inflicting any undue hurt. When they heard Janine's scream, Sumiko said, 'What is he doing to her? She is a good person. I'm sure she would not be involved in anything untoward.'

Sumiko was really frightened now. She came from a culture where one deferred to those in authority and did not question what the police did. However, she was sure this was irregular treatment and she was not going to cooperate with them.

'What is your relationship with her?' Thwaites asked.

She realised she would have to be careful in answering any questions. She remembered that Janine had described them as *evil* and that they were after Leo.

'We just met at an embassy party and arranged to go out for coffee.'

'If you just met, then how do you know she is a good person?'

'What I mean is, she seems to be a good person. And I *have* just met her.'

The Director called from the other room, 'Bring the Nip bitch in here.'

Harry picked her up, chair and all, and carried her into the room setting her down next to Janine. Before anyone could blink an eye, the Director slapped Sumiko across the cheek. He raised his right foot and pushed it roughly into her chest. This caused her to fall over backward, painfully pinning her arms under the chair back and banging her head on the wooden floor.

He stepped forward, and with his heavy boot, kicked the underside of the seat bottom. This sent an excruciating shock wave from her groin throughout her entire body. Apart from a gasp for air, she made no other utterance. Janine looked down at her newly found sister and marvelled at her bravery.

'Dad would be very proud of you,' she thought.

'Pick her up,' snarled the Director.

Harry lifted her upright again. He didn't voice any disagreement at this treatment; however, Janine noticed his body language. It was extremely negative.

She could not stand to see this lovely person suffer any more.

'What do you want?' she asked.

'I want you to tell me where your father is.'

'I told you. I don't know.'

The Director moved toward Sumiko drawing his pistol. He raised it as if to shoot her in the head and fired a shot. Sumiko screamed as the bullet missed her ear by a couple of centimetres. Janine realised that if she didn't act, then Sumi was going to be more viciously attacked or probably killed. She assessed that this miserable excuse for a man would stop at nothing to get what he wanted.

Her only hope now was that Leo, or Uncle Jim,

would find them and save them from whatever horrible end they would experience in the clutches of this beast.

'You could call him, his number's in my phone.'

The Director's face almost glowed in an evil grin. He moved to the table where Thwaites had emptied the contents of the girls' handbags. He picked up one of the two mobiles there.

'Is this it?'

Janine nodded. He saw that it was still turned on and checked the *Recent Calls* register. They had all been deleted.

He yelled, 'What's the listing?'

She answered dully, 'It's just *Dad*.'

Scrolling through to *Dad*, he pushed the call button.

41

As Leo waited for the knockout dose to completely immobilise Heinrich, he formulated a quick plan of action. Given that the attack was to take place in the Capital and Janine was probably in the clutches of the Director, he must get down to Canberra ASAP. He called an old pilot colleague who had gone into semi-retirement and now operated a helicopter rescue service from the nearby docks. He had two *Dauphin* AS365N3 machines that Leo himself was qualified to fly. He had used them for several high profile jobs in the past. He knew his old buddy could be up and running in an hour, no questions asked.

Leo briefed him on his need to be dropped off in Canberra on a matter of national security. He would be taking a trail bike and backpack. He didn't mention the weapons.

'No problem Leo,' said his friend. 'Do you need to be picked up again?'

'No,' Leo replied. 'But I may call you again in a few days. Usual arrangement, I'll pay on the spot in *green*; OK?'

'That's fine,' said the pilot. 'I'll check the weather, file a flight note for SAR with my operations room, and be ready in about an hour. Where do you want to be dropped, and what's our ETD?'

'Let's make it midnight. I'll give you the coordinates en route,' Leo responded.

'That'll be OK Leo,' said his friend. 'I'll be ready to pull pitch at twenty four hundred.'

Leo bundled Heinrich into the van, took him to a park near the river in Five Dock and laid him out on a bench to sleep off the effects of the drug. If he were lucky, the boys in blue wouldn't pick him up and complicate matters.

Then he hurried back to his base and packed his usual gear, including the Uzi and the Beretta. He made himself an energy-rich eggnog and was almost through drinking it when the sat-phone rang. Half-expecting it to be Jim calling again, he almost didn't bother looking at the screen, and then he saw it was Janine's number. Expectantly he answered.

The Director's unmistakable voice said, 'Hello Leonard, surprise, surprise.'

'You bastard!' exclaimed Leo. 'What have you done with my daughter?'

'Well, Leonard, don't lose your cool. She's here, visiting with Thwaites and me. Together with this Nip friend of hers, we make quite a happy foursome.'

'What friend?' asked Leo, feigning ignorance.

'I haven't figured that one out yet Kirkland, I was hoping you could enlighten me.'

'Let me speak to Janine,' said Leo.

The Director held the phone to her ear.

She quickly blurted out, 'I'm sorry Dad, I couldn't get away from them. They are torturing us and –.'

He whipped the phone away from her ear and delivered a vicious slap to her cheek. She cried out in pain.

The Director yelled into the phone, 'She doesn't know yet what torture is.'

'What do you want to release them?'

'I want you, Leonard.'

'What do you want me to do?'

'I want you to give yourself up to me, then I'll let them go.'

'How can I be sure you will do that?'

'You can't, but I don't believe you have any alternative Kirkland. Be assured, if you don't come, or if you send help, I'll do them in.'

That, Leo believed.

'Where are you Leonard?'

'I'm in Sydney.'

'Do you remember where SH 6 is?'

'Of course.'

'Where are you in Sydney?'

'I'm just near Pittwater,' lied Leo.

'So it will take you,' he paused thoughtfully, 'About four hours to get here at this time of night, right?'

'More like four and a half.'

'Well don't get picked up for speeding will you,' the Director sneered.

'You come straight to the front door and knock twice and remember, any funny business and they both get it, no questions asked. I mean it Kirkland. They'll be gone in a flash.'

'You have no more reason to harm them. I'm on my way.'

Leo hung up. He immediately called his pilot friend.

'Change of plan. I'll be there in fifteen. Can you be running and ready to go? It's extremely urgent Ben.'

'I'm walking out there now,' Ben replied.

42

At the Terrorists' holding camp it was time to go. The teams all wished each other success and loaded into the two vehicles. It was 2230 precisely. They launched up the road to the Capital. Their spirits were high after getting their final pep talk from Smith, combined with various substances, depending on personal choices, of pot, speed or whisky. The leader was careful to monitor their intake; he wanted them hyped up, but not to the point where their efficiency was impaired

It was a bumpy ride up over the range, but they made the first drop point right on time. Making sure there was no traffic to spot them, Team One disappeared into the bush at the start of the trail to begin their hike to the south.

Smith made a U-turn and proceeded to Caswell Drive, dropping off the next trio ten minutes later. He then drove to a spot near the last drop point and waited to assure himself that all four sections were safely delivered.

In similar fashion, the deputy leader dropped off his two teams at the eastern and southwestern entrances. Smith observed the last drop and, satisfied with this progress, drove to Capital Hill as planned. The deputy leader in the truck headed back toward their camp in the National Park. Neither of them observed the unmarked police cars, which attached to their tails as they exited Rani Road.

43

Jim and the SAS Colonel were in the command post, which they had set up in ADF HQ at Russell Offices to control the anti-terrorist operation. Things were beginning to happen.

Firstly, those watching the satellite images reported a vehicle discharging a few persons, possibly four, into the walking trail that starts on Belconnen Way, north of the Black Mountain nature reserve. The command post dispatched one of the SAS patrols to intercept them and check out their credentials. If they happened to be innocent night hikers, then they were in for a rude shock.

Secondly, as near as was possible, given that there was some traffic on those surrounding roads, they figured the drop vehicle had made a *U* turn and headed back to the west. Then, ten minutes on, they observed the same type of incident on the western side of the reserve, near an entrance to the reserve.

This was it. The attack set-up was surely commencing.

An unmarked police car was diverted to Caswell Drive where it picked up a white van turning into Rani road. The officers followed at a safe distance, lights out. They saw it stop suspiciously near the end of the road, where its lights were switched off. This was near the start point of one of the walking tracks. No one alighted, so they moved off the road with lights still out and waited to see what was going on.

About fifteen minutes later, a military type vehicle went past, stopped at the entrance to the trail and discharged three soldiers carrying a long object and backpacks. They quickly disappeared. The officers assumed they must have been SAS and reported this fact on the police net.

The military truck made a *U* turn and departed. As it turned south into Caswell Drive it was observed by another unmarked patrol car, just as the message came through that there were no SAS drops in the area. Obviously this was another group of terrorists. The second car was instructed to tail the truck. After a few minutes the white van departed the scene and headed off down the Tuggeranong Parkway with the police tail in stealthy pursuit.

Those in the command centre now had three groups of what they assessed as three person teams under satellite infrared surveillance. They were all making their way toward the summit from the north, west and southwest. The three SAS patrols were being directed to intercept them. Extra troops were being sent to the area to assist, and those at the tower were now on full alert.

44

As soon as Leo had loaded his bike and pack into the chopper and strapped himself into the co-pilot's seat, Ben lifted off and headed out to the southwest. He climbed to the next appropriate level above his calculated lowest safe altitude for the flight to the capital. It was a cloudless moonlit night so he was following Night Visual Flight Rules. He told Leo he had advised Air Traffic Control that this was a NOSAR medevac flight. Canberra tower would not be manned at this time of night, so they would have minimum communication requirements. Leo was already punching coordinates into the Global Positioning System satellite navigator. He planned to land at a point about ten *clicks* southeast of SH 6, out of hearing range. He would then proceed on his silent motorbike to the house with the aim of effecting the rescue of his daughter and his old friend, Sumiko.

The flight would only take about an hour; he had already indicated to Ben that he needed maximum cruise speed. This would give him a decided advantage of surprise over the Director, now his arch-enemy.

Ben handed over control of the helicopter to Leo while he double-checked Leo's waypoint on the map and the coordinates in the GPS. Although Leo was now in a fairly high state of tension, given the current circumstances, he always felt relaxed with the joint feelings of command and freedom, when at the controls of a powerful flying machine. Flying would always be his prime love and his first passion in that arena was the helicopter, particularly a slick ship like this Dauphin. He reflected momentarily on the word, *slick*. This was the term given to the troop carrying *Hueys* he had flown in the Vietnam war, all those decades ago. He always marvelled on the fact that, even though he hardly ever had the chance to fly much these days, it was still like *riding a bike.* One never forgets how.

Ben could see in the dim lighting that his old friend was looking more relaxed now. When he came scurrying across the helipad, loaded-up with his gear, he looked fairly red-faced and almost flustered. In all the years he had known Leo, he had never seen him so distraught. He suspected something very serious must be afoot, but he knew better than to ask what was going on.

As they approached the boundary of the Air Traffic Control Area steps, which surrounded the capital's Fairbairn Airport, Ben called Melbourne Centre. He reported his position and altitude and requested clearance. They were given a clearance to enter the Control Area at six miles.

They were then told that the Canberra Control Zone was active. A separate clearance was required to enter it and a Prohibited Area had been established in the zone. This included the whole area to the west of the airfield out to ten miles. Under no circumstances were aircraft to proceed west of the north-south runway. Ben acknowledged this and reported their intention to land four miles to the south of Hoskinstown. They had no requirements to go near the circuit area.

Then he said on the intercom, 'What the hell is that about? A temporary prohibited area. I don't think I've experienced one in-country before.'

'Christ! It's on.' Leo let the expletive pass his lips and his *hot mike* allowed Ben to hear.

'Is this to do with your need to get here in such a rush?'

'Not directly Ben, and you know I can't talk to you about it.'

'I know.'

'You may read about it tomorrow. If not, I'll tell you what I can at a later date.'

'OK,' said Ben as he copied down the explicit clearance that came through from Centre. When he transferred to the Approach Control frequency, the controller reiterated the clearance and required a read-back of the instruction not to fly west of the airfield. Ben confirmed his previous advice.

They donned the night vision goggles, *NVG*, for the landing. Ben let Leo to fly the approach. This was Leo's old air force helicopter training area, and he knew it like the back of his hand.

Nearing their final approach, they had to cross a high-tension power line. Leo knew that the lines themselves were invisible, even with the NVG. However, the towers stood out well and as all helicopter pilots know, the wires are always lower; so he flew over one of the towers. He chose a large clearing next to the Captain's Flat Road and gently set the machine down on its wheels.

'I think you've done this before,' complimented Ben.

Leo nodded and thought, 'It *is* just like riding a bike – unless you fall off.'

Leo unloaded his equipment and waved goodbye as Ben climbed away into the moonlit night. He figured it would take him about twenty minutes to get to the safe-house, which seemed to be rather misnamed at this time.

45

Smith's Team One quickly unlocked the gate at the entrance to the maintenance trail with their skeleton keys, and proceeded south. After a few hundred metres they came to a T intersection. They took the track to the left and set off at a good pace, taking advantage of the full moon and cloudless sky. After they had covered about a kilometre, the man in front suddenly stopped and 'shushed' the other two.

'Did you hear something?' he whispered.

Before either could answer, the SAS patrol pounced on them. As they quickly disarmed, bound and gagged the terrorists, the sergeant radioed for a vehicle to whisk them away for interrogation.

When this task was completed, they headed off to the southwest to help find the others. This should not be too difficult, given that they were receiving constant updates from the command post on the satellite imagery. This showed the positions of the other two parties and the SAS progress. They knew the satellite window would be lost in less than half an hour, so they wanted to have it all wrapped up as soon as possible.

The last team, which the police patrol had reported

on, had not moved very far along the bush track before a five-man SAS squad was dropped at the entrance behind them. Moving rapidly with their night vision equipment, they swiftly overtook the assailants. When they closed to within fifty metres, the Nazi leader of the team heard a stick snap behind them. He quickly ordered the others, the husband and wife team, to go to ground beside the trail.

Control picked up the cessation of movement from the satellite data about a minute later.

'They've stopped,' they informed the sergeant. The patrol stopped. The female terrorist thought she saw a movement along the track from where she had come. She immediately opened fire with her AK 47, hitting one of the SAS troops in the abdomen. As he fell, fatally wounded, the rest of the patrol opened fire in the direction of the shooter. She fell screaming as her companions opened up with their sidearms. One of the SAS troops hurled a hand grenade. The explosion was followed by a deathly silence. The exchange was over in less than two minutes. All three terrorists were dead. But the price paid, was the life of one of Australia's finest.

Team Two heard the fire fight off to their right. Their leader assessed from the sound of the exchange that the army must be involved and Team Four had probably been wiped out. Somehow the operation had been discovered, and they were probably in serious trouble. They were not far from the Summit now and he decided to press on and try to get their missile launched. They moved off the path and made their way up the last steep slope under the cover of the trees. On the basis that their attack was now under threat, the leader decided to inform Smith of this latest development. He called Smith's mobile number. Smith answered gruffly.

'Why are you breaking comms silence?'

'We heard shooting and an explosion from the direction of Team Four, I think they may have been whacked.'

'Shit!' Smith yelled. 'How did they get onto us? Let me think.'

After a moment's pause he added, 'You'll just have to press on. Be prepared to meet opposition and don't wait for rendezvous. Attack the target as soon as you can get the shot away.'

'OK, wish us luck. Signing off.'

Smith knew he could not give them any help and he didn't want to expose himself personally to danger anyway.

46

After ending his call to Leo, the Director sat down with a contented look on his face. Then he started haranguing Janine.

'I suppose you thought you were being smart, bitch. Well you only made it worse with that little outburst.'

She made no response.

'Well, we'll all just wait now,' he said in an almost calm voice. Then he went over to the window, sat on a chair and started cleaning and re-loading his snub-nosed .38 revolver. Not a word was spoken for about an hour.

Janine was almost reaching breaking point now as she contemplated their fate. How ironic it was, she thought. Just when things were starting to look wonderful for the three of them, and probably for Michiko too, they should now be on the brink of death. Sumiko was in a similar state. This whole affair had been such a shock to her. It had now taken on a surreal quality.

'Could this actually be happening?' she thought. 'It's surely some horrible nightmare and I'll soon wake up and find that all is well.'

Harry was getting very worried now about his boss' state of mind. He had never seen him act in such a vile manner before. He sat down and pondered what the outcome of all this might be.

Harry was the first to break the silence. He asked how the Director planned to make the hostage exchange.

'What exchange!' exclaimed the Director. 'You naive fool. What makes you think I'd let these two get away to spill the beans?'

Harry blurted out, 'But they couldn't do us much harm once we arrest Leo. No one would believe them once we make our case against him.'

'Thwaites, I sometimes wonder how you got this far in the organisation,' the Director said disdainfully. Then he snarled, 'We are not arresting Kirkland, we are going to do what we tried to do the first time, eliminate him.'

Sumiko gasped.

Janine said, 'He's never done you any harm. He's always been a diligent worker. Apart from his alcohol problem, I'm sure he would have always acted in a professional manner.'

'That may be so, but it would appear as though he has been engaging in some extra-curricular activities, in which you are also involved. If my guess is correct, the content of the encrypted message he sent you was of material which may be injurious to Harry and me.'

Janine hid her surprise.

'How did they intercept the Fax?' she thought. 'At least they obviously had not deciphered it.'

Perhaps there was some way here to make a deal. She didn't think they knew anything about the terrorist plot. Maybe she could bargain their way out of this.

'I can assure you that the message had nothing to do with you. I didn't even know of your existence before today.'

Before he could react, she continued, 'It was about a serious threat to national security and Leo was trying to circumvent a catastrophic event.'

The Director had had a long experience in the assessment of verbal evidence and interrogation. He knew immediately that she was, at least in part, lying. He stepped toward her and slapped her again, hard, across the cheek.

'Lying bitch! That's it! I would have liked you to watch us eliminate your bastard of a father, but I'm not going to listen to this claptrap any longer. You are through!'

He quickly retaped her mouth before she could make another utterance. He signalled to Harry to take the same action with Sumiko.

Harry was looking rather distressed.

As he taped Sumiko's mouth, he asked nervously, 'What are we going to do with them now sir?'

'What we are going to do with them now, is have a little fun.'

'How do you mean?'

The Director reached at Janine and ripped open the front of her blouse, exposing her brassiere.

'I *mean*, that we have a few hours to fill in before Kirkland gets here, so; before we bump them, I'm going to have my way with this piece of goods first. You can take the Nip bitch.'

That was the breaking point for Harry. He realised the Director had completely lost his mind.

'We can't do this sir,' he yelled as he reached for his pistol.

Before he could un-holster it, the Director swung around, his gun still in his hand and fired two shots in rapid succession right at the centre of body mass. Harry uttered no sound as he reeled back through the door into the now darkened second room and fell lifeless on his back. The Director walked quickly to the doorway and looked down at the inert, bleeding body.

'Stupid bastard,' he uttered, with a snigger in his voice, 'Now I've got them both to myself.'

47

At the command post, the surveillance group had lost the satellite imagery. The next window would not open for about forty-five minutes. Jim had been monitoring closely the progress of the insurgents and the intercepting SAS patrols. He was greatly saddened by the death of the soldier in the southern patrol. His body had been removed, as had those of his killers.

The remainder of the patrol, determined to see the job through, proceeded east to pick up the main access road to the summit. They would join the troops around the tower and hopefully assist in the neutralisation of the last terrorist unit. This group, advancing from the west, should soon be intercepted and hopefully taken alive. Additional patrols had now entered the nature reserve on all sides and those in the command and control post were confident it would soon be over; mission accomplished.

It was now two o'clock. It appeared as though the terrorists were sticking to their original time frame, so their helicopter should appear on the radar soon. They had no idea from which direction to expect it, but assumed it would be from the remote mountainous areas to the west.

Four Tiger attack helicopters had been positioned at

the Fairbairn RAAF Base nearby, and were now on full alert. They would become airborne at 0230 and patrol the perimeter of the zone, ready to intercept any intruder.

There had been an alert about half an hour before, when a relatively fast civilian helicopter identifying itself as a medevac, approached the zone from the northeast. However, before the ambulance service could be contacted for verification of its bona fides, it had landed, outside the control zone. It departed shortly after and headed back toward Sydney; no longer a potential threat.

48

Team Two made it to within fifty metres of the western edge of the Tower carpark before they were detected. As they crept stealthily through the under-brush, they literally bumped into the perimeter guards who quickly placed them in custody.

What Jim and his party did not know was that terrorist team number three had escaped satellite detection as they entered the reserve on the eastern side of the mountain. Because the active satellite's polar orbit was transitioning to the west, they were in the *shadow* of the mountain and their progress had gone unobserved. The team was now approaching their objective, the lookout near the barbeque area off the main access road. They detected no movement as they crept onto the low-railed viewing deck.

There was no response to their pre-arranged *cricket call*. It was almost zero hour and Team Four should have been here already. They had not heard the fire fight on the other side of the mountain, so had no idea that Team Four had been annihilated. Their instruction was to launch on time, rendezvous or not. Once they had hit their target, they had to be ready for the chopper uplift.

Without further ado, the missile firer set himself up at the aiming point. The remote aimer was already in place, about fifty metres to his right. The little red strobe light on the pole opposite the embassy was quite visible to the firer through his sighting device.

'Are you ready?' he called out softly.

The aimer said, 'Not yet, I can't make out the strobe, hang on; yes I've got it now. Fire when ready.'

The firer was quite excited now. The adrenaline was pumping. The third member switched the weapon to ARM and steadied the firer. The firer squeezed the trigger and the missile exited the launch tube with a *Whoosh* on its way to the intended target.

49

Leo approached the house on his bike, stopping fifty metres away to ensure that he was not heard. He left his pack and the Uzi and crept through the scrub toward the back of the house. He had his Beretta drawn, with a round in the chamber and cocked. They wouldn't be expecting him for at least two hours, so he was fairly certain they would not be keeping vigil yet. The only light from the house shone through a front window, so he moved stealthily around the side of the building until he could see partially into the room.

There was the Director, moving toward Janine who was gagged and bound, sitting on a chair. He appeared to be talking to someone aside, but Leo couldn't make out what he was saying or see anyone else. As he watched, the Director, who had a revolver in his right hand, reached for Janine and ripped the front off her blouse. He wanted to charge through the window and strangle the bastard. He restrained the urge because he that knew if he did, someone would be shot.

He returned quickly to the rear of the house and lifted a carefully disguised loose brick from the gully trap near the back door. This is where they had secreted a key for emergency access many years before. As he expected, it was gone. He moved to the back door to see if he could silently pick the lock. Now he could hear voices from inside. Two males. He couldn't make what was being said. They started yelling, presumably at each other. Then two shots rang out in rapid succession, followed by a heavy thump.

He could mess with the lock no longer. He drew back from the door slightly. Then, with adrenalin pumping, he gave the door a mighty kick with the sole of his boot. The lock smashed and the door flew inwards with a resounding crash.

He heard the Director yell, 'What the hell!'

He rushed through the darkened house, leaping over Harry's supine shape toward the lit doorway, weapon at the cover position, safety off.

As he charged into the room, the Director pulled Janine upright in front of him as a shield, and placed his gun at her temple. He saw Sumi bound and gagged on a chair in front of, and facing away from him.

'Well Leonard, that *was* quick. You never cease to amaze me. You must have flown down. Or were you a lot closer than you said?'

'The game's up Director, the Feds are on their way, so don't make it worse for yourself than it already is.'

'Move across there away from the doorway or I'll shoot her right now,' ordered the Director. Leo moved as instructed, keeping a bead on the Director's right ear.

'If you shoot her, you know I'll instantly kill you,' Leo said forcefully.

He noticed that Janine was blinking strangely; two quick blinks; one quick, one long, two quick … .

She was saying something in Morse code.

'I L L D R O P I L L D R O P.'

'That's my girl,' he thought.

He acknowledged with one long blink. He couldn't afford to tip off this cunning, evil person.

As Leo completed his move as instructed, tensions rising in all present, the Director said, 'You know very well that I can assess lying very accurately Leonard, so why don't we cut the bullshit. No one's coming. If you put down your gun, I promise to let them go.'

Leo paused before answering, reading as Janine Morsed, 'H E I S G O I N G T O K I L L U S A L L.'

'That's not an option Director,' said Leo.

'Then what would you suggest Kirkland?' the Director sneered.

'If you want to live, and face the music, you drop your gun,' Leo ordered.

The Director hesitated a moment and with a most evil grin on his face said, 'You give me no choice then. I'm really going to enjoy this. Goodbye Mister Kirkland.'

The memory of Captain Wang's attempt to shoot him flashed through Leo's brain. But there was no Abdul to save him this time.

The Director's gun started to turn from Janine's temple toward him. The tension within him rose to fever pitch. Leo sensed that everything seemed to be happening in slow motion.

Suddenly, Janine let her legs collapse beneath her. She dead-fell to her left. Before the Director could react, or Leo could fire, two rapid shots rang out. The Director's head exploded. It was all over in a flash. He fell in a crumpled heap without uttering a sound. Blood poured out.

There in the doorway, now lying on his stomach was Harry; the smoking gun falling from his hands as his head lowered to the floor.

'I'm sorry Leo,' he gasped.

Leo rushed to pick up his beloved girl.

'Are you all right?' he blurted out as he sat her on the chair and removed the tape from her mouth.

'Daddy,' she said. 'I'm so sorry I got us into this mess.'

'Honey,' Leo responded, 'It doesn't matter. We've all survived, that's all that counts.'

Sumi sat in stunned silence staring at the bloody body in front of her.

Looking toward Harry, Janine said, 'Look out for him first. He's been hit twice, and he did try to save us both before.'

Leo moved to Harry's side and checked his vital signs as best he could. He was breathing, albeit rather shallowly and his pulse was weak. There was little external bleeding now. Leo felt sure that internally he must be a mess. He had taken both slugs in the solar plexus.

'At least, that must be better than the upper thorax,' thought Leo. 'Wonder why he didn't go for a head shot?'

He grabbed his phone and dialled 000, asking the operator for ambulance and police for serious gunshot wounds. He gave his name, and the address, and stressed the urgency of the situation. Then he examined Harry again.

Both shots had passed right through him and missed his spine. Leo rolled him gently onto his right side into the recovery position and covered him with a blanket from the bed.

Leo moved to Sumi next and slowly removed the tape

from her mouth. He had already noticed her hair was a brilliant black with no grey. As he removed the covering from her face, he could see that this was not Sumiko; at least not the one he had known. She looked into his eyes and smiled at his bewildered look. Leo was silent as he untied the ropes from her ankles and wrists. Then he knelt in front of her again, gazing into her beautiful face.

'Dad, may I introduce Michiko's daughter and my sister, Sumi.' said Janine softly.

Leo almost swooned as Sumi reached out, put her arms around his neck and tenderly said, 'Hello, my long lost father.'

A stunned Leo slowly placed his arms around this lovely girl and hugged her. They must have stayed holding each other for a full minute as tears of comprehension ran down Leo's face.

'May I join this family circle too?' asked Janine.

'I'm sorry honey.'

He rose and moved to untie her. The two bruised and battered women came, one either side of him, and they all embraced in a circle of love.

'Where is your mother?' asked Leo.

'Waiting for you at the embassy,' said both women together.

The ambulance and police arrived. One of the paramedics examined Harry and said, 'Seems like nothing too vital has been hit in there, he'll live.'

As they loaded him into the ambulance, Harry came to again and indicated to the police and Leo that he was prepared to confess, and to clear Leo of any wrongdoing. He apologised to Janine and Sumiko for the way they had been treated.

'Thank you for saving us from that madman,' said Janine.

The three of them stood on the west-facing veranda, waiting for the police to finish and take them to town. As they chatted excitedly about all the recent events, they saw a large flash over the horizon, followed a few seconds later by a dull *Tharrump*.

'My god!' exclaimed Leo. 'They've done it.'

'Done what?' asked Sumi.

'Bombed the US Embassy,' said Janine as the tears welled up and streamed down her face.

'That's not far from our embassy,' Sumi cried. 'I hope my mother is safe.'

50

The now four-man southern SAS patrol moved silently up the entrance road toward the tower. While passing the barbeque area, they heard someone call out softly. They raced toward the sound. As they came over the rise of the carpark, they saw, silhouetted in the moonlight, the two terrorists with the missile launcher aimed to the south. A voice, slightly to their right was saying.

'… hang on, yes I've got it now. Fire when ready.' There was a bright flash and a loud *Whoosh* sound as the missile launched.

The patrol opened fire downing the pair instantly. The missile continued on its path. They were too late!

Then one of the troops made out the shape of the second aimer, who was still directing the missile, at another low-railed viewing deck about thirty metres to their right. He put a burst of rounds into the figure. As he pitched forward over the railing, taking his guidance device with him, the missile arced over and to the right, down into Lake Burley Griffin. It landed with a massive explosion on Spinnaker Island. It was all over. The attack had been stymied.

Moments later, when the news reached the command post, they all cheered and clapped their hands, just as if it were a successful NASA lift-off.

Ten minutes later, the approach controller picked up a *primary paint* on his radar screen. It was thirty miles to the northwest and tracking toward Black Mountain. Its ground speed was ninety-five knots, helicopter speed. There had been no calls from it and its *transponder* was not registering on the *secondary radar*.

The Tiger helicopters were immediately vectored to intercept. Calls were broadcast on all frequencies in an attempt to establish communication, to no avail. It veered to the south, toward higher ground and the radar *paint* started to break-up. Two of the Tigers were very close now and were monitoring the *bogey* on their own radar. The intruder's track changed again and it was now heading straight for Capital Hill. The command post personnel were monitoring the action closely on their screens. The colonel figured the pilot must have been advised of the attack failure, and was apparently taking unilateral action. He ordered the Tigers to intercept and illuminate the intruder in an attempt to identify, and dissuade him from advancing any further.

Two minutes later both Tigers reported, 'Target acquisition'. They formed up in trail; slightly behind, and on either side of the aircraft, training their searchlights onto it. It was a dun coloured Huey with no markings and no navigation lights. The lead ship called on all frequencies, ordering it to land immediately or risk offensive action. He also used the aircraft's EmSID equipment. This **E**lectro**m**agnetic **S**ystems **I**ntrusion **D**evice enabled the interceptor to beam high powered radio signals directly into the target aircraft's wiring systems to achieve various outcomes.

This older machine did not have digital engine control so the EmSID could not be used to shut down its engine. Therefore, on this occasion the operator used it to send voice communications into the aircraft's intercom system. The pilot ignored all attempts to contact him. He would neither divert from his course, nor follow visual signals to land.

The aircraft was getting closer to built-up areas now so the command centre ordered the Tiger leader to fire a burst of tracer in front of him. If this brought no response, then he was to shoot it down. The leader fired his warning shots but the pilot pressed on doggedly toward the Capital. So the lead Tiger fired cannon to take out the power plant without hitting the cabin or the rotors. This action succeeded and the intruder put his aircraft into autorotation to make an emergency landing. Unfortunately, he apparently was not well practised at performing this manoeuvre in the dark and fatally crashed.

Later, when the authorities investigated the accident, they found that the pilot, the only one on board, belonged to Smith's organisation. The aircraft was an ex-Philippines Army machine that had been smuggled into the country.

51

Leo stood there with a weeping daughter on each side of him as he phoned Jim Harrison. Jim answered immediately.

'Where are you?' he asked.

'I'm standing on the Molonglo range and I just witnessed a gigantic explosion in the Capital. What's the situation?'

'Its OK Leo,' Jim answered. 'We got all of the attackers and as we speak, the rest of them are being picked up. They got one round away but an SAS squad hit the aimer mid-launch and the missile landed on one of the islands in the lake. No casualties, unless someone was on the island.'

Leo said, 'That's great; well I have some great news too. I have rescued Janine and Sumiko and they are not too much the worse for wear.'

Jim sounded greatly elated as he responded to the news. 'That's wonderful; I can't wait to hear the details. Helen will be so relieved; I'll call her right away. Who is the Japanese girl?'

'It's a long story. I'll tell you all about it when I see you.'

'Do you want me to call her embassy?'

'No thanks Jim, she's just about to call them herself.'

'We had to shoot down their helicopter as well. Apparently when their leader realised the attack had failed, he ordered the pilot to make a kamikaze attack. Also – bad news, we lost one SAS soldier during engagement.'

'Good grief!' Leo exclaimed. 'That's bad. What a night it's been. I'll get with you tomorrow and we can fill each other in on all the happenings.'

Jim replied, 'I somehow have the feeling it will take more than tomorrow to do that.'

'Yes, "tomorrow and tomorrow".'

'I'll wait to hear from you good friend. 'Bye for now, give my love to Janine.'

'And ours to Helen,' replied Leo. 'But just before you

go, a heads up on the Director's fate, before you hear it all on the news.'

'Yes?' said Jim in anticipation.

'He's been shot dead by number nine. The Director shot *him* earlier. But I think he'll recover to testify. It's like something out of a movie, Jim. More about that tomorrow.'

They both hung up.

Now it was Sumiko's turn to bring the glad tidings to her mother. She pressed the speed-dial for her mother's phone. Michiko answered immediately as she saw Sumi's name pop up on the screen.

'Oh darling! Are you all right?'

'I'm fine now mother, Janine and I were kidnapped by some evil people, but Leo has rescued us, and we three are now together. Leo has just found out about us.'

'How is he and how did he take your news?'

'He's fine and he accepted me wonderfully, he's everything you always said about him, and quite handsome.' Leo felt himself blushing. Janine squeezed his hand.

'Would you like to speak to him?' said Sumi to her mother.

'Not now Sumi. You bring him to me. Where are you?'

'We're out in the country somewhere.'

Then she asked aside, 'How long will it take to get back?'

'About half an hour, but we probably should get cleaned up a bit before we see your mother,' Leo said.

'Why don't we go back to the US embassy first?' offered Janine.

Michiko was following the conversation and said, 'All the streets between here and the US embassy are blocked off and they've all been evacuated. There was a big explosion a little while ago, but I don't know what was hit. You all just come over here.'

Sumi told her about the attempted attack on the US embassy. It had failed, she said, and she didn't think anyone had been hurt.

After a brief discussion they decided that as soon as they were finished with the police they would go directly to Michiko.

52

The reunion went off wonderfully. All four realised very quickly that there was much love to be shared between them. There was a good deal of catching up to be done. Leo discovered that his first love was as beautiful as when he first met her, and the embers of their lost love were soon rekindled.

For Michiko's part, she had always held him deep in her heart and even though it took the diligence of her tenacious daughter to finally bring about the reunion, she had always known there would never be another man for her. This was especially so as she still physically retained a part of him in her loving daughter.

Two months after that terrible, yet wonderful night, all the loose ends surrounding the Director's and Harry's plot had been tidied up. Their anachronistic office had been closed down and the staff suspended, pending further investigations and the inevitable *bloodletting*.

Leo visited Mrs Dorevitch at Cullen Bullen and explained to her, the sad demise of her father. He told her that the main culprit was dead and his accomplice would be brought to trial. Leo apologised for his deception at the time. After she had heard the whole story, she told him she understood and forgave him.

He completed his debriefing of the terrorist attack with Colonel Harrison and the US and Australian authorities. Then he retired on a generous redundancy package; his government position having disappeared with the demise of MO 10.

Leo realised his life had now come full circle. No longer would he need to chase after real, or imagined, evils. Neither would he have to worry about being pursued by real, or imagined, ogres.

There was just one more major thing to be done to put away old ghosts. He *must* go to Turkey.

Several weeks later, Michiko and Leo were married in a simple garden ceremony, with their two beautiful daughters as bridesmaids. The weather on the day of their wedding was typical of a Canberra Spring, late afternoon. Sunshine, interspersed with fluffy white clouds and light intermittent showers. Michiko did not want a church wedding. So they celebrated in a simple civil service with just the four of them and the Harrisons.

After the ceremony, Leo and Michiko strolled hand in hand down the garden path. Janine and Sumi followed, arm in arm, their backs to the soon to be setting sun. Janine pointed out to Sumi that their parents were perfectly arched by a brilliant rainbow. Sumi responded.

'I think they have already found their pot of gold.'

Janine suddenly recalled something her father had shown her many years before, on one of their frequent flights when he was helping her gain her pilot licence. They had been flying down-sun toward a light rain shower. He pointed to the brilliant light ahead of them. It contained all the spectral colours of the rainbow, but it was a complete circle. Her father had philosophised about the image.

He pointed out how all thinking people know you cannot reach the end of the rainbow to find the pot of gold. Because, even if there was one there, the rainbow always elusively moves away from you as you proceed. Then he had explained how terrestrial creatures only see half of the picture.

What the earthbound may not appreciate is the fact that the ground beneath their limited horizon inhibits their view. Only when one ascends to greater heights, can he or she discover that there is no *bow*, but a circle.

She now understood the parabolic significance of the vision. Love, life and indeed, the whole universe move in circles.

She thought, 'What is the old saying? "What goes around comes around".'

53

Leo had always wanted to attend the Australian and New Zealand commemorative services at Gallipoli, Turkey. Many Australians made this annual pilgrimage to honour the thousands of young Australian, New Zealand and Turkish soldiers who had made the supreme sacrifice at that place in 1915. Janine had tried for years to encourage him to go and had offered to accompany him.

He never talked much about his other war experiences, but on many occasions had told her about his time imprisoned with Abdul. During these periods of story telling, he had explained to her what a wonderful friend Abdul had been. He related how they had overcome so many tribulations and what a deep admiration and love he held for his friend.

He had also told her of the solemn vow he had made on the death of this wonderful Turk. He had shown her Abdul's *dog tag*, which he had treasured all these years, and expressed how he wanted to present it to whatever surviving kin he could find. For reasons he could not explain, he had kept putting this off. They had discussed the possibility of combining both of these objectives into a wonderful trip one day.

He decided it was now time for them to do just that.

However, if he wanted to attend the April 25 ANZAC Day Dawn Service, this would mean waiting for almost another year. He did not want to defer his long overdue, avowed journey to Abdul's home. He decided to make it a more private quest with his new family.

So, shortly after the wedding, the four of them, Leo and Michiko, Janine and Sumi, who had both taken extended leave, set off one June day to fly halfway round the world to Istanbul.

They hired a car at the airport, checked into a neat little hotel on the south side of the West City and retired early.

The next morning they had an early breakfast, and with Janine driving, headed off on the first part of their Turkish adventure. The first two hours of their journey took them along the northern shore of the Sea of Marmara with its picturesque villages, splendid mosques and thriving population.

They stopped for lunch at a busy little town called Tekirdaz. It was situated right on the coast. There was a small port for the fishing fleet; but that was rather empty at this time of day. Janine had taught herself a smattering of Turkish, and Leo was quite impressed with the way she was able to communicate with the local people. After a rather tasty kebab meal and some strong black coffee, at a quaint *lokanta*, a simple restaurant, by the waterfront, they did a little shopping along the main street. Leo wasn't too interested in this activity, but tagged along quietly while his ladies satisfied their curiosity and picked out a couple of souvenirs.

The travel agent back at their Istanbul hotel had tried to talk them into taking a conducted bus tour. Leo had said he wasn't interested, shaking his head from side to side. When the agent continued to explain how the tour included a ferry trip across the Dardenelles to Canakkale, Leo had looked a little annoyed. But before he could say more Janine, who had picked up on the situation, explained to her father that shaking the head in Turkish body language didn't mean 'no'. It meant you didn't understand.

With the misunderstanding resolved, they found out that most of the tourists make the crossing of this narrow waterway, which joins the Sea of Marmara with the Aegean, because the accommodation is better. However, Leo suggested they spend the next two nights in a small Turkish style hotel in Gelibolu, the Turkish name for Gallipoli. From there it would be a simple matter to make their own way to Anzac Cove and the other points of interest.

They had pre-arranged to meet a local guide at the hotel the next morning. So after a light meal of kofte, a delicious form of meatball, with cous cous, washed down with a most acceptable local red wine, they turned in early. The hotel, although quite plain, was clean and comfortable and the folk who ran it were very friendly and attentive.

They woke early, bathed, dressed and had breakfast;

then left as soon as Mehmet, their guide showed up. At Anzac Cove they were all very moved by the stories of the brave young men who had given their all in this futile campaign. Leo was certainly emotionally affected as he cast his mind back to the loss of friends and colleagues during both of the wars in which he had served. He became particularly sad thinking of Abdul and wondering if he would find any of his relatives.

As they were leaving to see the other sites, Janine showed Leo a poignant inscription on the monument erected by Kemal Ataturk in 1935. It was a poem to the soldiers who had fallen there, written by that great leader. It read:

> *Those heroes that shed their blood*
> *and lost their lives*
> *You are now lying in the soil of a friendly country*
> *Therefore rest in peace*
> *There is no difference between the Johnnies*
> *and the Mehmets where they lie side by side*
> *here in this country of ours*
> *You the mothers*
> *who sent their sons from far away countries*
> *Wipe away your tears*
> *Your sons are now lying in our bosom*
> *and are in peace*
> *After having lost their lives on this land they have*
> *become our sons as well*

Now *their* Mehmet continued to conduct them around the historic sites at Lone Pine, The Nek, and The Sphinx. He showed them the remains and reconstructions of the original trenches, some of them only eight metres apart. The graveyards were neatly kept and the monuments and statues, awe inspiring. It was a very fitting tribute to all of the young men who had fought in that place, especially to those whose remains were still there.

One particular statue caught Leo's attention. It was a large bronze depicting a tall Turkish soldier in his fez type cap, holding in his arms what appeared to be a British officer. Mehmet told them the story surrounding this work of art.

During one of the charges between trenches, which were only twenty metres apart, a British officer was hit and fell severely wounded, halfway between the lines. When the heavy Turkish fire forced the troops to fall back to their trench, he was left behind. As the firing continued over his head between the lines, he lay there crying out for help.

After a while a white flag appeared above the Turkish position. When the shooting stopped this Turk climbed out of his trench and went to the aid of the young officer. He lifted him, and his weapon and delivered him back to the British lines. Then he went back to his trench and the fighting re-commenced.

Leo felt the hairs on the back of his neck stand up. Tears welled up as he identified with the soldier's brave act. He had to sit down on the grass. Janine looked at him, concerned at his paleness.

'Do you feel ill Dad?'

'No,' he replied quietly. 'I just need a moment.'

She sat down next to him and placed her arm about his shoulders. Michiko and Sumi stood by looking a little perplexed. Leo had shared to some extent, the stories about Abdul with them, but this was all so new and they were unsure how to handle the situation. Leo looked at Michiko with a most forlorn look.

She asked, 'What's wrong?'

'I'm really OK honey,' he answered. 'It's just that, well, this statue depicts to a tee, the two times Abdul carried me to safety after I had been beaten and tortured. It brings back powerful memories that I have been dreaming about for the last couple of months.'

Janine understood immediately how his feeling of déjà vu created such an impact. They sat there, she with her head resting on his shoulder. Sumi and Michiko joined them on the grass and they rested there awhile, gazing up at the wonderful image the statue projected.

Mehmet discretely watched the spectacle of this tall, middle-aged European man demonstrating such a deep state of emotion. He was fairly used to such outpourings, so he just waited patiently for them to continue with the tour of the sites. He obviously wondered at Leo's tale, but did not intrude with any questions.

On several occasions during the tour, their guide praised Kemal Ataturk for the wonderful leader he had been.

Leo was most impressed when Mehmet said, 'What Gallipoli gave Australia was its sense of nationhood and comradeship, and what it gave Turkey, was Kemal.'

That night the four of them had a quiet time discussing the day's events and thinking about the terrors of war. They returned to the city the next day.

Over the following three days they checked out the sites in downtown Istanbul and Uskudar, the oriental part of the city, across the Bosporus. This narrow strait actually separates Asia and Europe, and joins the Sea of Marmara with the Black Sea to the north.

Places such as the Topkapi Palace and the Blue Mosque with their unique Islamic architecture and colourfully artistic décor, were of great interest to them. In the Topkapi Palace, in glass encasements stood two magnificent giant jars. They were beautifully carved from solid amber-coloured marble and stood about two metres tall. They were almost spherical and had rounded lids made from the same material.

'Ali Baba would have loved those,' said Janine.

'Maybe the thieves wouldn't have coped with those heavy lids though,' rejoined Leo.

The pavilions and the covered bazaar or bedesten, with its row upon row of gold and jewellery merchants, were exciting. The girls were certainly tempted to spend. All marvelled at the ancient sites. The City Walls, once impenetrable barriers to the attacking enemies, dated back to the fifth century. It was all so different, and grandiose.

Australia has less than a quarter of a millennium of advanced culture to exhibit, so for Leo and Janine these places were an awe-inspiring spectacle. Being so different from the sites of Japan, they drew a few 'oohs' and 'aahs' from Michiko and Sumi as well.

They crossed over the Bosporus Bridge, one of the world's longest suspension bridges, to the oriental part of the city. Here they enjoyed the many sites of everything from fish markets to glorious palaces.

They would have liked to stay longer, but Leo was keen to move on to achieve the main aim of the venture, to visit Akkisla and find Abdul's relatives. So, on the eighth day they flew to Ankara, the capital.

They spent two nights there, the ladies checking out the historic sites while Leo visited the Australian Embassy. Here he confirmed their previously notified travel arrangements and checked on security requirements. Leo had explained the purpose of his trip to the authorities before departure, and had received a special briefing from his colleagues in External Affairs. At the embassy they assured him it should be safe going to the planned places.

54

On day ten, they set off on the final section of their quest, travelling east by train to Kayseri in the Cappadocia region. Apart from the initial winding track through the mountains to Kirikkale, the journey was mainly across plains country. The train was particularly comfortable and the service fine. It moved along at a steady pace enabling them to take in the beautiful scenery. This was varied and magnificent, particularly along the Karanlik River. Each town they stopped at or passed by, exhibited varying styles of architecture, from ancient Byzantine churches to more modern Islamic mosques.

The last hour of the all-day trip, was across an area with large patches that looked almost like a moonscape. This effect was caused by the fall-out from large eruptions of the two major volcanos, now extinct, of Hasan and Erciyrs. The latter loomed ahead as they approached their destination, which lay at the foot of the impressive peak. They planned to spend a couple of days in Kayseri. Leo needed to organise transport to go to Akkisla, which was about seventy-five kilometres up the Kizil Irmak Valley to the northeast. Before doing so, he thought he should check in with the local constabulary.

He had two reasons for this. One was to make sure the police knew the purpose of their visit. They were closer now to the more dangerous eastern areas of the country, where Kurdish problems existed. Leo wanted to ensure that a group of foreigners such as they did not raise any suspicions or worries.

The second was to make some initial enquiries about the Akkisla family to see if this might shorten the search. Up to this point he had not tried to search for, or make prior contact with, any relatives for fear of misunderstanding or causing apprehension. The Desk Sergeant, who spoke very good English, was most appreciative of Leo's advice and told him that, although he had no personal knowledge of them, he would make enquiries and see what he could find out.

Leo left the police station, then arranged the hire of a large Range Rover and driver for the next few days and returned to the hotel. The ladies, who had gone off sight seeing, met him back there for lunch.

During the meal the three briefed Leo on their findings of the morning. The city was a student's dream. Janine told him that this place was the Caesarea of Roman times and is steeped in Eastern Roman Empire history. She and Sumi planned to spend the whole of tomorrow visiting places such as the Ethnography Museum and the wonderful Medical History Museum, dating back to the thirteenth century.

Michiko smiled at their girlish enthusiasm and whispered to Leo.

'So, I'll be able to spend some time alone with my new husband.'

Leo realised that ever since they had left home, his mind had been almost fully occupied with thoughts of the Anzac pilgrimage and finding Abdul's kin.

'You bet!' he said and squeezed her hand.

It was after all their *honeymoon*, albeit accompanied. He told her that apart from checking to see if the police had any information for him, they would spend the whole day together. So they told their daughters to look after all of their own needs tomorrow, including the evening meal. The girls got the message.

55

The next morning Leo called at the police station. The same sergeant was manning the desk and greeted him in a friendly manner.

'Good morning Mr Kirkland, I have some news for you.'

'Goo-nay-dihn,' said Leo.

The sergeant looked impressed with his attempt at the language.

Leo was trained in Mandarin and had a smattering of Russian and Spanish. He'd never been in a situation where his English didn't suffice, except in the back woods of Malaya and Indonesia. However, that was no problem because he was fluent in Bahasa Melayu. He found Turkish a little more difficult, and hadn't felt like putting in the extra effort at this stage of his life, especially as Janine had. So he planned to rely on her expertise if needed.

The sergeant had discovered there were two separate families in Akkisla with that name. At Leo's behest he had not spoken directly to any members of either family. He suggested enquiring at the town library. The manager was a Mr Akkisla.

Leo felt a spark of excitement at hearing the name

and said, 'Thank you very much, teh-shehk-kyoor eh-deh-reem.'

'You're welcome,' the sergeant smilingly responded. 'Beer shehy deh-eel.'

Leo hurried back to the hotel; thrilled at the idea that tomorrow they would probably find Abdul's clan. The girls had already left for their day of sightseeing, and probably shopping as well. Before going to the room, Leo had the hotel clerk organise accommodation in Akkisla for the next few days and arranged to check some of their luggage.

As he entered their room, Michiko asked, 'How did you go?'

'Really well I think; the local library is managed by a man named Akkisla, so that looks like a good starting point.'

'Sounds wonderful! You must be getting a little excited now.'

'I sure am! I feel like going today. But we won't. I'm all yours for today.'

Michiko came close and smiled up at him. Leo took her in his arms, bent over and placed his lips on hers in a lingering passionate kiss. She responded fully then pulled back slightly, looked into his eyes and said, 'I'm so happy I found you again my love. I always hoped I would, but for so long I was sure you were dead.'

Leo said, 'I've often remembered our time together back then and wondered what might have become of you. I certainly never thought of you having my child though.

'It is wonderful how Sumi was so sure she would find you one day,' Michiko observed. 'The world turns in strange ways doesn't it?'

'It certainly does,' he sighed.

So Leo and Michiko had a wonderful day all to themselves. Their lovemaking was now perfect, each knowing just how to please the other, and themselves. It was as if they had been together all those separate years and had each, silently come to know it was a union made in Heaven.

After a light lunch they went for a walk around the town, the girls having taken the car. They were both fairly fit considering their ages and hiked over to the Cumhuriyet quarter. Their first stop was the Resit Aga Mansion. Here, Kemal Ataturk's museum displays many of his maps, artefacts and personal belongings. They both found the history of this place enthralling. They visited a few more places of interest, including the thirteenth century Seljuk mausoleum. The architecture was classically simple and the decoration elegant, with colours of mainly gold and red. Then they returned to the hotel to freshen up before dinner, which took the form of a romantic tete-a-tete in their room.

They had arranged with the girls and the driver to leave early the next morning, allowing a couple of hours to reach Akkisla. So they retired early.

56

The pleasant early spring weather the next morning was perfect for the drive up the valley. Once they traversed the initial barren landscape in the vicinity of the volcano, the roadside was a splendid mix of brightly coloured flowers. Janine and Sumi chattered away in the back, more like a couple of teenagers than forty and fifty-year olds. They had by now become the strongest of friends and continued to find new areas of common interest and joy.

They told their parents that the day before, they had found a beautiful variety of rugs and kilim, a sort of finely woven shawl. They didn't make any purchases because John, the driver told them he could take them all to Bunyan, which was between Kayseri and Akkisla. This is where they are made. Of course he had the inevitable cousin in the business who would give them a good price and arrange shipping as well. Leo and Michiko expressed their interest in also being involved. John looked most pleased.

Around mid-morning they arrived in Akkisla. It was an attractive little town nestled in the foothills on the western side of another tall and steep mountain. It may have been an extinct volcano too, judging by its shape. They quickly found the library and Janine accompanied her father in to help him make enquiries. A young lady sat at a desk just inside the front door. She was busily stamping the inside covers of an assortment of books.

She looked up and smiled as they approached.

'Do you speak English please?' asked Leo.

'Of course,' she replied. 'How may I help you?'

'We are visitors from Australia and I am trying to locate the relatives of a man named Abdul Akkisla.'

Before Leo could continue, or the girl could answer, a deep voice behind them said, 'I am Abdul Akkisla.'

Janine and Leo turned, startled by the utterance of this man, who had come out of an office opposite the desk. Leo couldn't believe his eyes. It *was* Abdul as he remembered him, with the same droopy moustache, but obviously not looking as bedraggled. Leo paled as if he had seen a ghost. Janine, slightly confused by the sudden turn of events, could see that her father was at a loss for words.

'Are you a relative of Abdul Akkisla who served in the army in Korea?' she asked.

Now it was the man's turn to be surprised.

'Yes! Yes!' he exclaimed. 'He was my uncle.'

There was a moment's silence as they all composed themselves, then he added, 'Please come into my office?'

'Would you mind if I brought in my wife and other daughter?' asked Leo.

'Not at all. Please do. Would you like some tea?'

'Yes please,' said Leo, as he and Janine went out to get the others.

Leo asked John to fill in time for maybe an hour and told Michiko and Sumi that he had found Abdul's nephew. They followed him excitedly back into the building.

When they had all settled down in Abdul's office with their tea, Leo began explaining who he was and the purpose of their visit. When Leo told how his uncle and he had been prisoners together, Abdul was awe struck. He explained how he had never known his uncle, for whom he had been named.

'You are the image of the Abdul whom I knew in 1952.'

'Yes, my family always said that. My father is Abdul's younger brother and remembers much of their youth up to the time he went off to war. My grandfather and grandmother are both gone now.'

'So how many of your family are here in Akkisla?' Janine asked.

'There are only my father, Yasher and my mother, Ayse, my older brother Muhammad and his family. I am not married and live with my parents in the old family home. There is another family here with the same name. They are second cousins.'

They all chatted on for about an hour and Abdul called his mother to arrange for them all to visit for lunch. Leo thought this was on too short notice, but Abdul insisted.

'They will be most excited to meet you and hear of your time with uncle Abdul.'

57

Abdul took the rest of the day off and around noon drove them all to his family's house. This was about twenty kilometres out of town down in the valley. John said he would visit some friends in town and gave Leo a number to call when they needed to be picked up.

Yasher greeted them at the door and gave Leo a warm welcome. He ushered them into the comfortable lounge room and seated them.

Ayse and her daughter-in-law, Rebecca, came in from the kitchen. They had been preparing a sumptuous meal ever since Abdul's call. After all the introductions, Leo briefly explained his relationship to Yasher's brother.

'We only received three letters from Abdul during the whole time he was a prisoner. They were heavily censored with whole sections cut out,' said Yasher.

He had taken them out and now showed them to Leo. They were in Turkish so quite illegible to him, but he could see the many holes in the pages. Yasher pointed to one.

'In this, the last one sent around the end of 1952, he tells of a wonderful friendship that had developed between himself and a younger prisoner,' said Yasher. 'Because of all the censoring, we could only establish that he was a pilot, but there was no reference to his name or nationality. We assumed he must have been an American. But it was obviously you.'

'Yes,' replied Leo. 'Because of what we went through

together, and our need to protect each other, he was the best friend I ever had.'

Leo had to wipe a tear from his eye as he related this, and all started to get into a state of expectancy as to what Leo might tell them next. Michiko and Sumi had heard very little about Abdul, and even Janine had not heard the whole story.

So, for the next hour Leo told the assembled group virtually everything that had happened back then. As he continued with the story he could feel a great weight lifting from his whole being. He realised that for all those years since Abdul's death, he had carried feelings of great loss; and of guilt at not being able to save Abdul in the final phase of their relatively short relationship. Now he felt he was coming to a point where he could at least lay to rest that part of Abdul's spirit, the part remaining in his own bosom. Leo had not mentioned Abdul's actual death. He felt he had not known these people long enough to subject them to that knowledge yet.

Around one thirty, Ayse and Rebecca started to bring in all manner of mixed dishes and lay them on the large coffee table in the centre of the room. There was a variety of kebaps including spicy-hot grilled kofte, small filet beefsteak and tasty lamb doner. Side dishes of chopped salad and roasted aubergine, cucumber and pickled vegetables abounded. Added to all of this was a large circular dish with about eight different compartments containing assorted dips. And of course, there was the more-ish ekmek, flat bread. To finish off they had baklava, dripping with honey, cold baked rice custard, Turkish delights and delicious Turkish coffee.

Yasher told them tales of Abdul's youth and described their family business, which up to his recent retirement had been sheep farming. Abdul was a graduate in philosophy and while completing a thesis in history for his professorship, was managing the library to supplement his income.

Janine was very interested in this information and told him she would like to know more about his work. Abdul appeared keen to tell her more when they had the chance.

Leo hadn't mentioned Abdul's dog tag yet, and was wondering how best to raise the subject when Yasher said, 'We have a small shrine to Abdul's memory in his old room. Would you like to see it?'

'Why yes,' replied Leo. 'I would like to pay my respects.'

Yasher and Leo rose from their chairs. Leo looked around and saw that none of the others had moved. He looked at Janine.

'Just you go dad,' she said.

Michiko and Sumi both nodded. Leo followed Yasher out into the hall, down to its end and through a door into a small, darkened bedroom. It had obviously been kept, as Abdul had known it. The bed was made up, and on the walls was a collection of faded photographs of his college football team. Abdul was obviously the captain for one year.

There were various items of sporting equipment and on a side table, a large sepia coloured photograph of Abdul in his army uniform. Leo took a long look at the face that had meant so much to him. In front of the photo were medals and badges laid out in orderly fashion and a small Turkish flag. The flag draped from a short staff, which protruded from a bronze urn.

Yasher lit the candles on either end of the table. As the light increased, Leo was surprised to see, hanging from the top of the small flagstaff, on a faded nylon cord, a dog tag. A cold shiver ran down his spine, his legs felt weak as he vividly recalled removing Abdul's second dog tag before covering his face and burying him. He had to sit down on the bed.

Yasher looked concerned and said, 'What is wrong Leo?'

Silently Leo reached into his pocket, took out the dog tag and held it in his open palm. Yasher took it from his hand, held it to the light, and read the inscription. He looked at the remains of the cut cord in the holes on each end and realised they matched the two ends of the cord on his brother's tag. He looked into Leo's eyes, which were now welling with tears.

'You were with him when my brother died?' Yasher asked.

'Yes, Yasher, he was my brother too,' Leo replied. 'We had come through so much together. He died in my arms during our escape and I buried him there in North Korea. I took his second tag to return it to you one day.'

Yasher held Leo's hands in his, the dog tag clasped between them, and with tears running down his cheeks also, said, 'You were truly Abdul's friend and brother.'

'But how did you get the dog tag from North Korea?' Leo asked in amazement. Yasher told him the story.

'Many years ago my father asked *The Red Crescent* to approach the North Korean Government to see if they could release Abdul's body to be brought home. Initially they had met a blank wall. Then, out of the blue the authorities suddenly acquiesced. We received a letter saying he had died whilst attempting to escape from custody. They pointed out that neither soldiers nor citizens of the Peoples' Democratic Republic were responsible for his death. The location of his body had been determined from information supplied by the UN Military Command. They exhumed his body and with due ceremony had returned it to Ankara. The family then arranged onward movement.' Yasher continued.

'Abdul's remains now lie in the Akkisla cemetery. The North Koreans also returned a wooden grave marker, which they had treated against decay.' Yasher asked, 'Did you make that?'

'Yes I did,' replied Leo.

'This is amazing Leo. Your marker has been incorporated into Abdul's monument. We shall go there tomorrow.'

'Yes,' Leo replied softly.

Then he told Yasher of all the circumstances surrounding his brother's death. He was thankful that he could do this in private with Abdul's nearest living relative. It seemed so appropriate that he could tell the story here, in Abdul's room.

Yasher listened in silence and when Leo had finished he said, 'Now we can all take rest in this knowledge that you have brought us. We will be forever grateful.'

Leo certainly felt a deep satisfaction in the fact that finally, he had been able to share the knowledge of his beloved friend with his family.

He privately acknowledged that not everything in The Peoples' Democratic Republic was evil.

The following morning Yasher, Abdul and Leo went to the cemetery. When Leo saw his roughly carved grave marker, all the memories of that final day with Abdul came flooding back: the horrific aerial attack on the convoy; Abdul's saving his life; the just and timely death of Captain Wang; the brave manner in which Abdul had concealed his injury so as not to delay their fleeing from that place; and finally, Leo laying his friend's body to rest.

Leo hadn't prayed in decades but now he dearly wanted to say something as a final parting. He asked Yasher if he would mind his reciting the twenty-third psalm, as he had done when he buried Abdul all those decades ago.

'By all means,' said Yasher. 'We too cherish the psalms of David.'

So together they stood at the foot of Abdul's grave, and repeated the beautiful eulogy.

58

Over the next few days they all shared some great times. Various members of the family accompanied them on several short sightseeing jaunts around the beautiful countryside. This included the trip to Bunyan, about thirty kilometres from Akkisla, for the ladies to order some rugs and shawls from John's cousin. True to his word they all made some good deals.

Janine and Abdul were really getting to know each other well now, a point that was not missed by Leo and Michiko. They even noticed that she was actively practising her Turkish with him, and he seemed to have organised at short notice, some leave of absence from his job.

She intimated to her father how she had been thinking of retiring from the navy for some time. She had served for twenty years and wanted to go back to studying. What could be a better place than this? Leo knew the feeling well and said he was sure she would consider all the pros and cons. He gave his tacit approval and verbal blessing to whatever course she chose to follow.

Their stay was coming to a close now and they prepared to make their goodbyes. Yasher said he would like to take them on one final excursion. This was up over Mount Erciyrs to Develi and the beautiful Kapuzbasi Waterfalls, which would be at their grandest after the spring rains. So the afternoon before their second last day, they moved back to Kayseri.

The next morning, Yasher, Ayse and Abdul turned up at their hotel about ten, and they all set off in the Range Rover to climb up over the mountain to the south. It was steep going to the peak, but the road was good. The grey moon-like rocks, spring flowers and snow patches made a beautiful sight.

Although the season had finished, several of the ski centre hotels were still operating, so they stopped at a rather pleasant one for refreshments and a comfort stop. Then up over the top to Develi.

They stopped there for a couple of hours looking at interesting Seljuk period buildings, the Ulu Mosque and the Develi Tomb. Janine was so impressed with the place that she blurted out to her father, 'I'll just *have* to come back here sometime. It's all so beautiful.'

He grinned at her and said, 'Well I'm sure you'll find someone to show you around.'

Abdul looked a little embarrassed and it all appeared to go over Yasher's and Ayse's heads.

After lunch they drove the thirty or so kilometres on to the falls. This was a breathtaking sight. Seven natural springs made separate cascades of differing heights down the mountain face. The highest was about one hundred metres. The spray was making a glorious quadrant of refracted colour. After the inevitable round of camera shots, they boarded the vehicle and set off for the last sight. Yasher insisted that they had to see the view from the rim of the volcano.

After about another hour's driving on their way back

to the north, they came to the turn-off to the summit. It was about another four kilometres from there to a parking area at the end of the road. From here they had a steep climb for a couple of hundred metres to the summit. There wasn't much snow on the ground now, but it was quite cold outside the car. They had come well rugged up and there was no wind. The sky was clear to the west, and there were a few rain showers off to the east of the mountain.

As they climbed the last few paces to the rim of the volcano, the vision of the plateau to the northwest materialised. The vast areas of *moonscape* were awe-inspiring. There was a gigantic saltpan or dried up lake to the west, and the rugged mountain ranges behind them to the east. The views were certainly all that Yasher had promised.

While they gazed around them at the breathtaking scenery, Janine pointed to the east and said, 'Look at that!'

There, stretching above the horizon was a large but faint rainbow. Inside this was a smaller brighter one, which, because of their height, almost formed a complete circle.

As they looked at the beautiful sight Janine reminded Michiko and Sumi, and told the others, of the experience of seeing the full circle when flying. She spoke of the parable that Leo had made, about the circle of life.

'Now,' she said, 'Another circle had been completed with this visit.' They all nodded in solemn agreement.

Michiko snuggled up to Leo and looking at the

rainbow said, 'You are probably right about the full circle Janine, but I think I prefer this one.'

'Why is that?' Sumi asked.

'Because,' she replied, 'I like to keep my feet on the ground, my head in the clouds, and still have some of the circle left to experience before I leave this planet.'

They all laughed and headed off down the track, and on to whatever life might bring them in the future.

Leo thought, 'Well, it can't get much better than this.'

no end

Epilogue

As the eagle soars on high
'Midst swirling clouds and rain
Free from any terrestrial tie
That may his spirit restrain
With the Sun at his back and showers before
He climbs ever upward his domain to explore
And views what earthman can not comprehend
The halo of light
The rainbow, no end

Lloyd Knight

Glossary

Ack Ack – WW II term for Anti-Aircraft fire.

ACT – Australian Capital Territory.

AK-47 – Russian designed assault rifle/sub-machine gun.

ADF HQ – Australian Defence Forces Head Quarters.

AFP – Australian Federal Police

ANZAC – Australian and New Zealand Army Corps - WW 1.

APB – All Points Bulletin.

ASIO – Australian Security Intelligence Organisation.

ASIS – Australian Secret Intelligence Service

ATC – Air Traffic Control.

Autorotation – Procedure that allows a helicopter to glide to a possible safe landing.

ASAP – As Soon As Possible.

'B' Girls – Bar girls employed to encourage drinkers to imbibe further, and perhaps indulge in less savoury activities as well.

BAFSV – British Armed Forces Special Voucher (military money).

Beretta – M9/92F, 9mm combat pistol.

Black box – Generic term for secret, or electronic aircraft equipment. Also describes a Flight Data Recorder or Cockpit Voice Recorder (which are actually coloured red).

Bluey – Hobo's or Swagman's bedroll, containing his possessions.

Blue Orchid – Derogatory or jocular army term for an air force person.

Bogey – Unidentified military aircraft.

CAP – Covering Air Patrol to locate the downed crew, guide rescuers and provide protection. Also, Combat Air Patrol,

CC – Canadian Club whisky.

Click – Military slang for kilometre, derived from an artillery term.

CO – Commanding Officer

Coms – Communications.

'DANEY' – Unique squadron call-sign. These were sometimes changed to confuse the enemy.

Anecdote: The original 77 Squadron call-sign, 'ANZAC' was re-assigned to a USAF 4th Fighter Wing Sabre Squadron. On the first day they used it they went out in force. When Chinese radar saw them approaching the Yalu River, they sent up a squadron of Mig 15s, thinking they were going to knock out a few old Meteors. The Yanks had a *turkey shoot* that day. The ploy had worked. Naturally it was a one-off win.

DC – Diplomatic Corps.

DMZ – Demilitarised Zone.

Echelon – Allied nations monitoring system that includes satellite surveillance over vast global areas.

ETD – Estimated Time of Departure.

Flack – Word describing anti-aircraft shells exploding.

Flight Note – An in-house flight following system that does not rely on the Air Traffic Control service.

Gettahs – Japanese sandals (thongs).

Gooney Bird – Affectionate term for the faithful WW II Douglas Dakota, C47 transport plane.

Goshu – Japanese name for Australia, which translates roughly as - Great Southern Island.

GPS – Global Positioning System, satellite navigation system.

Guard – Guard frequency. Universal emergency radio channels monitored by ATC, 121.5 MHz and 243 MHz.

Grease Gun – WW II, M-9, .45 cal sub-machine gun.

Hooch – Army slang for a one-man tent made with an army poncho. Also Hoochie.

Huey – Nickname for Bell UH-1 helicopter, derived from its original designation, HU-1 (Helicopter, Utility-1)

Hypoxia – Inadequate availability of oxygen in the blood.

HQ – Headquarters

IR – Infra Red camera etc for *seeing* heat generating objects in the dark, as distinct from Vision Enhancement devices for use in low-light situations.

Kamsa Hamnida – Thank you *Korean*.

May West – WW II expression used to describe the fairly bulky life jackets worn by sailors and airmen. They were named for a buxom American actress of that era.

Meteor – British Gloster Meteor Mk 8, twin jet fighter.

Mickey Finn – Knockout drops slipped into an unsuspecting victim's drink.

MO – Medical Officer.

MPC – US Military Payment Certificate, commonly called Scrip.

MP-5N – USMC, H&K 9mm sub-machine gun.

NCC – Australian National Crime Commission.

NOSAR – No Search and Rescue requirements. Notification used when the aircraft operator has an alternative means of flight following.

NSA – US National Security Agency.

NVG – Night Vision Goggles. Vision enhancing glasses used for night operations. Those depicted are also sensitive to IR light, with magnification, cine, photographic and range finding capabilities.

Obi – Broad waist sash worn with a kimono.

Old man – military slang term used to describe a commander or very senior officer.

Orderly Officer (OO) – Duty officer responsible for out of hours and off-base matters.

Primary Paint – The reflected data image of a target, produced on a radar screen as the scanner sweeps across its position.

Paraphrasing of Messages – It is normal to paraphrase the decoded text of a message to make it more difficult for an enemy to *break* the code, should both fall into his hands. A cryptographer would not release the acronymic name of the code as I have.

PM – Post Mortem. Examination after death. Autopsy.

POW or **PW** – Prisoner of war.

Pull Pitch – Helicopter control term - to initiate lift off.

RAAF – Royal Australian Air Force.

RAF – Royal Air Force (British).

R and R – Rest and Recuperation. Consisted of 2 weeks, including travel, after 3 months of active service.

R in C – Rest in Country. 4 days, including travel, each month.

Red Crescent – Islamic equivalent to the Red Cross, especially in Turkey.

Recce or **Recon** – Reconnaissance exercise.

REM – Rapid Eye Movement. A phase of sleep sometimes associated with dreaming.

ROKAF – Republic of Korea (South) Air Force.

Sake – Japanese rice wine.

SAM – Surface to Air Missile.

SAR – Search And Rescue.

SAS – Special Air Services (Australian).

Secondary Radar – That part of the radar system which receives data from the aircraft's *transponder*.

SI – Security Intelligence.

SOP – Standard Operating Procedure.

SP – USN Shore Patrol. RAAF Service Police. USAF term is AP, Air Police. All are equivalent to MP, Military Police.

TOW – Tube-launched, Optically tracked, Wire-guided (Missile).

Transponder – Aircraft device that transmits ATC information when interrogated by the controller.

USAF – United States Air Force.

USMC – United States Marine Corps.

USN – United States Navy.

Uzi – Israeli, 9mm machine pistol.

Waddy – Long stick (Aust Aboriginal) – Nightstick.

Yen – In 1952 £1 Sterling = ¥1008, US$1 = ¥420, which was about 10 Shillings Australian (now AU$1).

Acknowledgements

I would here like to thank all those family members and friends, who have read cut one, and offered encouragement and useful suggestions.

I particularly wish to thank Allana Corbin for the initial inspiration that I gained from reading her book, *The Best I Can Be, by Allana Arnott* and the help and guidance she has offered during my writing of this novel. Special thanks to Sandy Cahir for her excellent help with language and editing suggestions, and proof reading. A big thank you also, to Bob Macintosh, old friend and colleague, who helped straighten out some anomalies and errors.

Mustafa Kemal Ataturk composed the poem quoted in chapter 53. He was one of the leaders of the Turkish forces that overcame the invasion of his country by Allied forces in 1915. He became the first president of the Turkish republic in 1923. The poem is inscribed on a memorial erected by him, at Anzac Cove in 1935.

Of course, the recitation of the Twenty-third Psalm (AV) in chapter 34 doesn't infringe any copyright and may be enjoyed by all.

Personal Touch Products, Inc. California supplied the rainbow image on the cover. H & J Beste of Queensland supplied the eagle.

ABOUT THE AUTHOR

Lloyd Duncan Knight was born in Sydney, Australia in 1932. He left high school at a pre-matriculation level and joined the Royal Australian Air Force in 1951. His flying career spanned an unbroken period to his retirement in 2003. It comprised three approximately equal phases, as an air force pilot, commercial pilot and examiner of airmen. Apart from a home study course in Instrument Flying, published in 1980, this is his first literary endeavour. He now lives in Melbourne with his wife, Bonnie.

lloydknight@bigpond.com